PRINTS CHARMING

rebeca seitz

Published by
THOMAS NELSON™
Since 1798
www.thomasnelson.com

Published in Nashville, Tennessee, by Thomas Nelson, Inc.

Thomas Nelson, Inc. books may be purchased in bulk for educational, business, fund-raising, or sales promotional use. For information, please e-mail SpecialMarkets@ThomasNelson.com.

Publisher's Note: This novel is a work of fiction. Names, characters, places, and incidents are either products of the author's imagination or used fictitiously. All characters are fictional, and any similarity to people living or dead is purely coincidental.

Library of Congress Cataloging-in-Publication Data
Seitz, Rebeca, 1977-
   Prints charming / Rebeca Seitz.
       p. cm. -- (Sisters, ink ; book one)
   ISBN-13: 978-1-59554-271-7 (pbk.)
   ISBN-10: 1-59554-271-X (pbk.)
   1. Scrapbooks--Fiction. I. Title.
   PS3619.E427P75 2007
   813'.6--dc22

                                                        2006038739

Printed in the United States of America
07 08 09 10 RRD 6 5 4 3 2 1

For my precious Charlie.

*Thank you for loving this
broken woman. I love you.*

prologue 1

❁ · ❁ · ❁ · ❁ · ❁ · ❁ · ❁

"I'm telling you, Jane, this dog don't hunt."

"Keep your voice down, Lydia," Jane hissed, watching Lydia tuck a stray brown curl back into the wreath of baby's breath in her hair. "They'll hear you and wonder why I'm sitting in here listening to the one woman who's supposed to support me wholeheartedly on my wedding day, spouting country wisdom and down-home clichés like they're going out of style. Which they are." The big white train of her wedding dress swished around the floor in time to her nervous pacing on the baby blue carpet in the bride chamber of Grace Church. Satin white shoes with pearl-encrusted heels that had felt so perfect in the store now pinched her toes. Not that any shoe in the world would be comfortable after hours in front of a wedding photographer's lens, running back and forth behind trees to hide every time Bill came into view.

1

"Look, missy"—Lydia wagged a finger at Jane, other hand on her hip—"you can make all the excuses you want for him, but I know what I saw, and I saw him in the parking lot of Cadillac's with Lacy Champeign just last night." Lydia's righteous indignation made her seem taller than her five-foot-two frame.

"It was a *bachelor party.*" Jane looked to the door and lowered her voice. "I'm sure he did a lot of things I wouldn't approve of and I don't want to know about. That's what bachelor parties are for." She glanced in the mirror, grateful that every black hair was in place beneath the tiara. Her hair, at least, was performing as expected.

Lydia sniffed and turned her brown eyes to the window overlooking a parking lot crowded with cars. "Character is what we do when we think no one is watching."

"Cute one. Dr. Phil?"

Lydia turned back to Jane, fire in her eyes. "Don't you make fun of me, Jane Goodwin. I might use other people's words every now and then, but that's because they're truth. Bill Sandburg is a cheater, pure and simple. He doesn't have character, and you shouldn't be marrying him, I don't care what people say."

The door cracked open and a face caked with powder and rouge peeked around the corner. "Two minutes, Jane." The wedding coordinator tapped her clipboard. Her eyebrow arched at the stormy look on Lydia's face. "You gals need anything?"

"Yeah, a lobotomy," Lydia said under her breath, and Jane cut her eyes to her best friend since grade school.

"Nothing, Madge. Thanks." Madge nodded and shut the

door. Lydia walked over to Jane, reaching her hands up to Jane's shoulders.

"Look, I know this is your wedding day, and I know I'm supposed to be supportive. This day is all about you. That's what every magazine says, and I believe it. But you're making a mistake here. This man is not faithful. He's not loyal. I saw it with my own two eyes."

Jane looked out the window, debating. It seemed as if every single person in the Brentwood area had turned out for this wedding. Her clients, present and former, were out there. Bill's parents, their friends from college—heck, from high school. This was the wedding everyone knew would eventually happen. Months had been spent planning and preparing, right down to the shade of pale gold for the ribbons on each pew. Hours of cake tasting, band auditioning, and vow choosing were behind her. The finish line was within sight. She would not be the one to let down every beautifully dressed person sitting in that sanctuary, expecting to see a wedding over a decade in the making.

Lydia's hands fell away as Jane shook her shoulders a bit. "Lydia, thanks for your concern, but I'm going out there in two minutes and becoming Mrs. Bill Sandburg," *just like this entire community has expected since we were in junior high,* "and if you do or say anything to ruin this wedding, so help me, I will never speak to you again."

The door cracked open again. "Jane, it's time." Madge looked from Jane to Lydia and back again. "Or I can stall if you need me to."

"No need, Madge." Jane picked up her skirts and stepped to the door. "We were just coming out." She tilted her chin up and squared her shoulders. Bill and she would be fine together, had been fine together for years. Through Brentwood Academy and Vanderbilt University, they'd been the only ones to stick together through it all. She wasn't dumb in choosing a mate. Bill loved her with a quiet friendship that shouldn't be taken for granted. So what if he had a little fling at a bachelor party? That was the whole point of them. Lydia was probably blowing it way out of proportion anyway, since Jane was pretty sure Bill didn't have a passionate bone in his body. He just wasn't that kind of man. Solid, steady, dependable, yes. Passionate? No. Not once in all her years of knowing him.

She stood before the large oak doors, staring at the blue carpet, noting a footprint stain just to the right of the entrance. Why hadn't someone cleaned that stain? Only then did she realize Lydia was not in front of her, where she belonged as the matron of honor.

"Lydia?" She turned just in time to catch the bouncing brown ringlets as her best friend of forever ran from the church. The sounds of "Canon in D" by Pachelbel, an opening cue it had taken Jane three months to decide on, floated through the crack above the sanctuary doors.

prologue 2

TWO YEARS LATER

Coke fizzed in its glass as Jane settled herself in front of the com-
puter. The caffeine would keep her up for at least three hours,
plenty of time to finish up this publicity and fund-raiser proposal and e-mail it off to Sonya. Jane smiled at the memory of
Nashville's larger-than-life socialite. A diehard shopper and
president of Nashville's most prestigious nonprofit, many people
regarded Sonya as a force to be reckoned with. Her firm raised
millions each year, doling it out to various charities in town.
Jane knew the heart behind the name brands, though, and was
grateful such a formidable woman stood in the gap for those
less fortunate.

"Though they won't ever be more fortunate if I don't get
this crazy proposal done," she mumbled. Sometimes owning
her own publicity firm was more work than she'd bargained

for. But working from home had its perks. Putting fingers to keys, the first words were just flying onto the screen when a message box popped up. Jane sighed and snatched the mouse, x-ing out of the box. "Stupid pop-ups."

She typed a few more words, and another box popped up. Again, she x-ed out of it and went back to the proposal.

One minute later, the box popped up again, and Jane decided to see what product would endure her wrath from this point forward to eternity. It looked like an instant-messaging box.

Hey, hot thang. You're up late.

Ugh, some crazy cyberman had found her IM address. *Dateline* would love this guy. She x-ed out of the box and reread her last line of the proposal. The IM ding sounded, and another box popped up.

You there? Is the Boring One around?

Jane chuckled. This guy must know Bill. She thought about responding, her fingers hovering over the keys for a few brief seconds, but images from the *Dateline* online predators episode flashed through her mind, and once again she x-ed out of the box.

When ten minutes passed without another ding, she sighed. *Patience is a virtue.* She winced as the cliché reminded her of Lydia. Two years was a long time without a best friend.

The ding made her jump.

> Hey. I'm signing off. Is Jane around,
> or can you call me?

Jane read the message, chills coursing down her spine as she read her own name on the screen. Confusion raced through her brain. Her fingers flew to the keyboard before she could command them not to.

> Jane's not here.
> What do you want to talk about?

Her cursor blinked as the little window told her "Secrt1" was typing. What was she doing?

> You know. Tomorrow . . .

Bill had told her about the golf game he was playing in the morning with some of his old frat buddies. Why would this guy need to make sure she was gone to talk to Bill?

> What about tomorrow?

> Just making sure you can still come out to play.

> Why wouldn't I?

> So you told her?

Jane sat back from the screen, staring at a cursor that she was certain held secrets best left untold. This guy and Bill obviously shared a mystery she wasn't privy to. Not a big deal. Happened all the time in marriage. The twinge in her stomach forced her fingers back to the keys.

Told her what?

Bill! Don't you play me. Did you tell her
you were leaving or not? I'm not meeting
you if you're still a married man.

Her mind noted a searing pain in the general vicinity of her heart, but wouldn't admit the niggling of truth begging to surface.

Leaving? Why would I be leaving?

Seconds crawled by while the cursor blinked and bubbles fizzed in her glass. Had it only been minutes since she poured her caffeine kick?

LOL. You're so funny. I'll see you tomorrow.
Can't wait to get you off this screen and into
my bedroom. Hugs and kisses flying your
way, and a whole lot more when you
get here. Call me when you can.
xxxxxooooo

Jane stared at the screen, unwilling to accept what her mind was beginning to say. *Her* Bill was not having an affair. He couldn't be. Memories of Lydia pleading with her in the bride room at Grace Church flitted past her mind's eye. No. Jane shook her head, tiny stars of light beginning to flash, harbingers of the migraine to come.

Her hands pushed away from the desk, legs extending, feet walking. A rush of blood pounded through her ears, making it seem as if she was walking under water down the hallway to her bedroom, *their* bedroom.

Bill lay beneath the covers, his blue striped pajama top buttoned all the way up, just as it had been every night of their two-year marriage. She walked to the bed, looking down at this, her husband. Years of friendship shared, more of her life spent with him than not. He could not be cheating.

Her fingers massaged the temple pulsing with blood as she willed the headache away, refusing a reality that was not possible inside the Norman Rockwell painting that was her life. What would their friends think? Did they know already? Was Scrt1 a friend of theirs?

She stepped away and pulled her gown from the poster of the bed. Dropping her clothes, she paused a moment, willing Bill to wake up and find her naked. If he took her in his arms, it would mean this wasn't real.

Bill's steady breath kept on, wounding her with its rhythm.

The gown was soft as she pulled it on, a stark contrast to the shards of glass falling through her insides. Gingerly, scared now he would awaken, she crept into the bed. This was all a nightmare. In the morning, they would laugh about it over breakfast.

She counted the seconds, then minutes, as the vise around her head tightened. What if he was leaving her? What would she do? Who would she be? For almost as long as she'd been alive, her identity was being Bill Sandburg's girl. Could she be anything but?

Can a pope pray? Lydia's voice sounded in her head, the old wisecrack sounding just as if she sat beside her in the bed. Jane's heart twisted further. Her best friend had walked out of her life, abandoning their friendship the day Jane married Bill. *Or was it me who did the abandoning?*

Jane thought for one second more, then slid out of bed. Enough wasted moments already. A woman couldn't be a woman without her girlfriends. And there was one woman in the world who would get Jane through this.

She padded down the hall to the kitchen phone. Pressing buttons, praying Lydia wouldn't hang up on her.

"Hello?" The voice she hadn't heard in two years unleashed a torrent of tears.

"Lydia?"

chapter 1

❀ · ❀ · ❀ · ❀ · ❀ · ❀ · ❀

ONE YEAR LATER

Jane's tires screeched as she flew around a curve on Bluff Road.

"Girl, where are you?" The excitement in Lydia's voice came through loud and clear, and Jane pushed her foot down a bit harder on the accelerator.

"I'm coming, I'm coming." She kept one hand on the steering wheel while frantically sifting through the things in the passenger seat of her Blazer. There was a brush somewhere, she just knew it, but finding anything at seven in the morning after pulling an all-nighter was difficult at best. Exhaustion picked at her brain, but she took it for the victory it was. Her all-nighter had resulted (finally!) in a completed logo for Sisters, Ink. Bleary eyes gave testament to the long hours she'd put into creating the official representation of their scrapbooking group. A box of stationery rested in the passenger floorboard amid granola bar wrappers, a beautiful Sisters, Ink logo centered at the top. Four smaller boxes held their new business cards, printed on her laser printer at three a.m. The skeleton of their web site was even up and running, though none of the Sisters knew about it or the business idea she'd been brewing for weeks.

"Do I need to grab anything for you? This stuff is going fast. There are barely any of the foam alphabet sets left."

"Shoot, Lydia, I barely even know what I need. I'll be there in about two minutes." Jane lunged again, still searching for the brush while trying not to drop the cell phone from her shoulder.

"Okay, but don't let the grass grow under your tires. I'll be over in the baby girl section. I need to find something for Olivia's first bath pages and get ribbon for Mac. What's this big secret you have anyway?"

"I told you I'm not saying a word until we all get to Mac's. Be there in a flash." Jane snapped the phone together and slammed to a stop at the red light. Turning her attention to her still-searching hand, she finally found the elusive hairbrush and grabbed it. A blaring horn sounded, and she realized the green arrow had finally appeared. This business idea had monopolized her mind for weeks. And she had Bill to thank for it, in a way. Without him, she'd never have learned the value of girlfriends.

Jane pushed thoughts of her ex-husband out of her mind. Tires squealing again, she tore into the parking lot of The Savvy Scrapper. Tossing the hairbrush back into the passenger seat, she threw the car into Park, grabbed her purse, and flung open the door.

"Ouch!"

Jane looked up just as her door collided with the mid-section of one very tall man.

"Omigosh. I am so, so sorry. I'm just in a rush. The sale is happening, and I'm late and—"

"It's okay." Mr. Tall held his hands up as if to ward off any other car doors she might be hiding somewhere, and she noticed the coffee cup in one hand and bagel bag in the other. Bagels would be so heavenly right now. "I'm fine, really." He set the bag down on the ground and brushed the dust off of his olive green sweater, then looked at her. "I know how women can be when there's a sale involved." He grinned as he knelt to pick the bag back up.

She tried hard to ignore his sexist statement and not remind him of how many guys camp out at golf stores before a sale or sleep in the parking lot to get tickets to a concert.

"Are you sure you're okay? I mean, I have insurance, and we can call somebody." Jane shoved her hair behind her ears, willing herself to focus on the problem at hand rather than the sale happening about ten yards away or the way her stomach was now grumbling for coffee and a bagel.

"Really, go ahead. I'm fine."

"Okay, thanks." She turned and made her way around the back of the car. "I appreciate this. It's just that this only happens once a year, and my friend is waiting . . ." She stopped on the far side of the car and looked at him. He could sue if he was hurt, and her luck with men right now meant he would sue and she would lose to the tune of thousands of dollars. "You're certain you're fine?"

"Go." He made a shooing motion with the bag. "Happy shopping."

Her mother always said never to look a gift horse in the mouth, and this was one time Jane would be obeying Elizabeth rather than giving in to her own desire to argue. She practically sprinted to the front door of The Savvy Scrapper, yanked it open, and burst inside.

"Jane!" Lydia was in the front corner of the store, surrounded by pink, yellow, blue, lilac, and pale green. She waved a die-cut of a bathtub and bubbles above her head. "I found the perfect stuff for Olivia and Oliver's First Bath page."

"Great." Jane joined her, breathless. Her cheeks were tinged with pink.

"Okay, here's the deal." Lydia turned toward the back of the store and pointed. "All the Times letters are gone, the vellum is almost *finito*, and the dog section is getting riffled through as we speak. Where do you want to start?"

"Dog section." Jane stuffed her keys into her purse. "I took great pictures this morning of Mrs. Hannigan picking up poop while stepping in another pile."

"You are so gross. That poor woman, poop obsessed. To each his own, I guess."

Jane scanned the rest of the store, making a quick plan to get the most stuff. "What can you expect? She's lived there since before animals were allowed and tried to stop the changing of the rules. All she wants is a poop-free yard, and I can't say I blame her."

Lydia's eyebrows rose. "You're siding with Mrs. Hannigan?"

"I wouldn't say I was siding with her, just beginning to understand where she's coming from, that's all." Jane shrugged.

"Right. Go on over to the dog section. I'll come over there when I'm finished here. Can you grab me that new paper with the red stripes and dark brown bones? I've got some pictures of Otis with Olivia and Oliver from last week."

"Dale let that pug get near his precious twins? I thought you said the only thing he cared more about than SportsCenter was those babies."

"Dale hasn't seen the pictures yet. You know he never comes in my scrapbook studio. I think he gets hives when he thinks about how much money I spend on this stuff." Lydia waved her hand to encompass the store. "He's probably right."

"Oh, please. Men are never right." Jane turned toward the dog section. "Dogs, on the other hand, are wonderful companions who never cheat and can't even turn on a computer."

Lydia laughed and turned back to the wall of baby-themed paper in front of her, leaving Jane to take care of the dog paper. Stripes or flowers? She didn't want to make the scrapbook too babyish, but she also didn't want it to look too grownup. The papers were all on sale, so maybe she would just get both. Dale would never know, since he didn't come into her studio anyway, and she could give some of it to Mac for Kesa's baby book. She took two sheets of the pink and lime green-striped paper, then two of the blue rosebud ones.

"Men are never right," she muttered under her breath. Maybe Jane had a good point.

chapter 2

❋ · ❋ · ❋ · ❋ · ❋ · ❋ · ❋

"And then she pushed this woman out of the way and grabbed the last two sheets of the bone paper." Lydia laughed again as she and Jane settled into chairs at MacKenzie Allen's big oak kitchen table later that day and told her all about the sale.

"You pushed a woman?" Mac asked.

"Well, just a nudge," Jane admitted. "Anyway, let's not get hung up on this. I've got a surprise for you."

"Ah, finally, she spills the beans."

"Listen, girls, I've been thinking, and I'm pretty sure I've come up with a way for us to make some money at this scrapbooking thing while doing a very good deed at the same time."

"That's our Jane, always the entrepreneur," Lydia said.

"If it helps pay for my scrappin' habit, I'm all ears, chile."

Jane leaned into the table. Mac and Lydia followed suit. "Well, I was thinking about this past year and how I wouldn't have made it through without the two of you." She smiled at her old friend Lydia and her newly found girlfriend, Mac. "That's when I realized that I'd let my friendships slip when I got married. I'm not sure why, but it's like I let everything go but my relationship with Bill. And I think that made me less of the woman I wanted to be. I like my friendships with you, our conversations, our scrapping time, all of it. I don't know where I'd be without it."

"Okay, much as I'm loving the love fest, tell me how this helps other women," Lydia prodded.

"I'm getting there. I started thinking about why I had let my friendships go. And it occurred to me that, even if I had wanted to reach out to other scrappers in my area, I had no idea how to find them. Y'all know I don't like taking classes, and that seemed to be the only way to find other scrappers, which left me with no easy way to make other scrapping friends."

"You could go online," Lydia suggested.

Jane nodded. "I could, but then I'd be making friends that could be on the other side of the country just as easily as down the block. Having friends whose houses I can go to, or shop with, or just hug every now and then isn't something I could easily find online. So then it hit me." Her chair creaked as she leaned back in satisfaction.

"Um, *what* hit you?" Mac asked.

"A business idea—a way to connect scrappers with other scrappers in their area *and* across the country. To help women connect with other women rather than neglecting such an important part of being female."

"Okay, genius, I'll bite. How do we do that?"

Jane leaned forward again. "With a web site of our own." She grinned.

"But there are already a ton of scrapping web sites out there, Jane."

"I know, but they all exist to sell stuff—which is fine. Don't get me wrong. I'm happy to buy scrapping stuff all day long. But there needs to be a place that's all about building relationships first. So, I built us a web site and"—she reached into her tote bag resting on the floor—"incorporated us."

She set the boxes of letterhead and business cards on the table, pulling off the lids and watching her friends' faces. Would they balk?

Mac reached in and pulled out one of the business cards with her name on it. "MacKenzie Jones, Vice President of Class Development and Web Site Management. Now that sounds highfalutin for this country girl."

"Not really, Mac. It's just a title that puts you in charge of coordinating our online classes and maintaining the web site. Since you help teach at the Creating Keepsakes convention every year and you love classes so much, I thought you'd like to be in charge of that."

"Hmm, 'spose I might be able to do that."

Lydia pulled her own card from the box and read, "Lydia Whitehaven, Vice President of Creative Direction. What does that mean?"

"Since you're the one who loves to be creative and artsy, I thought you could be in charge of new products, techniques, and skills. You love the part of scrapping that is art form, and there's a large portion of scrappers out there who agree with you, so we need someone in charge of addressing their needs."

"So what's your title?"

"Since the relationship part of scrapping is the most important to me, I would be Vice President of Club Communications, helping our members connect with each other at the local and national level, making sure they get plugged in."

She watched as Jane and Mac looked at each other across the scarred table.

"You know, if my scrapping habit was helping to bring money in, Dale might take a little interest in it," Lydia said.

Mac looked at Jane, then nodded one time. "All right, chile, we're in. Tell us how to get this baby up and runnin'."

Jane squealed and pulled her business plan from the tote bag. "This is going to be so much fun!"

A few hours later, the leaders of Sisters, Ink sat around Mac's scrapping table. Paper and embellishments lay scattered about.

"You know, if we gonna be in business together, we gonna need to know each other's scrappin' history."

Jane looked up from her eyelet setter. "Scrapping history?"

"Mmm-hmm. Has Lydia told you about how she acquired her eyelet setter?"

Lydia looked up and rolled her eyes. "Oh, Mac, that's water

under the bridge by now. I'm sure everybody's forgotten it, and, besides, that woman started it."

"Started what? A fight?" Jane asked. "Two years I don't talk to you and you go completely to pot. It's a good thing I'm back in your life."

"It wasn't a fight, really—" Lydia started.

"Oh, yes, it was." Mac's voice was laced with laughter but brooked no argument. "Anytime somebody's hair is left lying on the floor, it's a fight."

"Well, how was I to know she was wearing a wig?" Lydia got up and made her way to Mac's wall of rubber stamps. "It looked real enough to me."

"That woman had the audacity to get between Lydia and the last Clikit. Mind you, this was the year when the Clikit first came out on the market. I'm telling you, I've never seen a situation go from peaceful to painful that quick." Mac snapped her fingers and laughed again. "Our Lydia pushed right back in front of the woman and grabbed that Clikit like it was the hem of Jesus' robe itself."

"Mac! Don't be blasphemous." Lydia snagged a baby bottle stamp and sat back down at the table, her dimple showing as she grinned. "I just got caught up in the moment."

"'Caught up' is sayin' it right, sister." Mac's eyes twinkled. "That woman tried to grab the Clikit from Lydia's own hand. Well, she messed with the wrong sister. Lydia snatched it back, and next thing you know, they're on the floor, pullin' and slappin' like there was no tomorrow. When the wig hit the floor, though, it was all over."

"You took her wig?" Jane couldn't quit laughing.

"Of course not. I left it lying right where it fell." She paused, tilting her head. "I would never take a woman's hair."

The room filled with laughter.

"My lands, that was some convention."

"It sure was. We've got to get our tickets to this year's. It's in four months, and you know if we don't get signed up, all the workshops will be full."

"Yes ma'am." Mac left the table and sat down in front of her laptop. "I'll get online and sign us up right now."

"Hey, so long as we're spilling scrapping secrets, I may have hurt a guy in the parking lot before the Savvy Scrapper sale."

"You hurt a guy? What happened?"

"I didn't see him coming and just opened my door right into his stomach. He wasn't hurt badly or anything. Not that his huge male ego would have let him admit it if he had been."

"He had a huge ego? How long did you talk to this man?" Mac asked from her place behind the laptop.

"Long enough to know he's probably the type that uses phrases like 'little woman' and such. He actually shooed me on into the store and told me he knew how women could be around sales." Jane mimicked the guy's shooing motion and rolled her eyes at the memory.

"Has he ever seen men around a TV during the draft pick or the Super Bowl?" Lydia asked. "Dale is just as rabid about sports as I am about my scrapbooks. Why do they think we're so crazy with our hobbies when they're just as crazy with theirs?"

"I know, I know. I let it go, though, so I could get on into the store. Arguing with a man right now just isn't an option."

"Yes!" Mac interrupted. "There are still tickets to the Creating Keepsakes show here in Nashville. Looks like 'bout half the workshops are sold out, including mine." She continued clicking through the web site. "Y'all wanna take any of the classes?"

"I wish I could." Lydia set out stacks of paper in varying shades of pink, blue, and green. "But I barely have time to get to the convention, much less take classes. I'll have Oliver and Olivia with me, anyway."

"I can't either. I've got three fund-raisers to conduct and publicize in the next six months." Jane chewed her lip and began placing her pictures of Wilson in groupings around the table. "I barely have time to scrap, much less sit down for others to tell me how. Besides, I'm not a class-taking kind of scrapper."

The light from the computer screen cast a blue glow on Mac's face. Jane rearranged a few of the pictures and assessed the new groupings.

"Oh, hey, did I tell y'all I finished the scrapbook of the Center's banquet?" Mac got up and headed over to a bookshelf. She ran her weathered hands over the spines of the scrapbooks there and pulled out a purple one. Coming back to the cropping table, she began thumbing through the pages.

"Jane, we oughta get on your calendar for next year. Much as I love helpin' those girls out in the midst of a crisis pregnancy, I don't think I can put together a banquet all by my lonesome again next year. It near did me in tryin' to take care of everythin' this year." She slid the scrapbook over to Jane.

"You've already scrapbooked that banquet?" Lydia asked. "It was in February, for goodness' sakes. When did you find time in the last month to scrap that?"

"I've been working on it by myself. I'd rather spend time on Tabby's baby's book when I'm working with y'all." She shrugged as if working on two scrapbooks at once was no big deal.

"Sister, you are one amazing person." Lydia shook her head. She pulled out her paper cutter and prepared to crop the pictures of the twins' first bath. "My babies are four months old, and I'm just now finished with the birth story pictures. I thought I'd never get to the ones from their first month at home. I'm so behind."

"Well, at least you're moving forward," Jane pulled out two 12x12 sheets of paper with white, yellow, and brown bones dancing across them. "All I've got to show for my scrapping efforts is an old wedding album I don't want to look at and a new album full of moving pictures. I need to get out more, I think. Just to have something to scrapbook."

"Been a year. Guess it's time." Mac slid the blade across a photo.

"You think?"

"To everything there is a season," Lydia said. "Maybe it's time for your season of starting over with a new guy."

"I've always liked that about you, my friend."

"What?"

"Your ability to come up with a quote or cliché for every single situation in life."

Lydia stuck out her tongue, then focused on her layout. "I need help with a title, ladies."

Mac and Jane came around to her side of the table and looked at the photos of little Olivia and Oliver lying in the kitchen sink. Each was surrounded by terry-cloth animals and a rubber ducky. Olivia was squalling like crazy, her face beet red, while Oliver had a sort of stunned expression on his face. Bath time had not been their favorite experience. Dale's big hands were around Olivia, emphasizing the frailty of the baby regardless of the passionate strength shown in her temper. His mom was holding on to Oliver, watching Dale's face.

Lydia had snapped a picture at the end of the bath as well. In this one, Olivia was sitting contentedly in her daddy's hands, staring at one of the plush animals floating nearby while Dale's mom wrapped Oliver in a yellow towel. The look of over-whelming love on both Dale and his mother's faces took Jane's breath. She stepped back over to her side of the table and picked up her pictures of Wilson, blinking back her tears before the others could notice. *Will I ever get married again? Hold a child in my arms? Maybe it is time to start dating again.*

"I'm gonna go see if I can't rustle us up something to munch on." Mac made her way to the stairs. "I'll be right back."

Jane picked up pictures of her and Wilson beside a moving truck. The dog's sad eyes and lowered head were as forlorn as Jane had felt that day. The tight plastic feel of bubble wrap around her china and the sound of packing tape still made her feel panicky sometimes, even after a year. Her twelve place settings of Noritake's Stoneleigh design still sat in their boxes, collecting dust in the spare bedroom closet. *What do women do with all of the things they acquired during a marriage when it ends? Post them on eBay?*

Now, there was an idea. If she sold some china, she could buy more scrapping supplies. Hmm, maybe there was a silver lining to this divorce business after all. Besides, scrapping was so much cheaper than therapy.

chapter 3

Jane rolled over and slapped the top of the alarm clock, groaning and praying for a bit more sleep. Why had she set it on a Sunday? She moaned when she remembered promising Lydia her presence at early service in church this morning. No way out. Who in their right minds got up at six-thirty in the morning on a Sunday on purpose?

She sat up and looked around the room. *Not bad for a year after the move.* No boxes remained in sight. Everything that could be unpacked was, and everything else was stuffed in the extra closet. Life, what remained anyway, was beginning to settle into a routine again. *Now if only the expectation that Bill would walk through the door at any moment would go away, then everything would be great.* Sometimes the empty key ring by the door still jarred her. Or the naked spot on the back of the couch, where he used to lay his coat. Even tripping over his big clunky shoes would be nice some days. The clutter could drive someone to madness and had done so to her the entire two years of their marriage, but the clutter also brought a sense of satisfaction. She'd been married, finally. *Yeah, time to get back out there.*

Jane jumped as her cell phone rang. Hopping up, she strode quickly to the front door and snatched her purse up off the floor. She plunged her hand in, grabbed the phone, and flipped it open.

"Jane Sandburg."

"Jane, it's Leota. With Sandpiper? Remember me?"

Jane grinned and pictured the petite lady with fake black hair piled into a beehive the size of Texas. The first time she'd met Leota, she'd known 1960 had put its hooks in and never let go.

"Hi, Leota. Of course I remember you. How are the kids doing?" Jane would never forget the day she'd spent working with the abandoned children Sandpiper took in. She'd cried for a week afterwards and begged Bill to come see them, maybe even provide a foster home or forever home to one or more. Bill had said they didn't have time. Now she knew what he'd spent his time doing.

"Oh, you know them. The older ones take the young 'uns under their wings and teach 'em the ropes. We've got a full house right now, but the house is fallin' down around our ears."

"Oh, no. What's wrong?"

"What's not?" Jane heard the exhaustion and resignation in Leota's laugh. "The roof is so old it's gonna cave in any day now.

The wood paneling on the walls has been painted so many times I can just about peel it off. The ruts in the driveway are so deep the gravel's more like dunes. The hot-water heater's got a rust spot on it the size of my knee. I can keep going on, but you get the drift."

"Oh, Leota. What can I do?" Jane leaned against the door, pulling up a knee and resting her foot behind her, nibbling the skin at the edge of her fingernail. And to think she'd been reflecting on how bad she had it. At least the roof over her head was sound, even if it was small.

"Now, those are words I like to hear. I think what we need is some community awareness. I can't think the town would let our house fall down if they knew about who it houses."

"Absolutely. I'll start crafting a press release tonight and get it out to the papers tomorrow. Can you do interviews? Maybe we should have an open house to let the public really see what repairs are needed." Jane pushed off the door with her foot and went to the kitchen. She jerked open the junk drawer and rummaged around inside for a notepad to start making a list.

"That's a good idea! I hadn't thought of that. Okay, let's see . . ." Jane heard pots and pans clanging and knew Leota had walked into the massive kitchen at Sandpiper, where some of the kids came together at night to make dinner and where a calendar hung on the massive refrigerator. She remembered the family feeling in the air when they all bustled around the kitchen, tossing spices and towels to each other, laughing as they made helpings big enough to feed a small army. "Would a month from now be too soon?"

"No, that's fine. That gives me a week or so to get the press materials together and out to the media, then a couple weeks for follow-up, then a week for interviews."

"Oh, Jane, thank you."

Jane smiled at the relief in Leota's voice. "Thank *you* for giving a home and love to those kids."

They talked over the details, and Jane hung up, having no idea how she would work this into an already full client load, but also knowing there was no way she'd say no to Leota. She thought again of the smiling faces of the kids.

Wilson's paws made a clicking sound on the linoleum as he joined her in the kitchen. She reached down and patted his smooth head. "It's just you and me now, buddy. But maybe that can change one day."

Wilson raised his head and looked at her with wide-open eyes.

"Okay, okay. Let's go outside."

At the word *outside* Wilson leaped up, wagging his black tail as he ran toward the door. Jane sighed and went for the red leash hanging in the hall closet.

Shuffling on her slippers, she snapped the leash on Wilson's collar and walked outside to the dog area. She let Wilson sniff all the trees while she tried to decide what to wear to church. Staying in her jammies and snuggling back into the warm bed sounded so much better than putting on makeup and fixing her hair. Hose and heels held no appeal at any time of the day, least of all at six-thirty in the morning.

"Come on, Wilson." Tugging him brought no amount of

movement from the dog. Instead, he pulled hard the other direction. Maybe she could tell Lydia she'd been hauled away by her dog and couldn't get back to the apartment in time to change. "Come *on*." She pulled harder. That story would be a true story if she didn't get a move on.

Wilson turned to look at her, then pulled against the leash again. "I'm not kidding. We're going inside." She turned and tugged him toward the apartment, but again he jerked the other way. She opened her mouth to scold him—and then she saw it.

A cat.

Horrified understanding flowed through her, "Oh no . . ."

But it was too late. With a mighty surge, Wilson jerked the leash out of Jane's hands and was off, running across the dog area, hot on the heels of the scrambling feline.

"Wilson!" Jane ran after him, praying no one else was up at such an ungodly hour on a Sunday to see her pajama-clad self running across the lawn. The dog kept running as Jane struggled not to slip on the dew-soaked grass in her house slippers. "Get back here."

The cat had run up a tree, and Wilson was at its base, barking his head off. "Hush. You'll wake up the whole apartment complex." Huffing and puffing, she caught up to the dog and snagged the edge of the leash. Her arms strained against Wilson's big basset hound muscles as she began pulling him backwards. And to think she had fought Bill for custody of this canine.

"Dog, you are in so much trouble. You better be really

happy that cat knew how to climb so fast, because if you had touched one inch of that little kitty's fur, so help me, I—"

Jane looked up at the sound of male laughter, and her heart hit her toes. Oh, no. There stood Mr. Tall from the parking lot of The Savvy Scrapper, his arms folded across a fabulous chest as he laughed at her. Her luck with men was getting better and better.

"Endangering cats now, are we?" He stood where he was, making no move whatsoever to help her, looking regal in his starched white shirt and way too put together for the early hour. He probably thought her dog would bite him or something, chauvinistic idiot. For a split second, she wished Wilson was a biting kind of dog.

"Excuse me?" She pushed her hair off her face and tried not to think about the image she was portraying.

"Well, you endanger innocent men with your car and now innocent cats with your dog. This is not the Southern hospitality I've heard so much about, I'll have to admit." He smiled and gestured toward Wilson.

"Perhaps those innocent men should watch where they're walking and, if they happen to see a cat in danger, alert the dog owner nearby. What are you doing out here anyway?"

"I was letting my cat have some outside time."

Jane's heart plummeted past her feet and into the dirt below. Was there any way in the cosmos that his cat could be any cat other than the one her dog had just treed? Of course not. Her universe didn't work that way.

"Who lets their cat out at six-thirty on a Sunday morning?

And shouldn't she be on a leash?" she asked, desperate to have his cat be any cat—any cat at all—other than the fluffy white one now meowing its head off, still hidden in the high branches of a very big elm.

"People who are trying to make it to early service at church." He walked toward the tree, giving her and Wilson a wide berth. "Which, I'll bet, is the same reason people let their dogs out at six-thirty on a Sunday morning. I'm leaving the leash question alone since the day isn't old enough yet for crazy questions. Have a good one, and thanks for a memorable welcome to the neighborhood." He waved over his shoulder before stopping at the base of the elm and calling to the cat.

Jane tugged Wilson toward the apartment, shaking her head the whole way. Of all the people in the entire town, she had to open her car door on one who lived in her building, had an ego the size of Texas, was dismissive, *and* owned a cat. A cat! The only thing that would have made the situation tolerable was if she had a camera to document the whole thing. At least then she would have a funny, if humiliating, story to scrapbook.

She walked through the door and unhooked Wilson's leash. The day was off to a poor start. Thank goodness she and Lydia were headed to Mac's after church to scrapbook. At least that was something to look forward to.

chapter 4

A couple of hours later, Jane uncrossed and crossed her legs for the umpteenth time. She racked her brain, but couldn't come up with a single instance of Lydia's having said they were going to Sunday school after the service. On her feet were beautiful Ferragamo black heels with patent-leather piping along the edges that led to a tiny bow running across her toes. They were some of her favorite Sunday-sermon shoes that now, having passed their comfortable time span, were beginning to rub blisters.

Lydia looked at her in understanding and slipped her own heels off. Jane smiled and did the same, tucking her feet behind the rungs of the folding chair. Both women turned toward the teacher at the front of the room, who was wrapping up announcements.

"Mari and John, any update on the adoption process?"

A short woman with sleek, dark brown hair that curled just under her chin looked up and smiled.

"Everything's moving along," she said. "They asked us to make a scrapbook that shows our family and home life. I'm going to start working on that this week. Since I have no idea what I'm doing, I'd appreciate your prayers."

"You've got it, Mari," the teacher said. "Any other updates or requests from the group?" He looked around and bounced on the balls of his feet for a minute, but no requests were forthcoming. "All right, then, let's pray."

Jane bowed her head with everyone else and tried to keep her mind on the words rather than her blisters. ". . . We ask all this in your Son's name. Amen," she finally heard. Lydia leaned over.

"Would you mind if I invited Mari to come with us this afternoon? She and her husband are adopting a little girl from Chile since they have secondary infertility," she whispered.

"What's secondary infertility?" Jane whispered back.

"It's when you have no problem having a first baby but for whatever reason you can't get pregnant again. They tried for a year and a half or so and then decided to adopt."

"That sounds strange. No, I don't mind at all if you invite her."

Jane grinned and began rummaging through her purse for some gum as the teacher talked about forgiveness. She most definitely did not need a lesson on forgiveness. After all, forgiving her cheating husband had required barely a thought. This lesson was one she had down cold. She could have stayed in her warm bed after all.

As soon as the lesson was over, Lydia shot up out of her chair and strode across the room toward the woman who had talked about making a scrapbook for a child in Chile. Jane grabbed her things and joined her.

"Hi, Mari," Lydia said as they approached.

"Lydia, *cómo estás?* How are the twins?" Mari's big brown eyes sparkled with life, and Jane felt a twinge of envy. Here was a woman who had happiness.

"We're all fine. Learning how to be a family, you know. I was wondering if I could talk to you a little about your scrapbook."

"Sure. I am so intimidated." She leaned forward and placed a small hand on Lydia's arm. "I went to the craft store yesterday and stood in the aisle for a good fifteen minutes, just staring at all the papers. *Ay, caramba.*" Mari threw up her hands in mock despair and laughed. "I don't even know where to start."

"Well, I'm not sure if you know, but a couple of friends and I scrapbook together all the time. We're actually meeting this afternoon, and I was wondering if you'd like to join us."

Lydia smiled as John came over and put his arm around his wife's waist. Jane's heart twisted.

"That sounds like fun." Mari turned to her husband, a thin man whom Jane noticed had been drawing in a journal. "Honey, Lydia was just telling me about some friends of hers who scrapbook. They're getting together this afternoon, and Lydia has invited me to join them. Maybe I *can* produce a scrapbook for the agency."

"Great. Anything that gets me out of learning how to work a

tape runner is fine by me," John said and laughed. "I'll handle all the paperwork, but I leave the creative stuff completely in Mari's hands." He patted Mari's back and headed over to the table where a cup of orange juice remained beside empty donut boxes.

"Well, then it's settled. You'll join us?" Lydia asked.

"Absolutely. Where and what time? Oh, and should I bring something? I bought a few things, but I have no idea how to put them together." Mari rolled her eyes at her own ignorance, and Lydia and Jane smiled.

"Just come over to my place around two. You remember how to get there?"

"I think so. You hosted the Christmas party for the married group last year, right?"

"That was us. I'll just wait on you there, and we'll go over to Mac's together. Sound good?"

"Sounds like a plan."

"See you then."

Lydia and Jane turned to leave the room but were stopped by the Sunday school teacher.

"Lydia, I wanted to come and welcome your friend," he said.

"Oh, sure. Jane, this is Lloyd Meshach," Lydia said. "Lloyd, Jane Sandburg. She's an old friend of mine who recently moved to our area of town. Lloyd moved to Nashville a few years ago."

Jane glanced over the rumpled shirt with its colorful designs and the well-worn Birkenstocks. Put this guy with Leota and she had a beautiful representation of two fabulous decades in recent American history. "Oh? What brought you to Music City?" Jane asked.

"Divorce," Lloyd said bluntly, and Jane stepped back as if she'd been slapped. "Excuse me?"

"Yep, the D word nobody in church is supposed to say." He leaned forward and winked conspiratorially. "It's been seven years and seems like another lifetime ago. Not a lot of folks know it, but I came here to get away from the gossip and rumor mill after my marriage broke up. Adultery makes for a tempting conversational topic for many, especially when you're living in a commune."

Jane shook her head in wonder. "A commune?"

"Oh, yeah. You know, it was the seventies. Peace, love, and the American way, right?" Lloyd said.

"Right." And that was plenty far for a trip down Memory Lane. "Well, it was nice meeting you. We need to go. I've got a dog at home who's probably trying to cross his legs by now."

Lloyd laughed, and Jane noticed a sparkle of mischief in his eye. Lloyd Meshach, she'd bet, kept folks on their toes.

"By all means, hurry home. It was nice meeting you."

"You, too."

"Good seeing you, too, Lydia," he said. "Everything going well with the twins? Are they sleeping through the night yet?"

"Not currently," Lydia said as she gathered up her purse and sermon notes from her chair. "Between them, they were awake most of last night, which is why Dale's not here. He did night duty last night."

Lloyd smiled. "Tell him we missed him, okay?"

"Will do."

Jane and Lydia made their way out of the classroom and into the busy hallway.

"Thanks for asking me to come with you today, by the way. I really didn't want to get out of bed this morning, and after the morning I had, I was pretty sure I needed to crawl back into it and hide, but this has been good."

"Oh, yeah. What happened this morning? You said Wilson got loose or something?"

"Sorry again for being late," Jane said, and Lydia waved her hand in forgiveness.

"Like that's something new." She winked. "Did Wilson get loose?"

"Yep, he treed a cat."

"No!"

"Yep. He took off running, and the leash just popped out of my hand, and off he went. He had that cat up a tree before I could blink. And, to top it all off, the cat's owner was that guy I hit with my car door in the parking lot at the Savvy Scrapper."

"You're kidding, right?" Lydia stopped walking and stared at her in disbelief.

"I wish. I was mortified for about two seconds, and then he opened his mouth. The guy's ego is truly the size of Mount Everest." Jane rolled her eyes as Lydia laughed and started walking again. "He accused me of endangering men and cats, or something like that," Jane continued. "I mean, honestly, what right does he have to accuse me of endangering anything?" Her voice took on an indignant tone.

"Well, you *did* hit him with your car door. And correct me if I'm wrong, but at the time of this conversation, his cat was up in a tree due to a race for its life from your dog?" Lydia tried to hold back laughter and failed miserably.

"Still. He could have been gracious about it. He could have been nice and apologized for not having his cat on a leash or something."

Lydia's laughter grew. "A leash? People don't put cats on leashes."

"Well, some of them do," Jane replied. "Even if he didn't, he could have pretended he should have. But no, he starts talking about me endangering him and his precious cat. I should've let Wilson loose again just to shut him up. Instead, he walks away from me before the conversation is finished, and no matter how nice his backside looked, that's just rude," she finished with triumph.

"He's got a nice butt?" Lydia asked as they arrived at the outside door and stepped into the beautiful sunshine.

"Hey, Mrs. Matchmaker, I'm outraged here. Can you focus on any part of this conversation other than my very brief commentary on the guy's anatomy?"

"Sure—you endanger a guy, he needles you for it and gets under your skin. I'm thinking I may like this guy. Tell me again what he looks like."

"You are so not funny," Jane said. "If I were in the market for a man—and after Mr. Wonderful it would have to be freezing in Dante's eighth before I would even think such a thing— but if I *were* in the market, there is no way on this green earth

I would consider that man for one second. Scratch that—one millisecond. No, one nanosecond of a millisecond." Reaching her car, Jane yanked open the door and threw her purse across to the passenger's seat.

"That's a lot of protesting," Lydia noted with a knowing look.

"I'm only trying to make it exceedingly, abundantly, crystal clear to you that I am not in the market and am in no way interested in this guy. Because I know you."

"Oh, you know me?"

"Yeah, I know you." Jane turned in the open doorway and faced Lydia as she shoved her hair behind her ear. "You think everybody needs to be married to be happy and that being single is akin to being sick. You want to cure everybody, but some of us see marriage as the sickness and want to stay far away from it."

"Marriage is not a sickness." Lydia straightened and turned serious. "Some people get into marriage and sicken it because they have a wrong perception of what it's about. But don't confuse the sick person with the quite healthy institution."

Jane saw the hurt look on Lydia's face and knew she had let her anger over her current situation spill over into her words. "I'm sorry, Lydia. I didn't mean to imply there was something wrong with you for being married."

"No, it's okay." Lydia softened, and her face took on a concerned expression. "I know what you meant. I just want to be sure you know what I meant. Don't give up on marriage just because your first husband was horrible at it, okay?"

"Yeah, yeah, okay." Jane sighed. "Geez, let's go scrap. I need some fun."

"Amen, Sister. I'll head over to Mac's as soon as Mari gets to my house."

chapter 5

Mac *hummed as she opened the drawer and took out a wooden* spoon. She loved baking. She loved everything about it. The work of putting all the ingredients together in just the right order, the waiting for things to rise or bake at the perfect temperature, the anticipation of warm sweetness on her tongue, the smell of baked goods permeating the house. It all made her feel as if there was, indeed, good in the world. For the time that treats were baking in her oven, there was the feeling of home.

She opened a bag of dark chocolate chips and another of mint chocolate chips and dumped them into the cookie batter sitting in a mixing bowl on the counter. As she stirred, Mac gazed out the window and thought back to when Tabby was just a baby and she'd been an eighteen-year-old widow. The feelings of terror and loneliness still came back when she thought about those days with a new baby and a dead husband she had loved with everything inside her. She'd have lost her mind if it hadn't been for the Center those first few weeks.

Mac chuckled as she continued turning the wooden spoon in the batter and thought about the long nights with little sleep that had left her wondering if she was simply living a nightmare that would end if only she could wake up. She remembered showing up at the grocery store wearing two different colored socks and two different kinds of shoes and not having a clue how she got there.

It had turned out all right, she supposed. Tabby was a good girl deep down, who just had a hard time staying on the right path when she was surrounded by the wrong people. But surely all that would change now that Tabby had Kesa.

"Yessir, Lord," Mac said aloud. "My Tabby's been plowin' some crooked rows, but she knows how to make 'em straight." Mac nodded her head. "Let this baby be her reason to plow straight, sweet Jesus. Keep my baby in Your hands while she raises this new baby, Kesa, and use me however you see fit." Mac stopped stirring and set the bowl down. Reaching under the counter, she pulled out two cookie sheets and began dropping the dough onto them in small clumps.

She hummed as her fingers pushed each new dollop of dough onto the sheet. All the ingredients were there; they just had to go through the fire to become complete. She filled the two sheets, then nodded in satisfaction and licked her fingers. After placing them into the oven, she bent low to look into its window. Yes, just a little heat and they would rise to the occasion, filling the room with the sweet scents of mint and home.

She straightened and headed to the sink to begin washing the dishes.

"Just a bit of fire, Jesus. That's all my Tabby needs. She'll come out the other side shinin' like gold, I just know. I'm askin' you to hold her hand through that fire, Lord. It ain't easy, but it's worth it, I sure do know. Just a bit of fire."

Mac picked up her humming again and tried to strengthen her resolve to let her baby fall a little bit so she would learn what it was like to hurt as a result of her own choices. This was going to be a hard row to hoe, letting Tabby fall without little Kesa having to hurt.

"And, Jesus," she added, "I'd really appreciate you holdin' my hand, too."

The phone rang, and Mac dried her hands on a dishtowel as she made her way to the phone hanging on the kitchen wall.

"Hello?"

"Will you accept a call from the Davidson County Jail?"

Mac's heart sank as the familiar words came through the line. When would Tabby get her act together?

"Yes, I will." She waited as the connection was made, and then her daughter's voice came through.

"Momma?"

"What happened, Tabby?" She waited for the sad tale that Tabby was sure to weave, just as she had done countless times before. The phone calls were getting fewer and farther between, but, Lord, when would they taper off completely?

"Momma, I swear I wasn't doing anything this time. I was with Leticia, and we decided to go get our nails done out at

Sammy's at the mall, but we had to wait 'cause the good guy had a line of women waitin' a mile long. So we went across and were looking at clothes, and Ticia grabbed a shirt when I wasn't looking. I swear I didn't know, Momma, but she put it in my bag, and the cop thought I did it."

"How much is bail?" The words changed, but the story stayed the same.

"Three hundred dollars," Tabby said.

"I'll be down in a little bit. I've got some cookies in the oven for the Sisters. They're comin' over this afternoon." She strung the telephone cord across the kitchen and opened the drawer for the Saran Wrap. No sense in letting the rest of the cookie dough go to waste.

"Oh, thank you, Momma. I promise I'm on the right path, and I wasn't doing anything this time, honest."

Mac heard cursing and yelling in the background and closed her eyes at the thought that once again her baby girl was amid criminals.

"It's just they're holding my past against me, and when the judge saw all that stuff from before Kesa, he just looked at me like he knew I was guilty and set the bail."

Mac rolled her eyes. As if Tabby had any reason to wonder why someone would hold her past against her. "Where's Kesa?"

"She's at Mama Ray's. They took her to church this morning."

Well, at least the baby was being exposed to the right path, even if her mama was spending Sunday morning in jail.

"Why weren't you in church this mornin'?"

"I *told* you, Momma. Me and Ticia wanted to get our nails done. Are you listening to me?"

"I'm listenin', child. I'm listenin' to way more than you seem to be listenin' to. I'll be down in a little while."

Mac sighed deeply as she hung up the phone. Tabby probably was innocent in this particular instance, which made her feel a little better about the situation. She'd been doing really well, staying off the drugs ever since finding out she was pregnant with Kesa. The phone calls for bail money had gotten fewer and farther between, a fact Mac was more than grateful for.

"She's just got no sense when it comes to friends, Jesus," Mac mumbled as she checked on the cookies. "Can you send her some new friends? Some that don't do drugs and who manage to pay for things before they walk out the store?" She reached into the drawer by the oven and pulled out a pot holder. A blast of heat hit her face as she opened the oven door and reached in for cookies that were just beginning to brown on top.

As she set the tray on a cooling rack by the sink, it occurred to her that timing really was everything. A few seconds longer, and the cookies would have been bitter and burned. A few seconds earlier would have given her a soggy mess. Maybe Tabby needed to sit for a few more minutes in that jail, though the thought of it made Mac's heart twist. Prostitutes and drug dealers were, no doubt, Tabby's cell mates.

She tossed the pot holder back into its drawer and slammed it closed. "Leave her be or rescue her again, Lord?" she asked out loud, knowing the blessing of a note with written instructions

47

dropping down from heaven wasn't going to come. She sighed and pulled a minispatula from the yellow ceramic pot by the stove.

Timing. Everything was about timing. Pull her out of jail too early and she might not learn the lesson the Almighty was trying to teach her by landing her there in the first place. Pull her out too late and her heart might harden.

She scooped the cookies onto a plate and made up her mind. "Just give me a flat tire, Lord, if You need a few minutes longer in that jail cell. Or else put a scrapbook sale right smack in my path. That worked before, remember? And I got my good Sister Lydia outta that deal."

chapter 6

Jane pulled up to her apartment building and put the car in Park.
She rubbed the blisters on her aching feet and picked her shoes
up out of the floorboard. There was no way she would be able
to put them back on, even to walk the few feet to her front
door. Looking around, she couldn't see anyone to witness her
barefooted dash across the sidewalk and down the open breezeway to her apartment. Bundling her purse up with her shoes,
she held everything close to her chest and stepped out of the car.

So far, so good.

Dashing to her door, she jammed the key into the lock,
already sending up words of thanks as she heard the deadbolt
snick back out of place.

"Lost your shoes?" Her heart hit her toes. Of course he
would be here. She turned, holding up her shoes as evidence.

"No, I have them right here. It seemed they were better on my hands than rubbing blisters on my feet, though."

He grinned and her heart flip-flopped. *He has a cat, Jane.*

"I see. Sunday-sermon shoes?"

"How do you know about Sunday-sermon shoes?"

"Now, if I answered that, how would I be the mysterious stranger living across the hall from you?"

"Oh, we're going for mysterious stranger status? Well, then I should go inside before I endanger the little story you've got going here." She waggled her fingers at him. "Ta ta."

Twisting the old knob, she entered her apartment and closed the door, eliciting barks from Wilson.

"I'm coming, Wilson. It's just me, no terrifying strangers to kill or maim." She struggled inside on her aching feet and walked into the bedroom, dropping the offending shoes on the bed and making her way around it to the dog crate. The latches creaked as she loosened them to free her Houdini mutt. "Guess crate number four did the trick, hmm, little guy? You thought you had me on those first three, but I've found the invincible crate now."

She let the last latch loose, and Wilson raced out of the room, tail wagging furiously all the way. Jane straightened and began changing out of her church clothes. *Ah, the bliss of being loosed from restrictive clothing.* Stretching, she reached for her jeans and a T-shirt as she heard Wilson scratching at the front door to go out.

"I'm coming, buddy. Just a second." She finished her quick change and grabbed the leash.

"Now, there will be no chasing of the cats this time, got it, mister?" she said with as much authority as she could. "Mommy's had just about enough embarrassment for one day." She was positive her feet sighed in relief and gratitude as she slipped them into comfy flip-flops and snapped the leash onto Wilson's collar. "I mean it, dog." She looked into Wilson's big brown eyes. "No funny business." Wilson panted at her and looked toward the door. "Oh, all right. Let's go."

As soon as she opened the heavy door, Wilson tugged her across the breezeway and toward the bright sunshine and grass. She scanned the field for any cats and, noting the lack of any other animal within viewing distance, loosened her grip on Wilson's leash as they walked toward the pond.

It was a beautiful day. March in Middle Tennessee was always a guessing game. Some days the skies were covered with gray and the wet was so heavy it seeped right down into a person's bones. But then there were days like today, when the sun was so bright it hurt, and there was the tiniest hint of warmth in the air, like a little whisper from spring that promised it would come soon. Jane tilted her head up toward the sun and smiled. Sunshine on her face. It seemed like eons had passed since she'd felt the sunshine on her face.

Stopping beneath the very tree Wilson had run the cat up earlier that morning, Jane folded her legs and sat down. The bark of the old tree felt rough against her T-shirt. Her fingers felt soft little shoots of grass, proof of spring's promise. The trees were showing the barest hint of life again. Tiny little buds would become huge canopies of leaves in another month.

A gaggle of geese flew over her head, honking loudly and flying in perfect *V* formation. "Bet their mates don't leave them," she muttered, hooking Wilson's leash on her flip-flop and folding her arms across her chest. "No e-mistresses to worry about. Just fly, eat, rest, and repeat." Jane sighed and shook her head. She was too young for this. Women in their twenties who had the world by the tail should not find themselves dumped for a virtual woman and left to start over with an empty apartment and a dog.

A breeze kicked up and blew strands of hair across her face. She reached up to jerk them behind her ear. Hearing her sigh, Wilson ceased his sniffing and came to sit beside her. As he nuzzled his way under her hand, Jane absentmindedly petted him and looked back up into the tree. Those little buds were easy to miss if a body didn't look closely. But they were there, just the same. It'd been a year, and maybe, just maybe, Sisters, Ink was a new bud of life for her.

"You know, we have to stop meeting like this," he called across the field and felt his heart flip when she turned. He had been watching her for a few minutes, noting the slump of defeat in her shoulders, the heavy sigh, and the comfort her dog was giving.

"What?"

Wow, she looked worn-out.

"I said, we have to stop meeting like this." He continued across the new grass, closing the distance between them. "People are going to start talking about us, and then I'll have to tell them about how dangerous you are, though I don't even know your name." He smiled and held out his hand as he came to a stop in front of her. "Hi, I'm Jake Cline."

She took his hand and shook it. He was pretty sure that was due to years of learned manners since her eyes telegraphed how unhappy she was with his presence.

"Jane." Her back straightened, and her eyes took on a wary look. "And this is Wilson." She let go of his hand and gestured toward the canine still sitting at her side. Though Wilson's gaze was now fixed on Jake, his stance was a mirror image of Jane's.

Her voice was like silk, even laced with tension and fatigue. He smiled, hoping to set her at ease.

"Where's your cat?"

"Major Carter? She's taking her afternoon siesta." He pointed back toward his apartment.

"Major Carter?" He noticed the little wrinkle of confusion that formed on her forehead, and his smile grew.

"As in *Stargate SG-1*?" Okay, so she wasn't a sci-fi buff. That could be remedied with a few Friday nights in front of the TV.

"Um, sure. I know a little about it. My ex watched it all the time."

There was definitely a land mine in there somewhere.

"Well, then, we must remedy the situation at the earliest possible convenience."

Her eyebrows rose up. "What situation, exactly, are we remedying?"

"Your flawed *Stargate* experience that has left you with the mistaken impression that it is anything less than a stellar show." He noticed the dog had dropped the wary look and was now licking his right shoe. That had to be a good sign.

Jane tilted her head and looked at him with what he hoped was amusement, and he hurried on. "*Stargate* is a really good show that should be viewed with an objective eye—not one clouded by the stench of the company, excuse me, *ex*-company, within viewing range." He knelt down and scratched the dog behind the ears.

"So what's your remedy?" She was laughing at him now. Laughing was good, much better than defeat. The sparkle in her eyes was amazing. Who had taken that from her?

"It's Sunday. *Stargate* will be on in five short days. It comes on Friday nights at seven p.m., so we'll need to start dinner around six. Sound good? I make a mean spaghetti."

She studied him for a few minutes, and he did his best to appear honest and trustworthy, opening his eyes wide just like all the detective novels said. After all, he was asking her out, and he'd barely even learned her name, though Wilson had now rolled onto his back and offered his tummy. He kept scratching, hoping the dog's approval would translate to hers.

"You're on." He opened his mouth, but she held up her hand and went on. "But only because I'm usually dead on my feet by Friday, and the idea of somebody else making dinner—no cleaning up after dinner—is worthy of suffering through some horrible sci-fi show."

She grinned at him, and his heart pounded a bit harder. Who

cared why she was coming, so long as she was coming? He'd give her a night off from all that stress and have some great company to boot. Not a bad trade-off for some cooking and cleaning.

"Great. See you at my place. I'm that door there." He pointed to the last door across the breezeway from her. "I better get back to Major Carter. Her claws and my couch aren't best friends."

He made a getaway before she could change her mind. At the edge of the field, he turned and noted with satisfaction the disappearance of defeat from her profile. It shouldn't matter that much to him—he knew he had no business letting a woman matter at all to him, much less one with a dog that might never be able to accept his cat.

She threw back her head, and that long black hair swung free.

Major Carter could deal.

Jane stared into the tree's maze of limbs and knew she had to be losing her ever-loving mind. Having interest in a man—*any* man, especially that *chauvinistic* man—was the last thing she needed. What was she thinking? And he was a sci-fi fan. Ugh. Bill had given her more than enough of those stupid shows with horrible makeup, bad acting, and unbelievable story lines. It had been one of the things she hadn't missed after her move. And now she was going back to it just for a free dinner and no cleaning? Yes, the mind had definitely taken a detour from reality.

But the show was only an hour. And she needed to get to know her neighbors anyway. The next time the bright idea of moving furniture came in the middle of the night or she was staring at Wilson's forty pounds of dog food, wondering how to get it from Blazer to apartment, he'd come in handy. Every girl needed a heavy lifter in her life, and since Bill had taken his muscles with him to the e-mistress, she might as well get to know her neighbor. One dinner and one more horrendous episode of *Stargate SG-1* would not kill her. Right after, she could be on her way, heavy labor secured for the future.

A smile crossed Jane's face. This was a pretty good idea.

"Don't get any ideas, boy." She looked into Wilson's sorrowful basset eyes and patted his head. "Your momma has no interest in men. She's happy and satisfied with her girlfriends. But you put me in a bad position by chasing his cat this morning, so I'm going to go make nice. We might need him to carry your dog food one day."

Wilson licked her hand as she stood up and began making her way back to the apartment, leash tightly in hand and thoughts firmly in place. At the breezeway, the dog stopped to sniff a rock just as she heard the University of Kentucky fight song. She rushed inside her apartment to the kitchen wall and grabbed the phone, cutting the battle cry off in midring.

"Hello?"

"Jane?"

"Yeah, Lydia. It's me." The leash clicked open as she pushed its lever and a freed Wilson walked over to his water bowl.

"Mari's here, and we're going to head on over to Mac's. Are you ready?" The SportsCenter music blared in the background.

"Sure. Let me put Wilson back in his crate, and I'll grab my stuff and head on over."

"Great. Be careful. See you there."

"You too. Bye."

She hung up the phone and turned the ringer volume down on the side. "No need making the whole apartment building listen to the UK fight song, right, Wilson?" He stopped lapping water and looked at her. "Crate, boy." Wilson turned and sauntered off toward the bedroom. Now, why couldn't men be that obedient?

Her cell phone rang just as she was securing the last latch on Wilson's crate. She dashed back into the living room and snatched it up off the end table.

"Jane Sandburg."

"Jane, darling, it's Sonya!"

Jane gritted her teeth and reminded herself to check the freaking caller ID before answering next time. "Hi, Sonya. How are things in Europe?"

"Marvelous, as usual; thank you for asking. I saw the most fabulous scarf in Hermès this morning and have just this minute decided I simply must go back for it. You would not *believe* how soft that silk is. I'll just have to get you one as well. Would you like blue or green?"

"Oh, Sonya, there's no need for that. But thank you for thinking of me. Was there something I could do for you?" Directing Sonya in a phone conversation was a lot like herding cats.

"I was just calling to check on your plans for our fall banquet, darling. Is everything in order for the most fabulous fund-raiser Nashville has seen this year?"

Jane tried not to panic as thousands of details pushed themselves up from the back of her brain. Nothing was confirmed yet, though telling Sonya that would come right after snow cones started being served in the lake of fire.

"Everything is on task, Sonya, no worries at all," she assured the heiress currently sitting as president of the board of Nashville's largest charity. "I should have some ideas to run by you when you get home."

"Marvelous. I knew I could count on you. I just couldn't get the fund-raiser off my mind, and Harry said, 'Sonya, call Jane, and she'll tell you everything's fine so you can enjoy your trip.' I suppose he was right. You'll let me know if anything arises that needs my attention?"

"Of course. Thank you so much for checking in with me."

"Ta ta."

"Bye, Sonya." Jane snapped the phone shut and wondered if spending time scrapping at Mac's was wise with so many details still left to handle for Sonya and work not even started for Leota. She looked longingly at her wheeled tote standing silent sentinel by the front door. It would just be a couple of hours, and pulling a late night wouldn't be bad payment for time spent with the Sisters.

chapter 7

✻ · ✻ · ✻ · ✻ · ✻ · ✻ · ✻

Mac saw Lydia's car turn in to her cul-de-sac and took a deep breath. Pushing thoughts of yesteryear into the recesses of her mind, she got up and checked on the second batch of mint chocolate-chip cookies in the oven. They were still a few minutes shy of light golden. She reached in the cupboard and pulled down four tall glasses, then turned to the refrigerator to get the milk.

The jail had been as dark and depressing as it was every time she went to bail out Tabby, and Mac knew few better ways to feel better than munching on one of her grandmother's mint chocolate-chip cookies with a tall glass of milk in the other hand and plans to scrap in the near future.

The energy to welcome a new woman into their scrapping group seemed far away right now. "You brought her here, Jesus. Give me the strength to let her know she's welcome."

"Mac? We're here," Lydia called out as she came through the cheery white front door.

"In the kitchen. Come on back." Mac smiled and stood as Lydia entered the kitchen, followed by a short, brown-haired woman with ruddy cheeks and a ready smile. "You must be Mari."

"Hi, MacKenzie," Mari said and came across the kitchen to shake Mac's hand. "Lydia has told me a lot about you. Thanks so much for having me in your home."

"Child, the pleasure is mine." Surprising, but true. "Sunday afternoon's a perfect time for work, in my book. There ain't no better way to rest, I say."

"Work? I thought we were going to scrapbook." She looked to Lydia for an explanation.

"Mac, Jane, and I have started a new business called Sisters, Ink." She explained the concept to Mari, and Mari giggled. "Count me in, *amigas!*"

"What smells so good? Are you making mint cookies?" Lydia's nose lifted as she sniffed the air. "All right, spill. What'd Tabby do now?"

Mac sighed, heading over to the oven to retrieve the cookies. "I was makin' 'em before she even called this time. Tabby called from the jail a couple hours ago."

"Oh, Mac." Sympathy laced Lydia's voice.

"I've already gone and gotten her out. I don't think she did anything this time, but you know I can't ever be sure with that child." Mac turned the dial on the oven to zero degrees and pulled the dishtowel from its hook. The blast of heat reminded her of that morning's conversation as she pulled the cookies out.

"She's gotten in trouble before?" Mari asked in a small voice.

Mac rolled her eyes, setting the tray on top of a cooling rack. "She got a rap sheet as long as this kitchen." She hung the towel back on its rack. "Tabby's been tryin' to fly right since she had baby Kesa. She just doin' right with the wrong people, and they bring her down. You know what I mean?"

"Yes, I do," Mari said.

"So what was it this time?" Lydia asked.

Mac told them both about the shoplifting charge and then shook her shoulders. "That's enough depressin' stuff for right now. It's a work day; let's work." She pulled glasses out of the cabinet. "You like milk with your cookies, Mari?"

"Oh, I really shouldn't." Mari rubbed her tummy. "This thing keeps expanding every day. If I don't watch it, people are going to think I *had* another baby instead of adopting one."

"Well, neither should I, but I pulled my baby outta jail just a little while ago, and I need some sugar to make it through my afternoon. Besides, I always drink milk with my cookies, and I haven't had any calcium yet today, so this is just a good way to take care of my health."

"Hmm, when you put it like that, then I see the wisdom of the cookie. Yes, I'd love some milk."

Mac winked at her. "Gotta take care of them bones, right?"

Mari smiled. "*Sí.*"

"Y'all go ahead and take your stuff upstairs while I get these out and on a plate. I'll bring 'em up with some cold milk, and we'll get started. Is Jane comin'?" She picked up a pot holder from the counter and turned to get the cookies out of the oven.

"I called her before I left." Lydia and Mari turned toward the stairs. "She was putting Wilson up and then heading this way. You know Jane, always late."

"Yoo-hoo. Are y'all talking about me?" Jane came into the kitchen, wheeling her tote behind just as Mac set the tray of cookies on the cooling rack. "Can't leave you girls alone for a minute and you're telling stories about me." Jane grinned at Lydia and then saw the tray of cookies.

"Oh, *yum*. I love cookies. They're horrible on my waistline but heaven for my taste buds. Mac, you're the absolute best in the world. My day just got infinitely better."

Mac laughed at Jane's childlike exuberance. "Go on up with Lydia and Mari and get your stuff settled. I'll bring these up with some milk."

"Whatever the cookie lady says, I do." Jane saluted and turned on her heel toward the stairs. "Can I bring anything up for you? I've got a free hand."

"Sure." Mac arranged the glasses on a tray in short order and handed it to Jane. "You sure you can handle this tray with one hand?" She gave Jane a doubtful look.

"No problem. I've got it." Jane began gingerly going up the stairs, balancing the tray in one hand and pulling her Tutto tote up each step so as not to topple the glasses.

"Okay, you be careful. I'll be right up." Mac watched for a few seconds to be sure Jane did, indeed, have it under control.

Then she turned back to the cookies, hesitated, and popped one into her mouth. "Guess this just means I need more milk!"

Jane entered the scrapping room and exhaled in relief as she handed the tray of glasses off to Lydia.

"Wow, a scrapper *and* glass balancer. You could take that show on the road," Lydia said.

"I think I'll keep my day job." Jane began unpacking all of her scrapbooking materials. She stopped and turned to Mari. "Hi, I'm Jane, by the way. I'm not sure if you remember, but I was with Lydia at church this morning."

Mari smiled and reached across the table to shake the hand Jane was offering. "Mari. I remember."

"So I understand you're starting a scrapbook for your adoption agency?" Jane asked as she turned back to the task of unpacking and began setting out paper, stamp sets, eyelets, rub-on words, and punches. As usual, she'd packed too much stuff.

"Mm-hmm. We're in the process of adopting a daughter from Chile. We need to create a scrapbook of our family life so the agency can give it to the orphanage to be shared with our prospective adoptee. That way, she'll be a little familiar with us by the time we pick her up."

"That is such an incredible idea," Jane said. "She'll know what faces to look for in the crowd when you get there. Brilliant."

"Well, brilliant in theory, I guess." Mari's voice was soft as she watched Jane and Lydia pull out their tools and materials.

"*Ave Maria!* All this stuff! I didn't realize scrapbooking could get so involved." Jane set a big punch on the table. "I have no idea where to start." Lydia plopped a stack of paper in three different shades of blue and pink on the table. "I just know I want to make the best scrapbook possible for *mi hija*. I'm hoping you girls can help me out with that."

"Where there's a will, there's a way." Lydia blew her hair out of her eyes. "Anything you see on this table or in this room is open for your use." She waved her hand to encompass everything. "Don't hesitate to use our stuff or ask questions. Mac is the most experienced of all of us, but we can each help you out."

"You bet." Jane tucked her hair behind her ears. "I've just done one other scrapbook, so I'm a great source for knowing what not to do." She laughed. "Have you settled on a color scheme yet? It will make things easier if you know which two or three colors you'd like to see on every page."

"I didn't even realize there *were* color schemes."

"No worries," Lydia replied. "You should see my first book. I go from bolds to pastels to earth tones to monochrome black as fast as you can turn the page. I cringe every time I look at the thing, but you've got to start somewhere, right?"

"*Exactamente.*"

"Okay, then let's pick two colors that will appear on every page." Both Lydia and Jane watched Mari as she tapped her fingers on the table and tilted her head in thought.

"When I think of Chile, I think of red and orange. You know, big bold colors, like the skirts the women wear that flow out when they're dancing," Mari said.

"Great." Lydia pulled two more stacks of paper from her tote and pushed them across the table to Mari. "Then we'll use those colors as the theme of the scrapbook."

"But aren't those two colors too bold for a little girl?" Mari picked up the packs of red and orange paper.

"Nah," Jane said. "They're the colors that her mommy thinks of when she thinks of her. I think that's a great reason to use them."

"Okay, then red and orange it is. Maybe we can mix some white and yellow in along the way to soften it up?"

"Perfect," Lydia said. "I have a ton of it, so grab what you want. Jane, Mac, and I can sort through our printed and textured papers to see if we have anything that would work with your color scheme."

Mari stared as Jane and Lydia began sliding more sheets of paper across the table to her. She reached down beside her chair and retrieved a box full of photos.

"Um, *chicas*, I think I need some help here." Mari gave a bewildered look at a box crammed with photos. "How do I know where to start?"

"That's always the hardest part for a new scrapper," Mac said as she arrived at the top of the stairs with a plate piled high with cookies in one hand and a gallon of milk in the other. "I always start by grouping and ordering."

"Grouping. Of course, grouping . . . What's grouping?"

"I put the pictures into groups according to events. Birthdays, anniversaries, parties, and other events. Then I arrange the events in the order they happened." Mac set the plate of cookies in the middle of the table and took the cap off of the gallon of milk. She began filling each glass and passing them around the table.

"Okay." Mari took her glass. "Most of my pictures are from the past month. Everywhere John, Emmy, and I went, I took a picture so little Andrea would get a chance to see our everyday lives. So I guess I need to put those in order now, yes?" She took a drink.

"Yes." Mac handed a glass to Jane.

"Got it. Then what do I do with these pictures of my parents and John's parents?" She waved them in the air.

"Did you take them this month?" Mac filled another glass and handed it across the table to Lydia.

"No, they're older pictures. I wanted to include them so Andrea can meet her *abuelos*." Mari reached out and took a cookie from the plate.

"How about putting them at the end?" Lydia said around a mouthful of cookie. "You could do a section of 'Meet Your Extended Family' or something and put pictures of grandparents, cousins, aunts, and uncles."

"Oh, I like that idea." Mari began pulling photos out of the box and putting them in the suggested groupings and order. "I don't know how in the world I would have done this without you ladies."

"Well, I'm glad you don't have to find out," Lydia said, taking a drink of milk as Jane and Mac nodded their agreement.

For a while, the sound of paper cutters and eyelet setters combined with Mac's humming as each woman worked on her scrapbook. Slowly, their layouts emerged from the different scraps of paper and embellishments. Jane looked up from her work and snagged another cookie from the plate in the middle of the table.

She sat back on her stool and took a drink of milk, considering the layout on which she was working. Wilson was lying beside her suitcase, his massive basset head resting on the handle. In the background of the photo her apartment seemed to be a state of chaos. There were blurry boxes and what looked like packing tape and markers.

Jane picked up the picture and contemplated the state of her scrapbook for the thousandth time. In twenty years, would she want to look back on this stuff? Would she even want to remember these dark days of packing up her entire existence and moving to a place of her own because her husband had chosen his e-mistress over her? And if she wouldn't want to look back on it, then why was she bothering to scrapbook it in the first place?

She sighed and put the picture back into its position in the layout. Wilson's expression didn't match the glee pronounced by the bones dancing across the paper in the background.

"Problem?" Lydia reached for a cookie of her own and looked at Jane's layout.

"No, I guess not." Jane tucked her hair behind her ear and sighed again.

"The layout looks good. Maybe add some black ribbon behind that main picture to tie it to the journaling."

Jane unzipped the pocket in her tote that held ribbon and pulled out the black. She measured across the page and cut the ribbon to its appropriate length, then put the ribbon in the place Lydia had suggested.

"You're right. That's an improvement."

"Good. Glad to help." Lydia brushed the cookie crumbs from her lap and went back to her own layout.

"So, have we gotten any hits on the Sisters, Ink site?" Lydia said.

Mac walked over to the laptop and sat down. "I'll check. I was just on here last night, puttin' in a new page about us. I thought other ladies might wanna know how this whole thing got started."

"Good idea, Mac!" Jane said. "We'll need to add Mari's picture to our little group. Did you see where I put a picture of the United States on the site? I'm hoping we can add little scrapping groups all over the country, and people visiting the site can just click on their part of the country to find each other. What do y'all think?"

"I think whatever we're doin' is workin'. We've got fifteen women signed up already. How'd word get out that fast?"

Jane grinned. "I may have made a few phone calls to some scrapbook store owners I know."

Lydia shook her head. "Our Jane, always the businesswoman."

"It's not just about business, though, Lydia. I don't know how I would have gotten through the past year without you and Mac cheering me on. I didn't realize how much I missed my girlfriends—needed my girlfriends—until I hooked back up with you gals."

"Well, then, I'm glad we were here for you." Lydia took a drink of milk. "So, Mari, do you know how long it will be until you get—what did you say her name would be?" Lydia reached for a package of silver baby booties to add to her page and pulled it open with her teeth. She picked out one of the pairs of booties and began running a pink ribbon through it.

"Andrea Marinilda. It's a tradition in our *familia.* My mother goes by Andrea, *mi abuela* by Nilda. I remember when we named Esmerelda, my mom threw a fit because I was breaking the tradition. I always thought I'd just name the next one after us. Who knew I wouldn't be able to have another? Anyway, now that we've gotten her picture, it won't be long at all." Mari kept sorting through pictures. "We should get our travel date in the next six weeks or so. Then we'll travel to Chile about four weeks after that."

"Wow! So you'll have her sometime in late spring or early summer?" Lydia ran a blue ribbon through another pair of silver booties and began fastening them to the page underneath Oliver's picture.

"Hopefully." Mari looked up from her pictures with a dreamy expression on her face. "I can't believe we're almost to the end of this process. It's been over a year since John and I first filled out the paperwork to adopt."

"Have you talked to Emmy about having a little sister?" Jane asked.

"We've tried to." A worried expression crossed Mari's face for an instant. Then she smiled. "I don't think she'll understand until we actually have her little sister. We've told her, though, that we'll all be going on a very long trip so that we can pick up her *hermanita.* And we've shown her Andrea's picture."

"Well, it sounds like you've covered all the bases," Lydia

said in a reassuring tone. She opened up a box full of alphabet brads and began picking out the letters to spell Olivia and Oliver. "I'm sure Emmy will welcome Andrea with open arms when you get to Chile."

"I hope so," Mari said. "She's in that stage where everything is hers and no one under the sun can help her do anything. I'm a little worried about her sharing her room. We've told her, of course, but we haven't put a baby bed or anything in the room yet, since we just got the details." Mari reached for a cookie and nibbled at its edge. "We'll pull Emmy's stuff down out of the attic next week and set it up for Andrea." She took a sip of milk. "I think that might be the reality check for Emmy."

"Now, there's a scrapbooking moment. Setting up the nursery," Lydia said. "Maybe I could bring the twins over just so Emmy gets an idea of what it's like to have other kiddos in the house."

"That might be a good idea. I'll talk it over with John. *Gracias.*"

"Done," Jane said with satisfaction as she began putting her layout of Moving Day into page protectors.

"Ooh, can I see?" Mari asked. Jane turned the pages around to Mari's side of the table and smiled when Mari pointed and laughed at Wilson's expression.

"I've never seen a dog with such an expressive face. He looks like he just lost his best friend. Were you going on a trip?"

"I was packing up and moving," Jane explained. "This was the day after I found out Bill had an e-mistress and the afternoon of the morning he decided to go to her. I just couldn't stomach staying in our home another night, so I packed it all up in a day and left that night."

"Oh, I'm so sorry." Mari's face radiated concern. "*Que idiota soy. No puedo creer que dije eso.*"

"Um, I was with you there until the end."

Mari smiled and ducked her head. "I was reminding myself I can be an idiot sometimes."

"No, it's okay. It's been a year, and I'm pretty sure I'm over the worst of it. Wilson and I are settling into our new life. I can't say I'm loving it yet or anything, but at least I have the bed all to myself, and if I want to dance naked in my living room, I just remember to close the blinds."

"Did you have kids?"

"Nope, just Wilson and me. It's the only thing we fought over when we split—who got to keep the dog." Jane smiled ruefully.

"Well, I'm glad you got him."

"Me too. He keeps my feet warm at night." Jane began putting her things away. "Speaking of which, I hate to run, but I need to get home and let him outside." She stuffed boxes of eyelets into the zippers on the side. She also needed to get to work on Sonya's fund-raiser.

"No problem," Mac said. "You know, you can bring him with you whenever you come to scrap. I'm bettin' we'll be spendin' lots of hours on this site"—she nodded at the laptop—"in the coming weeks."

"I hope you're right." Jane put away the last of her stuff and zipped up the tote. "Well, ladies, it's been a pleasure as always."

"Wait." Lydia put out her hand to stop Jane's exit. "We need to figure out when we're scrapping again. Is Friday okay with everybody?"

"I can't," Mari said. "That's John's sci-fi night, and I'll need to watch Emmy so he can watch his shows."

"John's a sci-fi guy?" Jane said.

"*Chica*, like you wouldn't believe. I'm just happy all the shows come on together in one night." Mari put the lid back on her now organized box of photos. "*Stargate SG-1*, *Stargate Atlantis*, then *Battlestar Galactica* and his television watching is all filled in one night." She patted the top of the photo box.

"What is it with guys and sci-fi?" Jane ran a hand through her hair. "I have to watch *SG-1* with my neighbor on Friday. I think he might be as fanatical as John."

"You're watching sci-fi with a man?" Lydia asked. "Explain, missy. Who's the mystery man?"

"Remember the guy I hit in the parking lot? The guy that lives in my building?"

"The one whose cat your dog terrorized?"

"He did not terrorize that cat." Jane smacked the tabletop. "I'm telling you, the cat should have been on a leash."

"Wait, wait, wait." Mac put her hands up to stop the volley of conversation. "I think Mari and I are a bit behind. What man? What cat? And why is this the first I'm hearing of either?"

Jane explained to them her mishaps with Jake. "So I agreed to watch sci-fi with him this Friday," she finished.

"You're watching sci-fi? Seriously? Have you gone over to

the Dark Side?" Lydia asked, her voice full of disbelief. "Can't you find some other way to befriend a man? Maybe take him cookies or something? I'm sure any guy would carry Wilson's dog food if he tasted your homemade lasagna. Or take him some of Mac's cookies." She gestured to the plate that now held precious few cookies. "Though you'd have to make some more to go with these."

Why didn't I leave that part out?

"It's not just that. It's a free dinner on Friday that I don't have to clean up after. The thought of not having the Inner Dinner Debate for one night is nothing to be sneezed at."

"Inner Dinner Debate?" Mari said.

"You know, 'Do I go out? Or do I stay in and try to make something, then have to clean it all up?'"

"Sure, sister, that's why you agreed to watch television with a guy whose rear end you've already decided isn't hard on the eyes," Lydia said. "Oh, what a tangled web we weave."

"You checked him out?" Mari asked incredulously. "You left that part out."

"No, I did not check him out." Jane glared at Lydia. "I categorically deny any and all references I may or may not have made to this man's body. He's good-looking, yes, but I am only doing this for the free meal."

"And possible future heavy lifting," Lydia added with a smirk.

"Yes, and that." Jane pulled the retractable handle up on her tote. "So I can't scrap on Friday because I'll be busy securing a solution to my future heavy-lifting needs." She tossed her hair back over her shoulder. "So how about Saturday?"

"Saturday works for me," Lydia said. "We'll of course want to know all about your nondate on Friday."

"Saturday's good," Mac said. "Let's say ten?"

Everyone agreed, and Jane made her way to the stairs, her Tutto trailing along behind.

"Have a good week, y'all."

"You too," they chorused, and Jane began walking down the stairs, realizing halfway down that balancing her vacillating emotions required much more skill than the tray of glasses had on the way up.

chapter 8

❋ · ❋ · ❋ · ❋ · ❋ · ❋ · ❋

Jane opened the freezer door and reached in for some ice cubes just as the beginning notes of the UK song sounded. She'd been home from Mac's for an hour and had made some pretty good headway on the fund-raiser for Sonya, even settling on a jungle theme. Maybe ignoring the call would be the best option. She dropped cubes into the glass, then pulled a pitcher of tea from the refrigerator door. Getting back into work and ignoring her personal life felt good.

A quick glance at the caller ID made Jane change her mind, and she snatched up the phone just as it was getting to the good part. "Hello?"

"Hey, Jane. It's Lydia."

"Hey, girl. Still scrapping?"

Lydia laughed. "I left Mac's about three minutes ago.

That's why I'm calling. I was wondering if you were home and would like some company for a little while."

Jane set her cold glass on the counter. Why wasn't Lydia going home after—Jane glanced at the clock on the wall—two and a half hours of scrapping at Mac's? Didn't the twins need to be fed? Or was there trouble in Lydia's paradise?

"Sure, I'm here the rest of the day, trying to get caught up with work. Is everything okay?"

"Oh, yeah, it's fine. I'm just needing a little more girlfriend time before heading home to Mr. Sports, you know?"

Jane remembered all the nights she had stayed up late with a book, waiting for Bill to come to bed and knowing it would be hours before he was finished with whatever computer game he was playing or sci-fi show he was watching. "Gotcha. Head on over."

"Great, thanks." Lydia's voice was full of relief, and Jane's gut twinged a bit. There was trouble in paradise.

Twenty minutes later, the knock at Jane's door set Wilson off to barking.

"Hush, dog." Jane dashed down the hallway from her office. "It's just Lydia. You know Lydia." Wilson held his position by the door, his wagging tail incongruous with a fearsome bark that reverberated off the walls. "You know, one of these days you really *will* scare off an intruder." She smiled at the dog and opened the door.

"Hi," Jake said, taking Jane's breath with his unexpected presence. "I was hoping you'd be home by now."

Okay, nevermind. He has a cat, and if it didn't work out, you'd

have to move. "Oh! Yeah, I'm home. Just, you know, getting caught up on work." Jane cringed at her own ineptitude. Why did all ability for intelligent conversation leave her mind the moment this man stepped into her sight?

Jake smiled and Jane fidgeted. "Was there something you needed?"

"What?" Jake's gaze traveled back up her body, and he shook his head as if coming out of a fog. "Yes, uh, I came over to see if you like garlic."

"Excuse me?"

"For our dinner. On Friday. Sci-fi. Remember? I'm making spaghetti, which means spaghetti bread has to be made, which means I need to know if you like garlic."

Jane stifled a giggle. Yes, he was rude, but he was also cute when he wasn't acting all sure of himself. "Yes, I like garlic." *And I love how it takes away the question of a good-night kiss. Thank you, Jake.*

Jake began backpedaling toward his own apartment door. "Great. Well then, I'll see you on Friday, I guess. I'm going to go back on in now." He jerked his thumb toward his door. "Major Carter's in there all by her lonesome."

"And the couch is in danger, I remember." She couldn't hold back a smile. "See you Friday." She watched as he went back into his apartment, shaking her head at his clumsiness. Where was Mr. Suave and Debonair from that morning? Was he feeling the same crazy flutters she had?

"Good grief, that man is into *you.*" Jane turned to see Lydia coming down the breezeway. "Is that Jake?"

"Yep, Mr. Sci-fi Cat Lover himself."

"And future carrier of all things heavy," Lydia reminded with a grin.

"Exactly. So, what's up at your house?" Jane motioned for Lydia to come in and make herself comfortable.

"I'd rather talk about you and that man." Lydia settled herself on the couch, kicking off her shoes and putting her feet up on the coffee table. "Nothing major happening at my house. I just needed a little more girlfriend time before heading there."

"Too much baby time, not enough woman time?"

Lydia nodded. "Exactly. I love the twins to death, but sometimes I forget I'm a woman, too. Now, quit skirting the issue and tell me everything about that beautiful specimen of manhood and why you're not over at his apartment right now."

"Well, let's see." Jane held up her fingers and ticked off the reasons. "He's a cat lover. He's a sci-fi fan. I've only been divorced a year and barely dated anyone besides my ex, so I have no idea how to do it. My dog hates his cat. If it didn't work out, I'd have to move, and I'm just getting settled in. How's that?"

Lydia nodded. "Some of those have merit, sure. But I just saw how he looked at you, and that's not something to be taken lightly."

Jane sighed and sat down on the couch by Lydia. "You did? What'd you see?"

"Nothing you don't already know is there. Now, are you going to admit this dinner on Friday might be a date?"

"Do you think he thinks of it as a date?"

"Could you sound any more like we're back in high school?" Lydia laughed, and Jane fell back into the couch cushions.

"I know. This reminds me of why I dated only Bill in high school and college. It's too much work to go out with new people all the time."

"Yeah, and that thought really made for an exciting, wonderful marriage, didn't it?" Jane shot Lydia a mean look, and Lydia held up her hands in defense. "I'm just saying, nothing ventured, nothing gained, right?"

"You're quoting Garth Brooks now?"

Lydia grinned. "I'm fairly certain he got it from someone else, and, besides, the best quotes usually come from country songs."

"No they don't."

"Sure they do. Think about it. Love can build a bridge, the Judds. There's gotta be something more, Sugarland. Nothing 'bout love makes sense, Lee Ann Rimes. Ain't no road too long when we meet in the middle. I forget who that one was."

"Okay, okay, you win. Country songs hold all the wisdom for life. Ooh!" She sat up and turned toward Lydia. "We need music on the Sisters, Ink site! You know, music to scrap by or something."

"Good idea! Love music to play if you're putting together a wedding album, fun dance music if you're just getting together with the girls. I like this idea!"

"We need to call Mac. She'll have to figure out how to put it on the site so the sisters can download it." Jane jumped up and headed for the phone.

"Hey, Jane?"

"Yeah, Lyd?" Jane dialed and looked at Lydia.

"I think you're doing a good thing here with Sisters, Ink, you know. Girlfriends are important, especially when the chips are down."

Jane held up a finger. "Hold that thought." She turned back to the phone. "Mac? Lydia and I have an idea for the Sisters, Ink site, and I'm wondering if you can figure out how to make it work. Can you find a way to put music on our site so that scrappers can download appropriate music to play while they're scrapping?" She listened for a minute.

"Yeah, that's the idea. We can come up with a list of songs and themes this weekend, okay?"

"Mmm-hmm. Sounds good. Thanks, Mac!" She hung up and returned to the couch.

"Mac will find out how to offer music on the site and what kind of cost is involved. Now tell me why the chips are down. Something wrong with Dale?"

"I don't know. I think so, but then maybe it's just my hormones still being out of whack, or me making a mountain out of a molehill. He's fine so long as there's not a game on." Jane grimaced at the loneliness in Lydia's voice.

"Isn't there always a game on somewhere?"

"With the number of sports channels we have now, yes." Lydia waved her hand as if shooing a fly away. "I'm sure it'll work itself out, though. I'm just in the doldrums. I need some chocolate and to cuddle my babies. Just making something out of nothing here."

Jane shook her head. "That's not the Lydia I know. I remember a woman who had great instincts about what mattered and what didn't and rarely went wrong when following those instincts."

Lydia chuckled. "I can think of one time they steered her wrong and she lost her best friend for two years."

"Those were *my* instincts steering *me* wrong. Yours were screaming a truth I should have paid attention to. Maybe I could have saved myself some wasted time and scrapbooking materials."

Lydia turned in her chair to face Jane head-on. "I don't know if I've said it before, but I'm sorry I was right about Bill."

Jane shrugged. "It wasn't your fault. I should have listened when you told me he was a cheater. I didn't, and I paid for it. Am still paying for it." Jane looked around the apartment.

"Maybe you can quit paying for it, starting this Friday."

"I wouldn't put too much stock in one dinner. He may be having me over to tell me he's suing me for mental distress on behalf of his cat. But forget my love life, or lack thereof, and tell me what's wrong between you and Dale. That's a marriage that deserves saving if it's in trouble."

Lydia smiled. "Don't worry about us. This is just a little glitch that will either go away or drive me to a lingerie store. I'd much prefer the former, but feel free to volunteer your services if it comes to the latter."

"I am *so* in on that. There's a great little shop out on West End. I went there to get everything for my honeymoon, and it was in the paper a while back that they were expanding. I'd love the chance to go out and see all the new products."

"Great, then I'll call you if the need arises. I guess I should be heading on home. The twins, I'm sure, are getting pretty hungry by now." She felt her chest. "I know their Mommy could use some relief."

Jane laughed. "You are such a nut. Kiss the kiddos for me, and tell Dale I said hi."

Lydia stood up and pulled her shoes on, then headed to the front door. "And you tell Jake I've got some heavy lifting at my house if he's ever bored." Jane rolled her eyes as Lydia winked and walked out.

"Honey, I'm home," Lydia called out as she entered the house. Dirty baby bottles and dishes littered the kitchen table; crumbs of food dusted the kitchen floor. A quick glance to the left revealed a sink full of dirty dishes. Lydia tamped down on her temper. Dale knew she preferred to feed the twins rather than use a breast pump and feed it to them in bottles, though it looked as though that knowledge hadn't prevented him from feeding them a bottle while she'd been out.

"We're in here, babe," Dale yelled. Lydia guessed "here" meant the living room—where Dale could be found more and more often these days. Coincidentally, it was where their new big-screen television was. Lydia knew the presence of one was the direct cause of the other. She walked through the dining room toward the hallway leading to the living room, leaving her tote in her scrapbooking room along the way.

"Did you feed the twins?" she asked as she came into the room. "And could you please get your dirty feet off the coffee table?"

"Well, nice to see you, too," Dale said, not taking his eyes off of the basketball game long enough to acknowledge her, but taking his feet off the table. "Yes, I fed them. What'd you think? They'd starve if you weren't here to feed them?"

"No, I thought their daddy could keep them happy for the three hours I was gone so that I could feed them when I got home. Do you have any idea how it feels to have two boulders full of milk sitting on your chest?" She pushed on the offending body parts as Dale looked up at the angry tone in her voice.

"Olivia was crying, Lydia." His tone let her know how confused he was. "Was I supposed to just let her cry until you decided to stop playing with your girlfriends long enough to feed her? I thought that's why you left some milk in the freezer—in case one of them got hungry before you got home."

She sighed. "I left the bottle in case of an emergency—like if I was gone for six hours, not three. Did you even try to give her a pacifier and rock her? Did you even think about what it might be like for me when I came home with breasts full of milk and the need to feed my children?" Lydia felt what little control she had over her temper falling away. She knew she was being a bit irrational, but she didn't care. This feeling of being last in a long line of priorities had been beating on her mind's door for months. It was about time to answer the pounding. It was either that or let the huge television screen sitting in front of Dale take over her marriage completely.

Maybe her hormones were out of whack, and maybe she had no reason to go off on him like this, but her bra was about to burst with milk, and he just sat there all comfortable with a remote in his hand.

Dale sighed and rolled his eyes. "No, I didn't think about your breasts. I thought about meeting our child's need so she would stop crying."

Lydia opened her mouth to reply but realized there wasn't much of a defense for her position. Which didn't mean, of course, that it was the wrong position to take. It just meant she was too tired to think of an argument right now. She pressed her lips together instead and headed for the bedroom and her favorite reading chair. Plopping down into the soft recliner, she picked up the breast pump and a copy of Karen Ball's latest release, praying she could lose herself in a good mystery while the horrible contraption sucked away at her body. If anybody could make her forget reality with a gripping story, it was Karen Ball.

"Don't fail me now, sister," she grumbled, opening the book and flipping the switch on the pump.

As her milk flowed, the thought of apologizing occurred to her. Dale was only doing what he thought was right at the time. Then the machine pulled a bit hard, and she bit her lip in pain. Forget apologizing. Hooking Dale up to this contraption sounded like a much better way to make sure he got the point.

chapter 9

*Across town, Mac was just putting away the last of her scrapbook-*ing supplies. She hadn't gotten nearly the number of layouts completed that she had hoped, but some hard work on Saturday should catch things back up. Kesa's birth book needed to get done so that when Easter rolled around, there would be plenty of free time to devote to an egg-themed layout and a gift scrapbook for Tabby.

Mac sat at her computer to check e-mail. Logging in, she smiled when she saw forty-two new messages. Between her scrapbookers group, the prayer circle, and a pretty big list of online friends, Mac never lacked for e-mail in her inbox. She deleted all the offers for Viagra and free money from Nigeria, shaking her head at the absurdity folks went to just because they had access to the World Wide Web.

She nibbled at the last cookie left and read through her

remaining e-mails. A little thrill of excitement and apprehension knifed through her when she saw Tabby's name in the Sent From column.

Dear Momma,

Just wanted to let you know Kesa and me are doing fine. Tonio's momma said she slept all through church today. She's taking a nap right now, so I'm catching up on my e-mail. I know you were having your ladies over today, so I didn't want to call and bother you, but Tonio came by again right after you dropped me off. Says he wants to see Kesa sometimes and maybe be her daddy. Not sure what to do about that. Well, I guess that's all for now. Thank you so much for helping me out today. I promise, Momma, I'm doing right now. I'll talk to you later.

Love,

Tabby

"Lord, help her." Mac shook her head. Tonio had no business being in anybody's life when he still had a problem with meth. Mac shuddered at the thought of precious baby Kesa getting anywhere near the dangerous meth kitchen Tonio went to so much. She'd need to have a talk with Tabby and make sure she knew that kitchen could blow up at any minute. But she knew Tabby wanted so much to believe Tonio could kick the habit. And who was Mac to say he couldn't? Why, just yesterday a lady had been on *Oprah* talking about how hard it was to kick meth but that it was possible with a lot of willpower.

"Lord, help him," she said. Mac wanted Kesa to have her daddy, but not so bad that she was willing to settle for a meth addict in her grandbaby's life, much less her daughter's. She clicked the Reply button and typed a quick message to Tabby.

> Dear Tabby,
>   You're welcome for the help today, baby. I'm real proud of the way you're trying to do right by Kesa. I'll be praying for Tonio if he's thinking about being a daddy. Sure would be nice for Kesa to have two parents to help raise her. I'll be home tonight if you want me to watch the baby for a while.
>   Love,
>   Momma

She clicked Send on the e-mail and then headed over to the Split Coast Stampers web site. Minutes ticked by as she read the latest posts on the message boards, making a few notes of new techniques other stampers and scrappers across the country had discovered. She absentmindedly reached toward the cookie plate and looked up when her hand met only crumbs.

"Now, how did that happen? I know I didn't sit here and eat every cookie that was left," she said to the empty room and checked the plate again. Sure enough, all that remained were crumbs and little bits of chocolate chip.

"I think it's 'bout time I started makin' popcorn instead of cookies. This waistline just keeps growin' and growin'."

Mac was just about to exit her in-box when another e-mail popped in, this one from Cecil Cloar. Mac recognized the name as the preacher who'd been down at the jail talking to Tabby when Mac had shown up. She double-clicked on the e-mail and read.

Dear MacKenzie,

I pray you and Tabitha made it home all right this afternoon and that things have settled down. Tabitha told me about her new little one as we talked at the jail. I'm praying for blessing on both you and the baby as Tabitha begins to walk the narrow road before her.

Tabitha told me that you had raised her alone, a task for which I commend you. She is a smart girl with a good head on her shoulders. I also wanted to let you know that, if you need to talk or need some help, I would be honored to offer assistance. The path Tabitha is walking is paved with potholes. Should she fall and you find that another set of hands would be helpful in bringing her out of the pit, please call or e-mail.

Sincerely,
Pastor Cecil Cloar

Mac sat back from the computer and read the e-mail again, seeing Pastor Cecil's kind face in her mind as she read his words. She wouldn't call him, of course. But having the option certainly helped to lighten her load. Her mind went back to the image of the tall, broad-shouldered man as he sat beside her daughter in a jail cell, Bible open in his hands. Nearly two long decades since Saul went home to His maker, and thoughts of being with another man hadn't entered her mind once.

But Pastor Cecil Cloar just might change all that.

Mac shook her head and refocused on the screen in front of her. "Silly old lady," she muttered. "He's just bein' nice 'cause your baby girl can't keep her head on straight." She clicked over to Google and began searching for ways to put music downloads on the Sisters, Ink site. As Lydia would say, idle hands were the devil's playground.

chapter 10

❀ · ❀ · ❀ · ❀ · ❀ · ❀ · ❀

Jane sat in the grass, holding Wilson's leash and tipping her face back to take in the sunshine, loving that it was so warm for this time of year. Like getting an unexpected and perfect gift. She pushed her sleeves up, closed her eyes, and imagined herself on an island somewhere that had no bills, no divorce papers, no looming to do lists, and no stranger across the hall. *Maybe he could come to the island with me.*

Now, where had that come from? One little invitation to dinner and she was carting them off to a secluded island.

Jane opened her eyes and stared out across the water. As long as she lived, she didn't think she would ever understand why Bill would prefer a cyberwoman to the real flesh-and-blood person sleeping in the next room. It had been a year, though, and no word from Bill since the day she signed the divorce papers and put them in his lawyer's hand. Time to move on.

"Oh, Wilson," she said as the dog came and lay down at her legs, "your momma is such a nutcase. Sitting out here talking to you when she should be inside working on Sonya's fundraiser." Wilson raised his dark brown eyes to her and licked her hand. "If I don't get it done, we'll lose that account. And then how will I pay for your dog food?" She stroked the dog's velvety ears as she talked.

"You could always beg Major Carter for her food, I guess." Wilson perked up his ears and barked. "I know. You're not a big fan of her. But I'm having dinner with her daddy, so you might want to think about making nice at some point." She sighed and fell backward to lie in the soft grass and stare up at the sky. Life seemed to be floating along with as little purpose as those wispy clouds overhead, and she didn't like it one tiny bit. Life's path and direction had always been very clear-cut.

"I followed all the right steps. I got an education, then married a nice man with whom I had a good friendship. I didn't go out searching for or chasing some stupid mythical, Hollywood-glam love thing. I said forever to solid friendship. And look where that got me. Alone in a little apartment. Guess it wasn't as solid a friendship as I thought. And if I couldn't make it work with him, what makes me think I should be starting up a new thing with my neighbor?" She wiped a tear as it rolled down into her ear.

Jake watched Jane from his side of the sliding glass door. Her long hair was splayed out across the grass, dog lying by her side.

He had no business getting involved with anyone—especially anyone walking around with her history. That right was lost after what he'd done.

He thought about going out to her, but she might start thinking he was stalking her, and what would he say anyway? The dinner invitation was about as far as he could go right now. Major Carter came and wound her way around his feet. He reached down and picked her up, scratching behind her ears until she emitted a low purr. She poked her paw at the glass in the door and looked up at him.

"Need to go outside, madam?" The cat turned to look out and back at Jake again. "You're the only cat I know that refuses to use a litter box indoors like normal cats. We can't go out there." *Because that would give me too good of an excuse to talk to a woman who can't be right for me.*

Major Carter pawed the door again and meowed.

Jake sighed. "All right, we'll go outside, but let me go and warn her first so that big ol' dog doesn't run you up a tree again." Major Carter looked through the glass with disdain for the dog lying by Jane, and Jake laughed. "Okay, Queen Bee, I'll be right back."

He set Major Carter down and slipped out the sliding glass door in time to see Jane wipe the side of her beautiful face. Was she crying? Maybe Major Carter should just hold it. His ignorant feet refused the message, though, and kept walking toward her.

"Jane?" he called out as soon as he got within hearing distance. She sat up and looked his way, her hair falling down her back.

"Hi, Jake." She swiped at her face again.

"Carter is begging to come outside, and I thought you might want to know in case Wilson is planning another chase." He nodded to the dog, whose ears had lifted at the sound of his voice or Major Carter's name, he couldn't tell which.

"Oh, sure. Um, thanks. We'll go on inside." She got up and brushed the dirt from her pants.

"I didn't mean to make you go in." In his rush to assure her, he forgot his resolve to leave it at dinner and reached out to touch her arm. She stared at his hand, and he wondered if she might bat him away.

"I just wanted to give you a little warning, that's all." He put his hand back in its pocket. "I don't have a leash for her, though someone recently told me I should get one." He was rewarded with a small smile.

"Well, I hear the women around here can be rather bossy, so you might want to take that advice with a grain of salt." His heart lifted with her banter. "Seriously, I'm sorry Wilson managed to tree Carter."

"Hey, no problem. The old girl needs a little run every now and then. Keeps her heart healthy. Plus, it's good for her to learn right off she won't rule this apartment complex." He leaned in close and winked. "You should have seen her at our last apartment. She ruled the place." Her smile grew, and he wondered at how much that meant to him.

"So what brought you here?"

"The usual." He shrugged. No use getting into it. "Just needed a change of scenery and had heard a lot of good things about Nashville. Thought I'd come check it out for myself."

"In that case, welcome to town."

"Thanks. I'll go get Carter. She's probably tearing apart the curtains by now." He started backing away from her.

"Right. Go save your curtains, and we'll just go inside for a while."

He stopped walking. "I thought we established I didn't mean for you to go inside."

"*You* established that. I still think we should go inside. I wouldn't want Wilson giving Carter a heart attack or anything." She leaned down and scratched the dog's floppy ears.

"If we're going to be sci-fi fans together, shouldn't our animals learn to coexist?"

"Oh, nice one. I am not about to become a sci-fi fan, so no worries there. Though you're right that our animals might need to learn to get along if we're going to live in the same building. Otherwise, we're going to have to work out a schedule for them." She tilted her head and thought for a minute. "All right, go ahead and get Carter. I'll stay here with Wilson, and we'll introduce them properly. Sound good?"

Anything that kept her there sounded good to him. He mentally bopped himself in the head. He was being an idiot over a complete stranger—a stranger he should stay at least twenty yards away from at all times, considering his history.

"Perfect. I'll be right back." He turned and jogged toward his apartment—which was less than twenty yards from hers, so his new rule didn't make sense anyway. He wondered if she would be there when he got back and hoped she was a woman of her word. Three encounters with her didn't give him enough to know. "As if there *is* a type for her," he mumbled as he dashed into his apartment and lifted Major Carter off the arm of one of the chairs.

Making his way back, he was heartened to see Jane sitting in the very spot she had been occupying before he came outside. She was holding Wilson in her lap—the parts of him that could fit in her lap—and talking to the dog about cats. He laughed when he got close enough to hear her.

"—and they keep the mice away, and they're sometimes great for cuddling, and—"

"Here we are." Jake knelt down about four feet away from Jane and Wilson, keeping a tight grip on Major Carter as the fur on her back began to rise. He noticed Wilson become very intent as he looked at his nemesis.

"Major Carter, may I introduce you to Wilson." He prayed Carter wouldn't slip loose and scratch a new eyeball for the dog.

"Wilson Wellington, may I introduce you to Major Carter," Jane rejoined with a laugh.

"Wellington?" Jake asked with a grin.

"He's a proper British mutt, so he needed a proper British name," she said with mock indignation and then relaxed. "Really, I just needed more than one name to yell out the back door when he was in trouble." He joined her in laughter, and the animals lowered their backs a bit.

"They seem to be declaring a truce."

"Maybe. Come a little closer and let's see what happens."

He tried to ignore the thrill her words brought and reminded himself she was talking about the animals. He moved within arm's reach of her and leaned forward to scratch Wilson's ears.

"There ya go, buddy. See, we cat lovers aren't all bad." Wilson turned his head in Jake's hand and stretched his neck out.

"He likes you." She reached out to pet the fluffy white cat in Jake's lap and was rewarded with a soft purr.

"Looks like the feeling's mutual." Jake envied the cat and felt stupid for doing so. "So, tell me what you have against sci-fi shows." He leaned back and crossed his legs at the ankles, petting Major Carter's fur to keep her still.

"Where should I start? The horrible acting, the unbelievable story lines, the ridiculous costumes and makeup, the fanatic viewers . . ." Jane ticked off each detail on her slender fingers.

"Hey, I'm a fanatic viewer."

"Precisely. You seem like a perfectly normal human being, but I'll bet you know every detail about some alien world and race, right?"

Jake ignored her adorable expression and thought about the extent of his knowledge of the Stargate, how it worked, and what worlds it had opened up to Major Carter, Colonel O'Neill, Daniel Jackson, T'ealq, and the crew. She had him there.

"All right, I'll give you that. But I'm sure it's no more than you know about your hobbies. What are your hobbies anyway?"

"Reading, scrapbooking, networking women, and getting through life."

"What do you read?"

"Romance, mystery, suspense. Anything fiction."

"I'm a fiction lover myself. Ever read *Dune*?"

"Just a few chapters over my ex's shoulder at the beach one summer."

"Ouch." He winced. "I'm two for two now."

"No, it's okay. No sense in trying to tiptoe around it." She looked out across the field, and he watched the war of emotion play out across her strong face.

"So . . . was 'it' recent, or in the past?" Jake knew he shouldn't pry, but he needed to understand her past if he was going to be a part of her present. Wait . . . when had he decided to be a part of her present? *When she knocked the breath out of your chest with her car door*, he thought. *Now, quit being an idiot and get to know her.*

Jane looked at him for a moment, as though considering the fact that they were strangers and he didn't really have any right to know the details. But then she shrugged. "I'm not sure how long it had been going on, but I found out a year ago. The day before I moved in here, actually. He found someone else. An e-mistress. He forgot to log off one night, and I couldn't sleep, so I went in the study to work on a proposal. His—um—partner was still online and thought I was him. Instant messages started popping up." Her voice was flippant, but the pain in her eyes revealed her inner thoughts.

"That must have been a shock." Now that she was talking, he wanted to do anything he could to keep the flow of information coming.

"At first I thought it was a mistake. I kept thinking some site was spamming me with IMs or something. I just clicked out of them as they popped up. But then she used my name, and I knew something was up."

He hated her ex. "Did you tell her you weren't him?"

"No, I carried on with her for a while just to make sure I wasn't jumping to conclusions."

"Nice of you."

She shrugged. "Not really. I think it was more disbelief than anything. Anyway, that's how I learned he was planning to leave me for her." She shook her head and stopped. Without thinking, he scooted around to her side and put his hand over hers in the grass, knowing it was stupid and dangerous, but desperate to offer some comfort.

"It's okay. You don't have to tell me."

She turned to face him, and the hurt in her eyes nearly took his breath.

"I just felt so stupid. They had been carrying on for *months*, and I never even suspected. My husband was about to leave me for a woman I didn't even know existed." She sniffed. "Most days, I'm over it. Some days it hits me again." She scooted a bit to make more room for Wilson.

"I turned off the computer, went to the bedroom, and tried to go back to sleep. I thought it must all be a terrible nightmare and I would wake up and laugh at how ridiculous the whole idea was. But he woke up before me the next morning and went to IM with her." She grimaced. "He knew I knew before I even got out of bed. He was so mad. He woke me up screaming at me that I had invaded his private life, and I had no right to do such a thing, and how could he trust me if I was going to go online masquerading as him."

Jake fought to keep the thousand horrible names he conjured up for her ex from escaping his lips.

"He told me he was leaving me for her and that he was glad I had found out." Jane looked out across the water and sighed. "I packed up that day and left. I just couldn't stick around to see him abandon everything, me." She hung her head for a moment, then patted Wilson's neck. "Wow, I didn't mean to dump all that on you. I just don't talk about it that often."

"Hey, don't you dare apologize. I've got two ears, no waiting, anytime you need 'em." She looked up at him and studied his face. He met her eyes and gave her a look he hoped was full of assurance and empathy. "And just for the record, I think your ex is the complete idiot."

Jane laughed a sad little laugh.

"Well, *idiot* is the tamest word I could use. I have a thousand others in my brain, but they're not fit for public consumption."

"Thank you." She touched his hand. He looked down at their hands and dragged his gaze up to hers.

"Like I said, anytime." They shared a moment of silence. "So, what kind of dog is Wilson anyway?"

She chuckled. "He's mostly basset hound, but he's got some corgi in him, too. At least, that's what they told me when I adopted him."

Jake leaned back and studied Wilson. "I can see that. His ears aren't as long as a regular basset. Is he really smart?"

"Oh, yeah. We're on our fourth crate, because he keeps figuring out how to work the latches."

"That's the corgi in him." Her eyebrows rose and he explained. "My parents had Welsh corgis for a while. Very smart dogs."

She patted his hand and put hers back in her lap, taking a deep breath. "So now that I've spilled my guts, care to share your life story?"

"If you make it through *Stargate*, I'll spill." Jake waggled his eyebrows in challenge.

She tilted her head and considered the offer. "All right, that's fair." She got up and once again dusted off her jeans, then wound the red leash around her wrist. "I should really go inside now. I've got a ton of stuff left to do today, and sitting out here talking wasn't on the list."

"No problem. I'll see you on Friday." Jake got up too, putting a sleeping Carter in the crook of his arm. He watched her start to walk away and called out, "Hey, Jane?"

She stopped and turned. "Yes?"

"Thanks for telling me."

She looked at him for a long moment. "You're welcome." Her voice was so quiet he wondered if he had misheard her. And then she turned and walked away.

chapter 11

✽ · ✽ · ✽ · ✽ · ✽ · ✽ · ✽

Mari slowly pulled into her organized garage and turned off the minivan, a silly grin splitting her face. The past three years had been full of raising Emmy. Finding time for other relationships was just too time-consuming most days. Laughing and talking about life with her Sisters, Ink group, though, had reminded her she was a woman—not just a mom and wife.

She gathered up her things and headed toward the kitchen, planning the evening's dinner in her mind. Maybe John wouldn't mind grilling since it was such a nice day outside. If he would grill some chicken and fresh vegetables, she would have some free time to play with her sweet Emmy.

"John?" she called out as she came through the door. "I'm home!" Little Emmy came streaking into the kitchen and nearly knocked her over with the force of her hug.

"Mommy! You're back!" She began tugging Mari toward the living room. "Daddy and I painted a picture for Andrea. Wanna see? We used lots of red and pink since she's a girl, and I drawed our house so she could find it."

"You *drew* our house?" Mari corrected gently, setting her things down on the table and allowing Emmy to pull her through the house.

"Yep. Come see, come see."

Mari came into the living room and took in her husband's tired but pleased expression. He was in old blue jeans and a faded T-shirt, drawing in his journal. It wasn't fair that men could look so good in clothes that should have been put in a yard sale years ago.

"Hi, honey. Did you have fun scrapping?" He set the journal aside and came to give her a hug.

"I had a blast. We're all meeting again on Saturday, okay?"

"Sure, no problem."

"Mommy, look." Emmy held up a white piece of cardboard full of red and pink paint, glitter, and buttons. "It's for Andrea." Pride made her face shine.

Mari smiled. "Oh, *hija*, it's just beautiful. Andrea's going to love it." She knelt down next to Emmy and took the picture from her, noting that Emmy had drawn a family of four rather than three. She looked up at John with tears in her eyes. "Did Daddy help you with this?"

"Yeah, a little. But I did the glitter all by myself. See? I put it on my window so Andrea can find our room."

"Well, that's the most perfect part of all." Mari stretched

back up. "Let's go put this in an envelope and put it in Andrea's Box, okay?"

Emmy nodded and took the painting back from Mari, then skipped her way out of the room.

"*Eso fue una idea increíble.*" Mari turned to John for a hug.

"It really wasn't my idea. We were watching cartoons, and one came on about sisters. She asked me if that's what Andrea was going to be for her, and I explained it as best I could. Then she decided she wanted to make Andrea something. I just sort of tagged along. It was all her adventure."

"I'm glad you were here for it, then. I was beginning to get a little worried that she might be too possessive and selfish right now."

"Nah." He squeezed around her waist and touched his forehead to hers. "I think she's getting to the other side of that phase. By the time we bring Andrea home, she'll be ready for a sister, I think."

Mari leaned into his embrace, grateful for him and Emmy, but longing for Andrea. The weeks of more paperwork and government bureaucracy stretched before her, and she wondered if, at the end of it, they would truly be handed their new little girl. And, if they did or didn't, would John continue treating her as if she were a fragile piece of china, ready to break at any moment?

"John, do you ever consider the possibility that we might not get Andrea?"

He pulled back from her and, taking her chin in his hand, forced her gaze up to meet his. "No," he said forcefully. "I thought that for a long time, but not anymore. We have her picture, and pretty soon we're going to have a travel date. I think we're definitely about to become a family of four, so just get ready, *mi muñeca.*"

Mari smiled. John's confidence was contagious, and she loved being called his little doll. "Okay, then. No more worries. We're getting a little girl."

"Yes, we are." He let go of her chin. "But right now, can we get dinner?" The playful light in his eyes made her smile grow.

She stepped out of his embrace, and he followed her to the kitchen. "I was thinking maybe you could grill some chicken and veggies. I'll get it all ready and then spend some time with Emmy while you grill. Does that work?"

"Sorry, didn't hear that. I was distracted by the view from back here."

She turned and swatted at his shoulder. "John Campbell, are you sexually harassing me? They have laws about that in this country."

"Absolutely. Is it working?" His devilish grin was adorable.

"You're too much." She leaned forward, intending to give him a peck on the lips, but his arms wound around her and pulled her tight, deepening the kiss. For a brief second, she thought about resisting. Dinner wasn't going to make itself. But then he moved his hand against her hip and she gave in to him, loving that he still wanted her like this after five years of marriage. She felt that wonderful spark she'd had ever since their first kiss and ran her fingers up his neck and through his golden hair.

"Mommy, I'm hungry." Emmy pulled on Mari's shirt top.

"Foiled again," John whispered as he released her with a

peck on her nose. She trailed her hand along his face and then turned to Emmy.

"Okay, sweetie. Mommy's going to make dinner right now. Want to help?"

"Yeah!" Emmy started bouncing up and down in excitement. Mari reached down and took her hand. "Then come with me, *mi princesa,* and let's see what's in the castle pantry."

"So tell me about these women you met with today." John followed her into the kitchen.

She pulled vegetables from the refrigerator and handed them to Emmy, who took them to the sink and began rinsing them. "They're great, John." Mari filled him in on the afternoon as she joined Emmy at the sink, rinsing the veggies. Together, they wrapped everything in aluminum foil and put it on a platter, along with chicken breasts.

John took the tray and headed out to the grill, Mari and Emmy following behind. Emmy headed for the swing set, her brown pigtails bouncing along, as Mari finished up the account of her afternoon.

"They sound like a really neat group of people," John said, putting everything onto the grill.

"They are. I had so much more fun than I thought I would." She watched as Emmy pumped her legs, swinging higher and higher.

"I'm glad you found some girlfriends."

"And I may have found you a friend in the process." She turned back to face John. "You know that guy Jane's having dinner with?"

"Jake?"

"Yeah. He's a sci-fi lover."

"Yes!" John punched a fist in the air.

Mari laughed as she went down the deck steps toward Emmy. It was definitely time for some mother-daughter fun. "You are such a sci-fi freak, *loco*," she called over her shoulder.

"That may be, but you love me anyway," he yelled out to her, and she shook her head as her daughter ran into her embrace.

chapter 12

❊ · ❊ · ❊ · ❊ · ❊ · ❊

*Jane dropped her head to her desk and rubbed her neck. It was mid-*night, and she had at least three more things to get out the door before calling it a night.

She glanced up at the screen and the latest publicity proposal and tried to get some inspiration to finish it. Bill would know exactly where to go with this. Since he was a night person, he could always come up with good ideas when she was pulling an all-nighter. Her internal clock had gone to sleep two hours ago.

She sighed. If she drank some caffeine now, it would keep her awake for at least four hours. Which was great except for the fact that she only needed about another two hours of work.

Maybe a quick walk outside would get the blood flowing again. Wilson jumped up from her feet as she pushed back from the desk and stood up. "Outside?"

He ran to the front door and paced back and forth in front of it. "Good idea."

Walking across grass heavy with dew, she breathed in the night air. A quick trip around the lake ought to get her brain energized. "Come on, boy." Tugging on Wilson's leash, they started a brisk walk around the water. The full moon reflected brilliantly off the water, lighting up the landscape and illuminating her path. She stepped along, keeping an eye on her surroundings like all the e-mail warnings to women advised, yet loving the feeling of walking through a dark night with no one to answer to. Singleness had a few advantages.

Now, what to do about this proposal? Coming up with fresh ideas for fund-raising was always the most difficult part of owning her own firm. There was no staff to consult or conference room in which to sit around a large table and brainstorm ideas. Her work becoming boring and stale was an unending battle to fight.

Their circuit around the lake finished, she turned her feet back toward the open breezeway. "At least I'm awake again, right, Wilson?" The dog woofed low and followed her back to their apartment, stopping to sniff at the base of Jake's door.

"Come on, buddy. Major Carter's probably in there sleeping soundly with Jake by her side." The mental image of him curled up in bed with a cat quickened her pulse. She allowed herself to dwell on it for two seconds, then tugged Wilson over to their door.

Time to buckle down and get some work done.

Lydia opened her eyes to bright sunshine streaming through the bedroom window. She felt a heaviness settle about her and couldn't quite remember what she was sad about until she turned over and saw Dale asleep beside her. He had come to bed after she fell asleep last night, no doubt staying up to watch some ball game on television. March Madness was living up to its name.

She swung her legs off the side of the bed, coming up to a sitting position and gazing out the window. The sun reflected off the aluminum swing set in the backyard and hurt her eyes. Would it be as warm today as yesterday? She picked the remote up off the bedside table and clicked on the news just in time for the ten-day forecast.

Her depressed feeling worsened when she took in the little snow flurry symbols on the screen. That was Tennessee weather for you. Beautiful and sunny one day, snowing the next. The forecast showed that today was the last day of temperatures in the seventies. Knowing another day of warmth might be weeks and weeks away, Lydia resolved to make the most of the day's beautiful weather.

"Dale, time to get up." She poked his arm. "Come on, it's the last warm day for a while. No rest for the weary. Let's take everyone to the park."

Dale grumbled a bit, but didn't even open his eyes.

"Dale, come on." She raised the volume of her voice. "It's

already"—she sneaked a glance at the TV screen—"after seven. The day's wasting away, and we're lying here in bed."

Dale opened his eyes a fraction of an inch and squinted at her. "Considering the fact that I just got in from work seven hours ago, I'm okay with that." He shut his eyes again.

Lydia huffed her impatience with him and slid off the bed. Why even bother? Maybe if she offered to bring a football to throw around, Dale would show some interest. She padded into the bathroom. How had he ever gotten his mind off of sports long enough to propose to her in the first place?

A quick turn of the lever and hot water gushed forth until she pulled the shower lever. As stall steamed up, she checked out her face in the big oval mirror hanging over her side of the vanity. Turning to each side and pulling back her natural curls let her take stock of the gray growing along the side of her head. Her hairdresser, Coytt, had offered to highlight it when the gray started popping up a few years ago at the ripe old age of twenty-five, but Lydia had refused. It gave her a sense of maturity.

"Wonder if he can still cover it?" She stuck her tongue out at her reflection. Who would even notice the effort? Dale certainly wouldn't notice, unless she took out an ad to run on ESPN. And it was more money out of their budget—money better spent on scrapping supplies.

She pulled her nightgown over her head and stepped into the warm shower, grateful for the steam that seeped its way into her bones. Soaping up her long brown hair took forever, which allowed plenty of time to mentally map out the day. Taking the twins to the park was a good idea. She could pack them a lunch and take Otis as well. The poor dog hadn't gotten much outside time lately and would go nuts as soon as they got in the car. Maybe Mari could join them with Emmy. Olivia and Oliver would be good exposure to babies for Emmy, and Lydia would have another adult to talk to since her husband was too busy sleeping the day away to spend time with her. She tilted her head back and rinsed the shampoo, then applied conditioner. Thank goodness for girlfriends.

Reaching for her razor, she debated pulling out some capri pants for the park. It was warm enough, after all. But, no, her legs might blind somebody. Better stick with jeans. She put the razor back in its hanger and leaned her head into the water to rinse the conditioner. She soaped up her body and rinsed quickly, looking forward to the day now that it had been planned.

Shutting off the water and grabbing a white towel from the hanger by the door, Lydia stepped out of the steamy shower. Her makeup and hair routine were quick and no-nonsense. Fifteen minutes later, jeans and a T-shirt were the order of the day. Grabbing her tennies from the back of the closet, she made her way through the house and upstairs to the nursery just as crying came from the baby monitor in the living room.

"Morning, precious ones." She bent and kissed each baby's forehead. "How about we go to the park today and soak up some of this gorgeous sunshine?" The green-and-yellow nursery was adorned with characters from *The Wind in the Willows*. Morning sunlight poured through the window blinds. Olivia would need to be fed, changed, and dressed first. Oliver was content to lie in his crib and watch. So long as she was in the room with him, he would be fine.

Lydia picked up Olivia from her white crib and took her over to the changing table. She rummaged around in the dresser drawer, pulling out a white romper with a big yellow daisy embroidered on the front, and yellow rickrack on the sleeves.

"Here we go, sweet girl. Daisies for you today." She changed the baby and got her dressed, keeping up a monologue while putting the little white socks with lace edging on Olivia's chubby feet. Olivia gurgled and cooed back at her, turning her head side to side on the changing table. Lydia picked her up and turned toward the big cherry rocker in the corner of the room. Settling into the massive chair, she raised her shirt and began feeding the baby. Pictures of Olivia in this outfit would be adorable on a layout of daisy paper. Had she gotten any at the Savvy Scrapper sale?

Twenty minutes later, Olivia pulled away, and Lydia went to lay her back in her crib. With a full tummy, Olivia would amuse herself with the little mirror hanging on the inside of her crib while Lydia got Oliver ready for the day.

"Hey, big guy." She scooped Oliver up and carried him to the changing table, pulling a yellow romper with a white train embroidered on it from the drawer below Olivia's. "Did you have good dreams last night? Were big trucks and trains rumbling through your nighttime stories?" She wiggled her fingers at him, and he smiled a toothless little grin. She finished up the changing, putting little yellow socks and white cloth shoes on his kicking feet. "How about some breakfast?"

She went through the same feeding routine in the rocker. Another twenty minutes later, both babies were full, happy, and wide awake. She put one in each arm and headed downstairs to call Mari about going to the park and snapping some good scrapping pics.

"Hello?" Mari tried to get her breath back before answering the bedside phone, pushing John's roaming hand away as he continued their early morning interlude. She never could just let a phone ring, no matter what was going on.

"Mari? Are you okay?" Lydia's voice rang with concern over the telephone line.

"*Buenos días,* Lydia. I'm fine." She pushed John's wandering hand away again and tried to give him a stern look, but his devilish grin was her undoing. Being married was really, really fun sometimes. "What's up?" She turned over onto her stomach, thinking if the temptation was removed, John would lose interest. His fingers walking up her bare calf said otherwise.

"I'm taking the twins and Otis to the park today and wondered if you and Emmy might like to join us. Can you take that long a lunch hour?"

"I took the day off today, and that sounds like fun." Mari captured John's hand in her own and gave a playfully disapproving look. "Which park?"

"Edwin Warner is the best, I think. Would that work for you?"

"Sure."

"Perfect. I was thinking a picnic lunch. How about we meet you there around eleven? I'll go early and scope out the best picnic table. Oh, and I'll bring my camera to capture some pics for Andrea's book."

"Sounds good. See ya then." She ended the phone call as gracefully as possible and turned back to her husband, sending up a prayer of thanks for this beautiful man in her bed whose last name she was blessed to bear. "You are incorrigible, mister."

"*Gracias.*" John brought his lips to hers. "I'm also insatiable, mesmerized, addicted, and overcome, but I'll settle for incorrigible." He trailed kisses down her neck and let his hand stray down her bare leg. She shivered with goose bumps.

"I've got to go get Emmy ready for the day. That was Lydia on the phone, asking us to join her and the twins in the park for a picnic lunch."

"But it's only eight," he said against her neck. "We've got hours to spend before lunchtime. I thought you took the day off from crazy bankers with suicidal career plans to spend with me. The office can run for a day without its head of Human Resources." She giggled and lost herself for a minute in his touch.

"Right, I did." She forced herself back to the conversation. "And I will spend time with you today, but I promised Lydia we'd meet her at the park by eleven, and it takes thirty minutes to get there. That means we have two and a half hours to get ready, and you know how long it takes to get Emmy ready for anything, and we haven't even started on breakfast." She blushed as he stopped his kisses to look at her directly.

"Okay, Madame Overplanner, how about this." He began kneading the small of her back as she turned on her side to face him. "I'll help you get Emmy ready. Together we can do it in a little over an hour, which leaves us about an hour for *us* while she's busy watching Veggie Tales now."

He kissed her again, deepening it as her body softened into his. She loved his warmth and how he could completely envelop her with his arms. She tilted her head back and enjoyed the magic as he once again trailed kisses down her neck and back up to her ear.

"Deal." She took his hand in hers, determined to show him just how much she loved him, even if her body wouldn't give him the second child he longed for.

"But after this picnic, you take Emmy over to Mom's and come home to me for the rest of the afternoon. No stopping at Wachovia on the way. There is no working before coming home. Still a deal?" He pulled her close to him and hooked his legs around hers.

"Deal," she said breathlessly and resolved to enjoy the next hour.

chapter 13

❋ · ❋ · ❋ · ❋ · ❋ · ❋ · ❋

The knock on Jane's front door set Wilson off to barking.

"Okay, okay, buddy. I've got it." She bent and looked through the peephole, then tamped down the happiness that spread through her at the sight of Jake. Taking Wilson's collar firmly in her hand, she opened the door.

"Hi." He looked unsure as he held out a large gift bag, and she tried to ignore the little flip her heart made. "I was thinking about our conversation yesterday and, well, thought maybe you would like this."

"Oh! Um, come on in." She opened the door further and pulled Wilson back, making room for him to enter her apartment. Closing the door, she released Wilson's collar, and he immediately began sniffing Jake's shoes.

"Wilson, stop it." She shooed the dog away, then looked up at Jake. "Sorry."

"No problem. Carter checks out everybody who comes through the door, too." He raised the gift bag again, and she took it from him, carrying it over to the kitchen table, excited that he had thought to get her something. Presents were so much fun.

"Shall I open it now, or would you like for me to wait?"

"Oh, no, go ahead." He gestured toward the gift. "I mean, I didn't mean for you to wait."

She reached in and began pulling white tissue paper out, wondering what in the world he had gotten her. Chocolate? Maybe a CD or DVD? Excitement turned to confusion as the end of the tissue paper unearthed a stack of at least fifty AOL CDs.

"Um, thanks so much. I'm not sure what to say." *Act happy. You can throw them away when he leaves.*

He chuckled. "There's more. Trust me; this will make sense in the end." He pulled another, smaller, gift bag from behind his back and handed it to her as well. "Now open this one."

Once again she pulled tissue paper out. Maybe the first one was a gag gift. She burst out laughing at a miniature sledge-hammer in the bottom of the bag.

"I thought we could go outside and spend some time smashing the Internet. Since your ex seems to have used it to hurt you, you might as well hurt it back, right?"

Her laughter grew with the thought of slamming the sledge-hammer into the CDs, little bits of Internet connection capability flying everywhere. This was *exactly* what she needed.

"Jake, thank you. It's perfect. Absolutely perfect."

"Whew. I was worried for a second that you might think I was crazy." He put his hands in his back pockets and rocked back and forth on his heels. "So, no time like the present, right? Let's get to smashing!"

"You bet. No time like the present. Just let me get my shoes on." She snatched up her tennies from beside the door and sat down in one of the Windsor chairs at the kitchen table to get them on, excited at the prospect of doing something destructive, and thrilled with such a fun gift.

"Okay, all set." She tied the last bow and slapped her jeans-clad legs before standing up. "Wilson, crate!" she called out and followed Wilson into the bedroom to latch his crate.

"Now, *that* is obedience," Jake called from the living room. "Does he actually walk all the way into his crate?"

"Oh yeah. Come watch." Jake walked down the hallway and into her bedroom. "I couldn't believe it when he first did it." She began latching the hooks. "It was totally by accident that he even learned it. I didn't realize that every time I put him up, I was telling him to get in his crate." She reached into the big jar of dog treats on her dresser and pulled out a peanut-butter-flavored one. "Until one day I was heading out and did my usual, 'Let's go get in your crate,' and he ran ahead of me." She poked the treat through the wires, and Wilson gingerly took it in his mouth.

"How amazing is that? So he's a pretty smart dog." They walked back toward the front door.

"Yeah, he's scary smart sometimes." She smiled at the pride in her voice and dusted dog-treat crumbs off of her hands onto her jeans. "Anyway, let's go smash some Internet!"

Jake picked up the red gift bag full of CDs with one hand and grabbed the mini-sledgehammer with the other.

"Where did you get so many AOL CDs anyway?" She followed him back out the front door and locked it behind them.

"After you told me yesterday what had happened with your ex, I wanted to give you a way to get back. When I saw the stack of AOL CDs piled by the mailboxes, I knew I had my answer. I waited around for a while and offered to take anybody else's as they checked their mail. Here I thought I was the only nut who checked his mail at eight a.m."

"Our mail runs at eight?"

"Yep! We're the first on the mail route. Anyway, it turns out a bunch of folks get their mail on the way to work in the morning. Within a couple of hours, I had enough weird looks to make my skin crawl, but I also had enough CDs."

She stopped walking and turned to look at him in disbelief. "You sat at the mailboxes for a couple of *hours?*"

"Well, yeah." He looked unsure again. "There were some stacked on the ledge already, but I wanted to have more. You know, enough to make a real smash party. I had a Chris Well book with me, so I wasn't bored." His eyebrows went up as he gave her a quizzical look. "Is that all right?"

Jane stood and stared. He had given several hours out of his day for her. He had sat and thought about what would bring her joy and then gone out and found it for her. She tried hard to remember the last time Bill had done something just to bring her pleasure, when there wasn't anything in it for him. It took a few seconds, but it finally came to her. It had been the night of their six-month wedding anniversary. He had brought home Stargazer lilies, her favorite. Had it really been just that one time? She nibbled her fingernail, oblivious to the concerned expression on Jake's face as she tried in vain to think of another instance of Bill showing affection toward her with a gift.

"Hey." He held up the bags in his hands. "I can take them back if you want. Say the word and they're trash."

Not only had he gone and gotten her the most thoughtful gift she had ever received, but he was willing to throw it out the window for her if she didn't like it. She opened her eyes wide to keep the stupid tears from falling.

"No, no, it's not that. I'm sorry. I just . . . It's just . . . Oh . . ." Losing the battle with tears, she tilted her head down in a vain attempt to hide them. Taking her elbow, he steered her over to the stairs that led to the upper-level apartments and sat her down on one. He set the gift bags down at their feet and waited silently as she got control of her emotions. He patted her back as her sniffling came to a close.

"Whew, sorry about that." She peeked up at him and nearly lost it again at the worry on his face. He barely knew her, and here she was, blubbering in his presence for the second time. Geez, what he must think of her?

"Not a problem. Want to talk about it?" He leaned back and rested his elbows on the stair above them, crossing his legs at the ankles and settling himself in.

"I was just trying to remember if or when Bill did anything nice for me."

"I take it Bill's the ex?"

"Yep."

"And?"

She grimaced. "I realized it was six months after we got married, but not a single time before or after. How dumb am I that I didn't catch on to that until now?" She shook her head.

"I don't think that means you're dumb. I think it means he is." He bounced his feet in rhythm.

"Where did you learn all the perfect lines?" she asked with a small smile.

"*Perfect Lines for Dummies.*" She jerked her eyes back to him, but saw the laughter in his face and grinned.

"I'll need to get that, I guess. Is it a Barnes & Noble staple, or will I have to special order it?"

"They try to keep it in stock, but for some reason it keeps selling out. Been on the *New York Times* list for weeks and weeks. I'm surprised you haven't heard of it by now." He laughed and stood up from the steps, offering her his hands. "So, you ready for that smashing party now?"

She put her hands into his big warm ones and jumped up from her position on the steps, snatching up the red gift bag again. "Absolutely." Hand in hand, they turned to go just as Jane heard the Kentucky fight song ring out from inside her apartment.

"Is that your phone?"

"Yeah, hang on just a second." She dropped his hand, missing its warmth, and dashed back inside the apartment, grabbing the kitchen phone just before the answering machine picked up.

"Hello?"

"Jane?"

"Hey, Lyd. What's up?"

"I was wondering if you were busy this afternoon. Mari and I are taking the kids to the park, and I thought you might want to join us."

"That sounds like fun. I was outside a minute ago and it's gorgeous out there."

"Were you, now? Any run-ins with Mr. Tall, Dark, and Neighborly?"

"As a matter of fact, yes."

"And?"

"And I'll let you know."

"You'll let me know? No time like the present, girl. Spill."

"I'd love to oblige, but I simply can't." Jane twirled the phone cord around her finger and smiled at Jake.

"You mean you can't talk right now?" Jake grinned back, and her heart flipped. *He's too far away.*

"You're so smart."

"He's *there?*"

"Yep." *And if he takes three steps he'll be right here beside me, and that's great with me, since he's holding the most perfect gift I've ever gotten in his hand.*

"What are you doing answering the phone?" Jane laughed. "Hang up and go find out all about him. Then meet Mari and me at the park to dish the details. You think he'll be gone by then?"

"I don't know." She shook her head to dispel the image of

a warm Jake, turning her back to the real one standing in her entryway. "What time are y'all meeting?"

"We're having lunch there, but we'll stay until you show up. Will that work?"

"Sure. I'll talk to you then."

"Bye. Oh, and be sure to remember every single second."

"I don't think that will be a problem" She hung up and turned back to Jake. "Sorry about that. Some friends are going to the park and wanted me to join them." *Which isn't any of his business, so why are you babbling?*

"Oh, do we need to do this another time?" He held up the bag of AOL CDs.

"No, no, that's not what I meant." *Geez, could you seem any more eager?* "I mean, they're meeting for lunch, and that's not for a couple of hours, so I'm free right now. I'll just need to be done in time to meet them for lunch. Or I can skip lunch. I just said I'd be there before they went home, which will probably be sometime after lunch." *But before I check myself into an asylum. Shut up already.*

He grinned and stepped closer to her.

If babbling gets you closer to me, I can keep going.

"Just to be clear, you don't have to be anywhere for a while. Right?"

"Right." She tilted her head back to look up at him and saw the sparkle in his eye. *Babbling was easier when my brain worked, which might happen again sometime in the next millennium.*

"So our choices are to go and smash these CDs right now

or stand here and"—he reached over and tucked a strand of hair behind her ear—"talk."

Not if it involves me being coherent. "Yes."

"Do you have a preference?" He cupped her chin and tilted her face to his.

Mmm-hmm. But it's hard to talk when your lips are otherwise engaged. She swallowed and took a deep breath. This was going faster than she'd planned. Did she know enough about this man to be kissing him in her apartment? "I suppose we could talk for a while."

He looked at her for a long moment, then put his hands in his back pockets and stepped backward. "Okay."

She cleared her throat, the ability to think returning in direct proportion to his distance from her. "Okay, so, um, tell me about you."

"Me? I'm boring. I live across the hall. I have a cat. I work on computers from home. That's it. Let's talk about you."

"Oh, I think you know more than enough about me already." She smiled and led him into the living room, her feet having regained their ability to move.

"I doubt it. What's your favorite ice cream?"

"Breyer's French Vanilla."

"See, I didn't know that." He sat on the couch as she took the big comfy chair. "Favorite movie?"

"Hmm, that's a hard one. Probably *What Dreams May Come*, though I like *Die Hard*—all of 'em—and *French Kiss*."

"*Die Hard?*"

"Hey, a girl can't resist Bruce Willis beating up the bad guys.

My dad and I watch the first *Die Hard* every Christmas. What about you?"

He leaned back, putting his hands behind his head just like on the stairwell. The sight of a gorgeous man stretched out across her couch was doing more things to her brain than she needed. "I think *Gladiator* would be at the top of my list."

"*Gladiator?* You're a Russell Crowe fan?"

"Not really. But it's a good story, and the fight choreography is fantastic."

"Ah, I get it. Man fights lion and wins. How could we resist?" She laughed, and he joined her.

"Back to you. Favorite band?"

She settled back into her chair. "Modern or old?"

"Let's start with modern—say, in the last fifteen years."

"Hmmm, if I had to pick just one band, it'd probably be Aerosmith."

He put his hand to his heart. "You've renewed my faith in women everywhere. Now for the bonus point—favorite Aerosmith song?"

"Just one? You're kidding, right?"

"Nope. Name one."

She thought for a long while. "Love in an Elevator" was great, but he'd probably read a lot into that answer. "Crazy" got nixed for the same reason. She went through the entire Aerosmith concert playlist, but the only one that seemed safe to mention was "Dude Looks Like a Lady," and no way was she claiming that as her favorite song.

"Well?"

"Um." She nibbled her fingernail.

He sat up and stared at her. "You do *know* some Aerosmith songs, right?"

"Of course I do. They're my favorite modern band. I know every single song they've ever played."

"Then name one."

She nibbled some more, tidbits of Aerosmith running through her brain like a 1-800 commercial for an Aerosmith boxed set. Surely there was one song that wouldn't make him think she was trying to get him to kiss her. *Which would be fine. Okay, better than fine, but he doesn't need to know that.*

"It can't be that hard. Doesn't even have to be your favorite. Just name one."

She nibbled harder. Inspiration struck.

"'Janie's Got a Gun'!"

He sat back and laughed. She sighed with relief. "You don't have to get violent."

"I wasn't. It's one of their songs—"

"I know. I was being funny." He shrugged. "Or not."

"Your turn. Favorite Aerosmith song?"

He stopped laughing and looked her straight in the eye. "It's a toss-up. 'Love in an Elevator' or 'Crazy.'"

She sucked in her breath, ignoring the pounding of her heart. Was he hinting at what she thought he was hinting at? "Those are good, too."

"Yeah, good subject matter." He held her gaze, and she felt her face heat up. He *was* hinting. Great, now what? It'd been too long since she dated. Should she say something? What? *Get*

a grip; he's just naming a song, Jane. He raised an eyebrow at her and got up from the couch. *Or not.* She sat transfixed as he crossed the short distance from couch to her.

He sat down on the footstool of her chair. "Favorite old band?"

She didn't even have to think. "Not band, singer. Etta James, with Otis Redding and Frank Sinatra tied for second."

"Hmm, an old school fan, I see. Favorite old song?"

Great. He would definitely draw conclusions from this, but she couldn't lie about the best song of all time.

"You can't laugh."

"*Moi?* Laugh? Of course not. Why would I laugh?"

"Because, well, just because."

He made an *x* over his heart. "Promise, cross my heart. No laughing. Song title, please."

"'At Last.'"

"At last?"

"Yeah." She stared at her hands in her lap.

"At last what?"

She looked up at him, eyes wide. "'At Last.' It's the name of the song."

"Oh, I don't think I know it. How's it go?"

"You don't know 'At Last'?" He seemed so perfect. It was almost a relief he didn't know the best love song ever written.

"Afraid not." He nodded to the CD player nearby. "Can you play it for me?"

Yeah, and I can also just tell you you're gorgeous and I'm ready to start dating again. I don't think so. "Um, I'm not sure where my CD is. And you didn't tell me your favorite old band."

He looked at her for a second. "Is there a reason you don't want to play this song for me?"

She shook her head. "Nope. Not a one. Now, spill. Favorite old band, please?"

She squirmed as he stared a second longer. "I don't have one."

"You don't have one?"

"I guess if I had to name one, I'd say Otis Redding, since I like 'Sittin' on the Dock of the Bay,' but I'm more of an '80s-band kinda guy."

"You poor, poor man." She shook her head. "You don't know what you're missing out on."

"Well, I would if somebody would play a certain CD for me."

"I'll search around for it and bring it with me on Friday if I remember, okay?"

He sighed. "Okay, you're off the hook. But I can't wait to hear what's so great about this song."

You'll wait if I can help it. Why didn't I just name another song? "Favorite food?"

"Pizza. You?"

"Chicken pie, my mom's."

"Favorite date?"

"Oh, gosh, I don't know."

"You don't know? Good. Slot's still open." He put his elbows on his knees and leaned closer to her.

She laughed. "Maybe I just have a bad memory."

"I doubt it. You'd remember a fantastic date."

"You give my long-term memory more credit than it deserves."

"Who was your second-grade teacher?"

She replied instantly. "Mrs. Darnell."

"Best subject in school?"

"English."

"First car?"

"Pontiac Grand Am."

"I don't think it's your memory." He leaned even closer and put his hand on her knee.

She blushed and ducked her head. "Okay, maybe I haven't had a great date."

His face was inches from hers as he put one finger below her chin, forcing her to look at him. "We'll see what can be done about that on Friday."

She held her breath. The tiny lines around his eyes mesmerized her. *He must smile a lot.* This close, she could even see a few gray hairs at his temple. *He'll be one of those gorgeous older men.*

"Jane?"

Her eyes shot to his, and she saw a tiny reflection of herself in his iris. "Yes?" She hadn't meant to sound that breathless.

The finger at her chin became a caress against her neck. "I—"

Wilson's sharp bark made them both jump apart. *That dog is dead meat.* "Sorry." She jumped up from the chair and held up a finger. "Hold that thought."

Rushing down the hall and into her bedroom, she bent low to undo the latch on Wilson's crate, then scratched his ears.

"Good boy," she whispered. "Momma was getting in over her head out there." She straightened, and the dog ran from the bedroom as she checked out her flushed face in the dresser mirror. *Moving a little fast there, Jane.* Her fingers trembled a bit as she smoothed her hair and headed back out toward the living room.

Jake was standing by the couch, watching Wilson jump at the hall closet door.

"I probably need to take him out, or I'll have a mess to clean up." She opened the door and pulled out his leash.

"No problem. I was thinking the same thing about Carter." He followed her and Wilson through the door outside. "So I'll see you on Friday, okay?"

"Okay." *Look anywhere but at him, or you'll pick right back up where you left off.*

"Have a good time at the park."

He went inside his apartment, and she tugged Wilson toward the grass, grateful again that she'd gotten the dog in the divorce.

chapter 14

❀ · ❀ · ❀ · ❀ · ❀ · ❀ · ❀

Jane slid her Blazer into a parking space just as Lydia was pulling a sleeping Olivia out of her pink plaid car seat. Lydia placed her peaceful daughter next to Oliver in the side-by-side stroller, buckled them in, and went around to the back of the Durango. She came back with Otis, a picnic basket, and a baby bag. Jane grabbed her own basket from the passenger seat and stepped out of the vehicle.

"Perfect timing, for once," Jane said. "See, I'm not late to *everything.*"

Lydia smiled back as she stuffed the huge diaper bag in the bottom of the stroller. "Well, will wonders never cease?" She picked up her wicker picnic basket in the same hand as Otis's retractable leash.

Jane followed Lydia across the park, eyeing the picnic tables on the far side for shade and suitability. Deciding on one below a great big grandfather elm, she led them to it and they set their baskets down on the worn, scarred tabletop. Two minutes later, a beautiful multicolored quilt was spread out on the ground, and both babies were lying contentedly, Oliver babbling up at the branches of the great elm while Otis settled his furry little body down into the grass with a snort.

"Wow, I'm hungry," Jane said. "And it's such a beautiful day for a picnic. Oh, look at that sweet little one, sleeping so soundly."

Lydia turned to look and saw that Oliver had fallen asleep.

"You've got to get a picture of that for your scrapbook. They're so adorable. And Otis is just lying there looking at them all serious. Did you bring your camera?"

"Honey, does the pope pray? Of course I'm prepared to capture any scrapbook-worthy moments!" Lydia pulled her Canon Rebel Ti from its carrying case. She snapped on the external flash and turned it on. Walking over to the twins, she lay down in the grass to be at their level, then snapped a few pictures.

Jane began unloading her goodies as Lydia stood back up. Unhooking the flash and placing the camera back in its bag, Lydia squinted into the sun's harsh glare as she studied the parking lot. "I think that's Mari and Emmy in the parking lot." She gestured to the far corner of the lot.

Jane turned and looked in the direction Lydia had pointed, straining to make out the figures now walking down the hill. "I think you're right. I'll go meet her and see if she needs any help."

Jane once again crossed the new grass, honest enough with herself to admit there was a new bounce to her step.

"*Hola, chica!*" Jane called out as she approached Mari and Emmy.

"*Hola!* Are we late? Have we missed anything?" Mari called back.

"Not a thing. We just got here a second ago. Lydia's over getting set up. Can I help carry something?" They walked together toward the picnic table.

"Nope, I'm good."

"Mommy, I want to play on the playground. Can I? Please?" Jane smiled down at the adorable little girl.

"Just a second, honey," Mari answered as they approached the picnic table.

"Hey, Mari! Hi, Emmy!" Lydia greeted Mari and the smiling little girl clutching Mari's hand, twirling a red-ribboned pigtail in her other hand.

"Hi. I hope we're not too late." Mari tucked her short hair behind her ear and deposited a big turquoise beach bag on the table.

"Oh, no, you're fine. We just got here."

"Mommy, can we go play on the swings, *por favor?*" Emmy tugged Mari in the direction of the nearby playground.

"*Un momento*, sweetheart. Mommy's got to get our food out first." Mari began unloading the beach bag with her free hand.

"I'll take her," Jane said. "You can stay here and get all set up."

"Would you mind?"

"Not at all. I'm done with the unloading anyway." She gestured at her things on the table, then bent down to Emmy's level. "Hi, I'm Jane."

Emmy stepped forward and grinned. "I'm Emmy."

Jane turned back to Mari. "We'll be back in a flash." Emmy's hopeful gaze swung back and forth between her mom and Jane.

"Okay, thanks." Mari bent down and tugged on one of Emmy's pigtails. "You be good for Ms. Jane, all right?"

"All right." Emmy grabbed Jane's hand and began pulling her toward the swings. "Come on, Ms. Jane! Let's get the purple one!" Jane trotted after her, tossing a bemused expression over her shoulder to Mari. Mari smiled back and, assured her little girl was in capable hands, turned back to unloading her bag.

"So, how's the scrapbook coming?" Lydia untwisted the tie on a loaf of bread. Pulling out two slices, she began tearing off the edges.

"Honestly, I haven't picked it up since we were at MacKenzie's." Mari watched her. "I just can't seem to find time for it at home. There's always so much to do. What are you doing?"

Lydia looked up in surprise and blushed. "I hate bread crusts. I know we're supposed to outgrow it, but I never did." Mari laughed as Lydia picked up the peanut butter and began unscrewing the lid.

"No need to explain. I feed Emmy green beans, and I won't touch the things."

Lydia shook her head. "Anyway, I know exactly what you mean about not scrapping at home. I get more accomplished at Mac's than I could ever dream about doing in my own studio at home. Usually, just as I get going, the phone rings or the dog throws up or something else happens."

"Yeah, or the husband decides it's time to remember that you're married." Mari jerked her gaze up as her hand flew to her mouth. "*Ave Maria!* I can't believe I just said that out loud."

Lydia threw back her head and laughed. "Honey, there's no need to apologize. I only *wish* that was one of the problems I had." She went back to spreading peanut butter on bread. "Dale seems to have forgotten that aspect of marriage ever since these little ones"—she nodded her head toward the still-sleeping twins—"made their entrance into the world."

"Oh, now I'm doubly sorry." Embarrassment flooded Mari's voice.

"Don't be. I'm trying to figure out if there's something I can do to make him notice me again. Sounds like whatever you're doing is working. Got any pointers?" Lydia threw the question out with as much nonchalance as she could muster. Sharing the fact that her husband no longer wanted her physically was appalling, but she was determined to find a solution, even if it meant humiliating herself.

Mari looked up into the branches of the old elm and bit her lip as she thought. "What's his favorite color?'

"Orange—Tennessee orange. If it's decorated with Vols, he'll love it."

"So we're dealing with a sports nut."

"That's the understatement of the century. His mistress is ESPN. How do I compete with that?" Lydia cringed at the desperation in her voice. How had they gotten into this conversation? She hadn't invited Mari to the picnic to air her dirty laundry.

"Vols lingerie," Mari said with a straight face, and Lydia dropped her knife.

"You cannot be serious."

Mari grinned. "Oh, yeah, it's made. You can find it online, or there's a cute little store out on West End that sells it."

"Do I even want to know how you have this information?"

"John has his favorite teams as well." Lydia gazed in surprise at the devilish smile that crossed Mari's face.

"You're kidding me."

"I'm not. You can find bras, teddies, garters, lots of stuff all made with the team's logo." Mari opened a bag of chips and dumped some onto a plate. She rolled the top of the bag and set it back on the table.

"Okay, but what if that doesn't work?" Lydia went back to the peanut butter. "I mean, it's one thing to be unnoticed when I'm not trying. It's a whole other thing to try, and get rebuffed."

"If it doesn't work, you try something else." Mari shrugged. "But it *will* work. I guarantee if you put on Vols lingerie and go stand in front of the television screen in the middle of SportsCenter, he'll notice."

"Stand in my living room in the middle of the day in only my lingerie?" Lydia's voice rose to a squeak. "Have you looked at me? I'm not exactly a supermodel."

Mari set down the soda can she had just opened and

stepped back. Slowly, she looked Lydia up and down with an appraising eye as a breeze blew across the table, rustling the leaves in the trees.

"Exactly what is your problem area? I see gorgeous curly hair, a beautiful olive complexion, and a great hourglass figure. Which part don't you like?"

Lydia snorted in disbelief. "Um, all of it? These hips?" She smacked the sides of her jeans. "These thighs? Or maybe these arms? I mean, come on. I wave, and the skin under my arms waves back."

Mari burst out laughing. "You really think if you step in front of the television in a push-up bra that he's going to be looking at your *arms?* Um, no, *chica.*" She waggled her finger at Lydia. "Trust me on this one."

Lydia took a deep breath and considered it for a minute. On the one hand, she would be mortified if this didn't work. The idea of Dale failing to notice her if she tried it was unbearable. But she also wasn't happy with the way things were. Either she could try this and at least know she had done something about the problem, or she could keep griping about it and waiting for some sportscaster to remind Dale to pay attention to her.

Oh, what the heck? "What's the web site and where's the store?"

Mari looked up and grinned again. "Good decision." She gave Lydia the web address and described where the store was, then turned toward the playground. "If you're ready, I'll go get Jane and Emmy so we can eat."

"I'm ready." Lydia sat down hard on the picnic bench. "Hey, Mari?" She rested her chin in her cupped hands.

"Yeah?"

"Thanks a lot."

Mari held up her ring finger and pointed to the diamond there. "*De nada.*"

She headed off to the playground, and Lydia stared out across the park. She had just decided not only to wear lingerie in the middle of the day, but to do so in her living room. She'd have to ask Mac if she could keep the twins for a few hours. But first things first: she had to visit that web site and see how long it took to get an order shipped. Lord knew her marriage was growing more and more stale by the day.

Emmy's giggle reached the picnic table a split second before Mari and Jane came around the trees with her.

"Okay, ladies. Lunch is served," Lydia said.

"Hey, is Mac coming?" Jane sat down and unscrewed the lid of her water bottle.

"She said she'd try. She's got Kesa this afternoon."

"Kesa's her granddaughter, right?" Mari said.

"Right."

"Who is her daughter married to?"

"She's not."

"Oh."

"It was a hard situation for her," Lydia said. "But she chose to parent rather than place Kesa for adoption since Mac promised to help. And it's been good for her. Tabby's straightened up her act a lot since Kesa."

"Really?"

"Oh yeah. It had gotten so bad that Mac and I joked she

should maybe start a scrapbook just for Tabby's legal papers."

"You're kidding. *Es loco.*"

"Crazy is right. But, like I said, it's getting better."

"Momma, I wanna go back to the swings. Can I go, please, pretty please?"

Mari tugged on one of Emmy's pigtails. "As soon as you finish up that sandwich, you can. But you have to stay on the swings that I can see from here, okay?"

Emmy crammed the rest of the sandwich in her mouth and bobbed her head up and down. She scrambled off the picnic bench and took off for the swings.

"She's adorable, Mari," Jane said.

"*Gracias.*"

"So are you going to tell us all about his visit, or do I have to pry it out of you?" Lydia asked.

"Whose visit?" Mari shifted on the bench to look at Jane. "Is this the *chico* you're having dinner with on Friday?"

"One and the same. He came over with a gift today." Jane couldn't stop the grin from spreading across her face.

"A gift? Ooooh, do tell."

"Yoo-hoo!" Mac's deep voice soared over the expanse of grass between parking lot and picnic area. "You girls startin' without me?"

"Wouldn't dream of it." Lydia scooted over to make room for Mac.

"Mmm-hmm. What'd I miss?" Mac snagged a potato chip.

"Nothing yet. Jane was just about to tell us the skinny on a gift Jake brought her."

Mac's eyes widened and she nodded. "Well, don't let me stop you." She gestured with the chip for Jane to continue.

"At first I wasn't sure what it was, because it was in two bags."

"*Two* presents?" Mari said.

"They went together. The first was a big bag of AOL CDs, and the second was a mini-sledgehammer." She took a drink of her Diet Mello Yello and waited for them to get it.

Lydia got there first. "To smash the Internet! How smart is that?" She slapped the table. "I *love* this guy."

Mari's forehead creased. "Smash the Internet? *No comprendo.*"

"Since my ex cheated through the Internet, Jake thought I might want to get back at it. So—get this, girls—he sat at our mailboxes for *two hours* getting enough CDs for me to smash."

"No way."

"That man is smitten with you, sure's I'm sittin' here."

"You think? Really? Maybe he was just being nice."

"Nice is a card or flowers," Lydia said. "I'm with Mac. He's smitten."

Jane grinned again. "I think he almost kissed me."

Mari squealed. "Oh, I love a good romance! Why 'almost,' though?"

"Wilson interrupted us." Jane explained what had happened.

"Did you kill the dog?" Lydia said.

"No, I thanked him."

"Thanked him? Why in the world did you do that?"

"This is all moving a little too fast, don't you think? I mean, we haven't even been on a date."

"But he's going to give you the best date you've had," Lydia said. "I'd bet on it."

"Mac, what do you think? You're the wise one of all of us."

Mac chuckled. "Now, I don't know 'bout that." She leveled a gaze at Jane. "But I wouldn't bet against it. You best be makin' sure you ready to be courted."

"Courted?" Mari said.

"Pursued," Lydia explained.

"Ah, got it."

"I think I am. By him, anyway. I'll admit, it's strange to be one-on-one with any man other than Bill. But when Jake's around, it's like I've never even dated. No, that's not right. I mean, it's like it's all new again." She shook her head. "Does that make any sense?"

"Makes good sense," Mac said. "Been a year now, ain't it?"

"Yeah."

Mac nodded her gray head. "'Bout time, then."

Jane began picking up her lunch mess. "I guess we'll find out on Friday. It'll either go great or put an end to this whole thing."

"I vote great." Lydia held up her hand.

"Me too." Mari raised her hand as well.

"I'll make it unanimous." Mac's hand joined the others in the air. "Now, which one of us it gonna be?" All the hands fell down.

"What?" Jane said.

"Which one of us you want to capture this on film for you?"

"You mean take pictures on my date with Jake?" Jane wadded up a napkin. "I don't think so."

"He ain't gonna know we're there. We'll just take pictures

while you get ready. That way, if it works out, you got some-thin' to scrapbook later."

"And if it doesn't work out?"

Mac shrugged. "We throw out a few dollahs in pictures."

Jane considered it for a second. If she and Jake did work out, it would be very cool to have pictures from the night of their first date in a scrapbook. On the other hand, wasn't this a bit like those women who bought a wedding dress before they ever had a boyfriend?

"I don't know, girls."

"Aw, come on, Jane." Lydia tossed a napkin ball in the nearby trash container. "Nobody but us has to know."

Jane walked her own trash over to the container, then turned and faced the Sisters. "Okay, how about this? I'm sup-posed to smash the AOL CDs with Jake that night. I'll ask him to take pictures with my camera. That way, even if it doesn't work out with us, I'll have some neat pictures."

"That's fine by me." Mac pointed a finger at Jane. "You just make sure you don't forget that camera, you hear?"

Jane nodded. "I hear."

chapter 15

❀ · ❀ · ❀ · ❀ · ❀ · ❀ · ❀

This was ridiculous. Jane threw yet another sweater onto a bed already heaping with them and blew out her breath in frustration. Every single sweater she owned was now crumpled on top of her bed, none of them having made the grade for pictures on her first date with Jake.

She put her hands on her hips and looked at herself in the mirror. "Get it together, Jane. Just grab something, anything, and put it on," she said to her reflection in the oval mirror framed in carved mahogany. A baby-blue sweater with a scooping cowl neck peeked from beneath the hill of wool and cotton. Snatching it, she pulled it over her head, smoothed it down, and turned to look back into the mirror. *Whatever.* She had to get out of here or she was going to be late for what was supposed to be the most fantastic date of her life that started in four—no, three—minutes, right across the breezeway. Her jewelry box slid a bit toward the edge of the dresser as she threw open the top and grabbed big silver hoops, putting them in on the go.

Wilson watched from the bed, only raising his head at the occasional slamming of a drawer. "You have it so easy, buddy." She put the second hoop's clasp into her earlobe. "All you have to do is eat and sleep all day." She walked over to the bed and pulled her black boots from underneath, then sat down beside the floppy-eared dog. He crawled his way up to her lap and rested his head on her leg. "You're a good dog, Wilson."

She patted him on the head and scratched his ears before pulling on her boots. Finishing the job, she sprang up from the bed and twirled in a circle. "How do I look?" Wilson raised his head and gave a short bark. "Good enough. Okay, Momma's gotta go, so head to your crate."

Wilson jumped down off the bed and walked over to his crate, nudged the door open with his nose, and went inside. Jane worked the latches, then headed for the door.

Grabbing the big red bag full of CDs to smash, she took a couple of deep breaths before opening her heavy door and stepping out into what had become frigid winter air. No trace lingered of the beautiful seventy-degree weather they had enjoyed at the beginning of the week. Now frost covered the ground, and fireplace smoke could be smelled in the air. Jane raised her head and sniffed the scent of winter. Hopefully, the chance to do that was disappearing. Enough of all this winter chill.

Jane knocked on Jake's door and turned to see the moon's

reflection on the pond. Despite the freezing temperatures, it was a beautiful night, and she didn't have to cook dinner. Life could be much worse.

"Hi, there. You're right on time," Jake said. "Come on in." He made a sweeping gesture into the apartment, and Jane stepped in and looked around. Dark leather club chairs sat facing a crackling fire, over which hung a plasma television. His coffee table seemed to be made of glass and iron. Underneath the entire arrangement ran an oriental carpet with reds and purples swirling amid golds and browns. A couch took up the side length of the room.

"Your place is lovely." She set the gift down and blew on her hands, rubbing them together in an effort to get warm.

"Thanks. How about I put those CDs somewhere and get you something to drink? Coke? Water?" He picked up the red bag and turned toward the kitchen.

"Oh, thanks. Water would be good."

"Not a problem." A timer buzzed in the kitchen. "That's the bread. I'll pull that out of the oven, and how about you take a seat in the living room?"

"Sure, go ahead." She walked over to one of the club chairs and sank down into its leathery softness. *Man, that feels good.* She had sat in a chair nearly identical to this one at Pottery Barn, and then gaped in sticker shock at the $1,799 price tag. The computer business must be doing well.

Major Carter stared at her from the arm of the other chair. Jane couldn't decide if the cat was sizing her up or just staying on guard in case Wilson came bounding in the door. Deciding on the latter, she reached out from her chair and petted the fluffy cat's head.

"Hey, there, Major Carter. You don't have to worry. No doggies are coming over tonight." The cat began a low, satisfied purr as Jane scratched around its ears. "But if your daddy and I are going to be friends, I think you two have to continue learning how to tolerate each other."

"Okay, we're all set." Jake came out of the small kitchen and gestured to the table in the dining nook just off the entryway. "We've got about forty-five minutes before *Stargate* starts, which should give us plenty of time to eat and smash some CDs, don't you think?"

She tried not to roll her eyes at his fanaticism as she pulled back from the cat. "Sure. Are we smashing or eating first?"

"Eating, definitely. You'll need your energy for the destruction." He grinned at her, and she felt the fluttery wings in her stomach again at the light in his eyes. *Steady, girl. The night is young.*

She walked over to the beautiful wrought-iron and glass table and took in his careful planning. He knew how to set a table. Or had looked it up somewhere. Gleaming silverware was placed on white linen napkins that had been expertly folded into little pockets. Her eye took in the small bowl of rosebuds with white taper candles placed on either side in crystal candlesticks. Her brows drew together as she tried to make sense of the scene before her. He was a sci-fi nut. Granted, he had a cat, and that was a bit out of the ordinary, but he also had real silver flatware and linen napkins. Something was rotten in the state of Denmark. Had she misread every signal? Was he gay?

"This is beautiful, Jake." She looked into his hopeful eyes.

"Great." He blew out his breath. "I should call my sister, then, and tell her the tutoring paid off."

"Excuse me?"

"Part of the best date you can remember should involve a unique dinner, right? Let's just say this isn't my normal Friday-evening fare." He nodded toward the extravagant table. "So I called my sister. She was so happy to hear I was having a woman to dinner, she rushed right over with all her stuff. Even drew me a diagram of where it all goes."

Oh, good. Not gay, just more thoughtful than any man she'd ever met. "Please thank her for me. It's beautiful."

"I'll pass the message along. Ready to eat?"

She nodded, and he pulled out her chair. Settling her in, he took out a match from the box on the table, struck it, and lit the candles.

"So, tell me about the rest of your week." He sat down across from her and placed his napkin in his lap. She told him about her trip to the park with Lydia and Mari and was thrilled when he laughed in all the right places. This sparkly feeling inside her was new. Not even with Bill had she had this. Their quiet friendship had never developed into a flaming romance like the ones she read about in novels. She didn't know what to do with the warmth stealing up her cheeks as Jake smiled at her across the table and regaled her with stories of Major Carter's antics.

"Never a dull moment, it sounds like," she said, and he chuckled.

"You said it."

"Where did you get Major Carter, anyway? Have you had her long?"

A shadow crossed his face. "Long story. Definitely longer than the"—she watched him steal a glance at the clock on the wall—"fifteen minutes we have before the show."

She shook her head. "Okay, then tell me about your sister. I already know she can set a mean table." She smiled and relaxed as the tension in his shoulders left.

"Meredith can be an hourlong story herself, but the condensed version is that she's amazing. I think you'd like her a lot." Jane took another bite of bread that melted in her mouth. "Mom and Dad adopted her when she was eight. Man, we hated each other that first year."

Jane chewed and swallowed. "How old were you when they adopted her?"

"Ten. She'd been in and out of foster homes for five years. Her birth mom died when she was three. They'd been living on the street. You've probably seen stories like hers on the evening news."

"Oh, how awful."

"Yeah, but she was so young that she doesn't have much memory of it, thank goodness." He looked up at her and put his fork down. "I still remember the day we decided to stop hating each other and start being siblings. It was recess, and we were both out on the playground. She'd only been with us about six months." He took a sip of water, and Jane waited.

"This kid came up to her and started yelling, calling her names, making fun of her for being an orphan. I couldn't help it; I just saw red. I went over and kicked the kid. Next thing I knew, we were all sitting in the principal's office, me holding a napkin to a bleeding lip and the other kid with a nasty black eye forming, just waiting on our parents to show up." Jake shook his head at the memory.

"Mom got there, took one look at us, and marched us out to the car. I thought we were in major trouble. She didn't say a word the whole way home, but as soon as we'd gotten into the garage, she turned around in her seat and stared at us with this look I'll never forget as long as I live. She said, 'Jacob, you know that we do not use fists in this house to solve disputes. However, sometimes a body is just too dumb to listen to words. Congratulations, son. It seems as if you know the difference.'"

Jane laughed.

"I sat there for a solid minute trying to make sure she wasn't going to come back and ground me." He sat back and wiped his mouth with the napkin from his lap. "But then Meredith reached over and took my hand, and I looked at her. And suddenly she wasn't just some kid that had come to live in our house. She's been my sister ever since." He pushed back from the table. "And that's enough of my boring stories. Let's go have some real fun and smash some CDs." He stood up. "Okay with you if we save dessert for after *Stargate*?"

"I guess."

"That way I know you'll stick around for the whole thing."

He leaned over the table and grinned devilishly at her, wiggling his eyebrows. She laughed and stood up as well.

"I'm sticking around for the spilling later," she reminded him. "I want to hear the story of Major Carter."

He grimaced, and she realized just how little she knew about him. "Right." He turned and went into the kitchen, coming back out with the red bag. "Let's go destruct!"

"Okay, but let me grab my camera first. I was running late and forgot it. This is definitely going to be a scrapbooking moment."

"Oh, right, you said you scrapbook." They stepped into the breezeway.

"Mm-hmm. Helps me stay sane. I can't believe you even know what it is." She inserted her key into her doorknob and opened the door, gesturing for Jake to come on in.

"In addition to setting a perfect table, Meredith also scrapbooks. She's always the one snapping pictures every time the family gets together."

"Yeah, well, when you're old and gray, you'll be happy she captured the youthful you on film." She grinned at him and picked her camera up off the shelf in the living room. "I'm good. Let's go smash!"

She followed him out to the pond and watched as he stacked the CDs up on one of the big gray rocks at the pond's edge. When he had them just so, he walked back over to her and ceremoniously handed over the miniature sledgehammer.

"Your weapon, m'lady." He bowed before her.

"Why, thank you, kind sir." She curtsied and grabbed the

tool as he took the camera from her hand and snapped a few pictures of the stack. Walking over to the CDs, she knelt down and looked at them. Such harmless little things, all shiny and innocent. To think this was the avenue by which her husband had turned her life upside down. She heard the click of the camera shutter and glanced back at Jake. She felt a little silly as she raised the hammer and smashed it down on one of the stacks. Bits of CD flew everywhere. *That felt good.*

"Hit 'em hard!" Jake cheered from the sidelines, snapping away as she raised the hammer again, bringing it down with enough force to jar her arm.

"Show 'em who's boss!"

She hit the third stack and felt the satisfaction flood her body at the sound of cracking CDs. *Should have done this a long time ago.* She raised the little hammer again and again, pounding the CDs into oblivion.

Pain shot up her arm, and hot tears coursed down her cheeks, though from her arm or her heart she couldn't say. Now that she had started, she couldn't seem to stop. Startled geese flew off the lake, honking at her as she slammed every little tiny bit of silver left on the rock. She hit the rock harder and harder, scaring herself with the depth of her own pain until Jake's arms came around her from behind.

"Hey, hey." His voice was gentle as he took the hammer from her and set it on the rock. "I think you killed AOL." She looked at the destruction around her, and the tears came even harder. He pulled her down to sit on the rock, speaking into her ear and rocking back and forth.

"Really, the Internet as we know it is now dead." She hic-cupped and relaxed her back against his chest. "That's better. Laughter is good." He kept holding her and rocking until the last little tear squeezed its way out of her eye. She took a deep breath and sighed, pushing her long hair behind her ears.

"Well, I must look a sight in those pictures." *How embar-rassing.* "I didn't know how mad I was until I started smashing. Sorry about that."

"No apologies needed." His head rested on top of hers, and she sighed. "I'm glad you feel safe enough to cry with me."

She turned a bit in his arms and looked up at him, not real-izing until that moment the depth of her trust. *And you barely know him.*

"Tell me about you."

He shifted on the rock a bit. "You want to be bored now? I thought we were going for fantastic date status here."

"Nice try, but not fair. I've told you my past." She turned back to stare out across the lake. "Tell me yours. I've been blub-bering on, and you still haven't dumped your story on me. So, your turn. Were you a Chippendale in another life? Come on. You can tell me."

He threw back his head and laughed. She felt the vibration in his chest. "Oh yeah, that's me, the original Chippendale."

"Okay, then tell me about your career as a hired assassin. You don't have to name all your marks, just a few so I know you're telling the truth."

"I probably couldn't hit the broad side of a barn if I was standing ten feet from it with a machine gun."

152

"Well, then, what is it?" She pulled away and turned to face him on the rock, pulling her legs up in front of her to sit Indian-style. "What'd you do before you became the guy across the hall who listens to all my problems and captures my major life moments on film?"

"I worked on computers all day and dreamt about the woman who would let me capture all her major life moments on film."

"Oh, nice. *Perfect Lines*?"

"Nope, that one was me."

"So you're not going to tell me?"

"There's nothing worth telling, Jane."

"How about letting me be the judge of that? Why'd you move here?"

"I told you, I wanted a change of scenery."

"Which is code for 'I'm not telling you the real reason.' Right?"

He sighed. "Which is code for 'I wanted a change of scenery.'" He pushed a button on his watch, and the face lit up green. "Come on. *Stargate* starts in one minute." He stood up and turned to go back to the apartment. She caught his arm.

"Um, we have a huge mess out here that I don't think the landlord will appreciate in the morning."

He looked around, seeming to notice the destruction again. "Oh, yeah. I'll clean it up in the morning. Come on, dessert and *Stargate* are waiting." He walked back toward the apartment, and she followed, picking up the camera from its spot on the grass and wondering at the real meaning of "change of scenery."

Jake headed to the living room as soon as they came inside.

He sat down in one of the club chairs, taking Carter from her perch on its arm and settling the ball of fluff in his lap. The remote controls clacked together in their basket on the coffee table as he reached in and took one. He pointed it to the television hanging above the fireplace, and the theme music for *Stargate SG-1* filled the room. Jane tried to ignore his change in mood.

"So, how much do you know about the series?" Jake said.

"Enough to know who the good guys are and what the Stargate is." She let him change the topic, grateful to be back on a neutral subject. "Well, and to know that all guys watch it just to see Major Carter in action." She laughed along with him.

"Well, she *is* one of the more attractive women on television these days."

They settled into their chairs and turned their attention to the screen as the storyline unfolded. Despite her previous contentions, Jane found herself interested in the characters, silently cheering them on as they did battle with the evil G'ould. Ah, to live in a world where everything was so black-and-white, where the bad guys said they were bad guys, and the good guys won in the end. That'd be nice.

Jake watched her from his seat. She had slipped down in the chair, curling her feet up under her in the process and laying her head on the arm of the chair. She would have to know about his past eventually, of course. But the way she looked at him took his breath away, and it was downright addictive. He doubted she'd look at him like that anymore when she found out how much he and her ex had in common.

What was so intriguing about Jane Sandburg? He rested his chin in his hand and allowed himself to gaze at her more openly. Of course she was great to look at, that was obvious. Who wouldn't want to stare at long black hair all day and wonder what it would feel like slipping through his fingers?

But it wasn't just that. There was something about her that made him want to take care of her, to talk with her, to argue with her, to just be near her. He'd even figure out a way to make Major Carter like that crazy mutt of hers if it meant he could be in her presence. His eye traveled over the beautiful skin on her neck to her sweater, and he smiled at the dog hair on her shoulder.

This was lunacy. That had to be it. Who smiled at dog hair on a sweater? He had finally lost his mind.

She laughed again at the screen, and his heart warmed at the sound of her happiness.

This was too much thinking. More than once he had been accused of overthinking, and he could admit he was doing that very thing right now. There were plenty of hours in the day tomorrow to analyze the wisdom of his actions. Tonight should be spent enjoying sci-fi in the company of a very intriguing woman with curves in all the right places. He turned back to the screen as the show went to commercial.

"How about I get us some dessert?"

"I thought I had to wait until after the show." Her smile was playful as she teased him.

"Well, you've only made fun of the acting twenty-two times, and you had to have burned at least a thousand calories obliterating those CDs, so I'm rewarding you." He got up from his chair and walked toward the kitchen. "I'm a bit disappointed; I was counting on more commentary from the peanut gallery."

"It's the blood sugar. If you hadn't withheld dessert, I'd be on my game."

"Ah, I see," he called from the kitchen, picturing her smile. "Then you'll have to stick around for *Stargate Atlantis* so I can see what I missed."

He tinkered around, fixing the desserts as fast as possible. In a moment, he came around the corner of the kitchen, a bowl in each hand piled high with chocolate cake and vanilla ice cream. Hot fudge sauce lay in a drizzle pattern over the entire concoction.

She stood and took her bowl from him. "You must have a lot of faith in this cake if you think it's going to make me sit through another hour of sci-fi."

He held out a spoon to her and, when she reached for it, pulled her to him. "It's Meredith's recipe." He looked down into her beautiful eyes and read the welcome in them. "Yeah, I've got faith in it." The thought of kissing her had dominated his mind all week. He let go of the spoon and ran his hand along the soft skin of her face, watching as her eyes closed in satisfaction and her head tilted upward to his. He set his bowl on the table at his knee. Took hers and did the same. She opened her eyes and looked at him.

"You're missing the end of *Stargate*." Her mouth turned up at the corners, and he traced it with his finger, slipping an arm around her waist.

"Something more important came up." Her smile grew, and his heart kicked up its pace. "Thanks for coming tonight. I know sci-fi isn't your thing."

She placed her hands on his chest and shrugged. "It wasn't as bad as I remembered. You were right. Must have been the company."

He held her two hands in his one, pulling her a bit closer. Bending his head, he brought her knuckles to his lips and kissed them. "Then you'll stay for *Atlantis*?"

"I guess I could be persuaded." He looked at her. The frantic pulse at her neck touched him in more ways than he cared to admit and reminded him to slow things down. He stepped back and picked up her bowl. Handing it to her, he said, "Then we'll see if I owe Meredith an even bigger debt of gratitude."

She smiled and spooned some ice cream and cake into her mouth, closing her eyes in bliss. He stared, transfixed by the look of pleasure on her face. He definitely needed to keep ice cream around at all times. And cake. Lots of cake.

"Mmm, this is my favorite dessert of all time," she said.

"Then you get as much as you want, provided you stick around for *Atlantis*." He resumed his seat as she settled back into her own, then he forgot his own dessert as she took another bite and closed her eyes again to savor it. Oh, yeah. She could have the entire gallon of ice cream and every single morsel of cake in the entire apartment complex.

Jane opened her eyes and looked straight at him. "*Atlantis.* Okay, I'm in. That's the one where humans found the Lost City of Atlantis in some faraway galaxy, but they can't enjoy it because some other alien or something needs to eat them. Is that right?

"Something like that," he said. "Sounds like you paid a little more attention to these shows than I thought."

"It was either listen to the shows or listen to Bill. I chose the one that had at least some small form of entertainment value. Bill is a great conversationalist, don't get me wrong, but long diatribes on the history of the Stargate do not constitute a pleasurable evening." She went back to her dessert. He noted her enthusiasm for chocolate again and then tried to remember what they were talking about.

"So, life with Bill wasn't a piece of cake?" Oops.

She screwed up her face. "Isn't it a cardinal rule not to talk about past relationships when on a first date? I'm sure I read that in some magazine."

"I wouldn't know. *Cosmo* isn't on my bedside table." He took a bite of the dessert.

"Well, it's a rule, and we've already talked about Bill at the smashing party." She nodded her head toward the lake outside. "So no more about my past until you spill yours."

The theme music for *Atlantis* filled the room, and he turned to the television in gratitude.

"How about I admit I have a past and we save it for our next date so we can enjoy *Atlantis*?"

She was silent through the theme music, and he turned to find her watching him. "Jane?"

She pointed her spoon. "Okay, I'll let you out of it tonight. But don't think I'm going to be so easily put off next time, mister. I don't care how good the dessert is, you're spilling. Got it?"

"Got it."

chapter 16

❉ · ❉ · ❉ · ❉ · ❉ · ❉ · ❉

Saturday morning, Jane rolled her tote down the breezeway and to her car, still puzzling over last night at Jake's. It definitely ranked at the top of her date list, hands down. But not knowing his past, or the reason he wouldn't share it, was killing her. *Welcome back to the world of dating.*

She opened the rear door of the Blazer and lifted the tote inside, reminding herself to run by the store for tape runners before going to Mac's. Thank heaven the Sisters were getting together to scrapbook. Maybe if she told them everything Jake had said, they could guess what he was holding back.

Her phone vibrated as she pulled out of the parking lot. "Jane Sandburg."

"Hi, Jane darling, it's Sonya." Jane rolled her eyes and tried not to panic. Between working on her ideas for Sisters, Ink and lost hours daydreaming about Jake, Sonya's project had taken a back burner.

She assured the heiress that the fund-raiser planning was on schedule and talked through her ideas for table decorations and entertainment. Flipping the phone closed as she pulled into the parking lot, Jane made a mental note to get some work done on Sonya's event.

She was still sorting through ideas in her mind as she walked through the automatic doors of the store and nearly fell over a shopping cart.

"Excuse me, I'm so sorry. I didn't see y—Jane?"

She'd know that voice anywhere. What woman wouldn't know the voice of the man whose last name she had for two years?

"Bill! Hi. Fancy meeting you here." Seeing his familiar face brought a rush of nostalgia she didn't want to think about.

"Yeah, what are the odds? How have you been?"

"Oh, good, good. And you?"

His voice was the same. He was even wearing a shirt she'd gotten him their last Christmas together. "I'm okay. How's Wilson?"

"He's fine. Look, I'd love to talk, but I'm in a rush, as usual." She turned to go, desperate to escape.

"Oh, okay. It was good to see you."

"You too. Bye now."

Of all the stores in all of Nashville, you have to walk into the one your ex-husband visits. Smart move, Jane. She berated herself all the way to the office supply section, through the check-out counter, back into the Blazer, and down the road to Mac's house.

By the time she arrived, Jane was certain that her subconscious had sought Bill out to make her feel guilty about a superb date with Jake.

She knocked on Mac's door and went inside. "Mac, girls, I'm here," she called out.

"In the kitchen." Mac yelled back.

Jane made her way through the living room, taking in the smell of chocolate in the air.

"Do I smell something yummy?" She parked her tote at the base of the stairs and sat down at the kitchen table.

"Mac made fudge." Mari cut a piece from the dark slab in the center of the table. "And it's heavenly."

"Thank goodness. I'm in bad need of chocolate right now." Jane cut herself a generous helping.

"Bad need?" Lydia pushed an empty glass and the gallon of milk toward Jane's end of the table. "What's going on? Was the date not good?"

"Oh, the date was excellent. Wonderful. Made the top of my date list of all time."

"Yay!" Mari clapped her hands. "I *love* love!"

"He was amazing." Jane took a big bite of fudge and moaned as it melted in her mouth. "Mac, you are a genius."

"Now, I don't know 'bout that, but I do know my meemaw could make some fudge in her day, and I happen to have her recipe." Mac finished drying a spoon and put it in its drawer. "So tell us 'bout this date. You seein' him again?"

"I have to. He won't tell me about his past until our next date."

"He has a past?" Lydia said.

"Don't get worried. I don't think it's anything major, but, yeah, he's hiding something. I tried twice to get him to tell me why he moved to this apartment, and he told me it was just for a change of scenery."

"Maybe it was."

"Mari, you're a hopeless romantic." Jane smiled. "He told me he'd spill on our second date. I assume he wouldn't say that if there wasn't something *to* spill."

"So other than finding out he has a past, how was the date?"

"Mmmm." Jane took another bite of Mac's sweet dessert. "Let's just say it was ten times better than this fudge."

"Details, *chica*, we need details."

Jane told them all about the smashing party and Jake's near kisses.

"It sounds exciting. Why the 'bad need' for chocolate?" Lydia said.

"I ran into Bill on the way here." Jane took another huge bite of fudge.

"Oh no. Was he with someone?"

"No, he was alone. But seeing him, well, I guess it was just unexpected."

"Unexpected bad, though, right?"

"Not really, no. That's what's so confusing. I thought if I ever saw him again, I'd . . . I'd . . . I don't know what I'd do. I never expected to see him again."

"Then let's pretend you never did." Lydia took a drink of milk. "You're on to bigger and better things with Jake. No sense in letting Bill put a wrench in a good thing you've got going, hmm?"

Jane thought about that for a second. "You know what? You're right. I'm being an idiot. Anybody would feel weird seeing their ex after a year, and the day after going on their first date, right?"

"Right."

"*Sí.*"

Jane slapped the table and stood up. "Right. Then enough about that. I've got pictures to scrap and more ideas for Sisters, Ink. Mac, have we gotten any more members?" She walked around the table, Mari and Lydia following her to the stairs.

"Got us ten more yesterday. You been makin' more calls and not tellin' us?"

"Those weren't me. I haven't had time to do anything but think about ideas. I guess word's getting around. What'd you find out about the music downloads?"

They made their way upstairs to the scrap room.

"We've gotta pay to put 'em on our site, but it's not too much. I think we should put up three or four downloads and see if the current members like 'em before we go investin' in a whole library of music, though.

"Good idea. How about a weddings download, an island one, and something for Christmas to start us off?"

"I like those." Lydia unpacked her tote onto the scrapping table. "Some Natalie Cole or Celine Dion for the weddings, Kenny Chesney and Jimmy Buffett for the island stuff, and maybe Nat King Cole or Bing Crosby for Christmas?"

"Oooh! Good choices!"

"Can we put some Spanish music up, too?" Mari said. "I listen to English music most of the time, but it'd be nice to have something in my native language, I think."

"That's a fine idea." Mac pulled a notepad out of a drawer. "You got some singers and songs I can look up on the Internet?"

"Sure." She gave Mac the information.

"This'll get us started. I should have it up by the end of next week, and then we can start trackin' to see if the members use it."

"Sounds like a plan. Thanks for handling that, Mac." Jane thumbed through a Stacy Julian book.

"My pleasure. Gives these old bones a reason to keep movin'."

"So, I've got a cat to let out of the bag." Lydia snipped off a piece of light blue ribbon as the Sisters looked at her. "Y'all know I don't like sharing too much personal stuff, but since that's what we're about, I think I should tell you that I've ordered some orange lingerie."

"Excuse me?"

"Oh, not for us. For me. For Dale." Lydia swallowed and started over. "Dale's been paying more attention to Sports-Center than me, so I thought I'd try something new." She spoke the words in a rush. "I found a company that makes lingerie in team garb and ordered some in Tennessee Volunteers patterns. It should be here tomorrow."

"Well, if that don't beat all, I sure don't know what does," Mac said.

"You go, girl!" Jane came around the table and high-fived Lydia. "Now, I think it's very important that we decide which of us will capture this moment on film for you."

"You're so funny." Lydia smirked. "And so insane. This one will have to be burned on the film in my memory."

"But, Lydia, I'm sure you'd agree a picture's worth a thousand words."

"Yep, and I'm not sure what this particular portrait would say, so no pictures."

"I'm kidding. Let us know if it works, though, okay?"

Lydia nodded.

"*Chicas*, I'm not sure I can do this." Mari spread her fingers across the layout in front of her and tried to figure out what to do. She had six pictures laid out.

"Here, this will help." Jane slid her layout design book across the table and Mari picked it up. "It's full of example layouts you can use in your own scrapbook. Just turn to the part that's for however many pictures you have, and you'll get some ideas for how to fit them all on a page."

Mari flipped through the glossy pages of the book. "So I do exactly what's in this book? Isn't that cheating?"

Lydia laughed. "Honey, if that's cheating, then I'm in serious trouble. I don't know how in the world I'd get a layout done without using Stacy's ideas." She went back to cutting another piece of ribbon.

"And you don't have to do exactly what's in there," Jane said. "You can just use it as a starting point and put your own embellishments so yours ends up looking a little different."

"But some of the pictures in here are a whole lot bigger than my little four 4x6s."

"No problem," Mac said from her side of the table. "Just take your picture over there to the computer and scan it in. Then we'll enlarge it and print out a bigger one for you." She pulled up the end of a Clikit and let go to make a hole for a pink eyelet in the shape of a flower.

"What's that thing you're using?" Mari asked.

"It's a Clikit." Mac pulled on the edge of the tool again and let it snap back into place. It made a loud popping sound, and Mari blinked. "It puts a little hole right where I need it so's I can set an eyelet there. When I've made the hole, I turn it to the other end and pop it down on the eyelet. That sets the eyelet in place." She demonstrated, then held the paper out to show Mari the finished product.

"So what are the little hammers for?"

"That's the old way of settin' eyelets. We used to have to pound 'em in place. You shoulda heard it at convention. Hundreds of women poundin' away on eyelets can give a body a deafenin' headache. Now you just click it once. No poundin' needed." Mac clicked another hole in the paper and placed an eyelet in the spot. "I think it might be the best thing since sliced bread."

Mari walked around to Mac's side of the table and watched as Mac continued setting eyelets in intervals down the page. "Can I try?"

"Sure!" Mac slid off her stool and handed the tool to Mari, then walked her through using it. Mari clicked her first eyelet into place and ran her finger over the finished product.

"I've got to get one of these." Awe filled Mari's voice, and the other girls laughed.

"Spoken like a true Sister," Lydia said.

Mari walked back over to her side of the table and looked again at her pictures. "I think I'm going to need a trip to the store before I can do much more with this scrapbook."

"Did I just hear a need for shopping?" Jane looked up from her layout. "When do we go?"

"What about tomorrow?" Mac said.

"I was wondering if any of you had time to help me out tomorrow," Mari said.

"Sure, what's up?"

"I'm going to get up in the attic and pull down Emmy's old nursery furniture so I can set it up for Andrea. John will help me get the furniture down, but I want someone who can take some pictures so that I can scrapbook the move-in. Is that crazy?"

"Not at all," Lydia said. "I can help out with that. Are you thinking around lunchtime?"

"Hmm, how about we grill burgers at my place for lunch? We'll eat and then get started on the nursery. If we finish in time, we can hit The Savvy Scrapper. Would that work?"

"I'm always in for a good scrapping moment followed by shopping," Jane said.

"Yep, count me in," Lydia said.

"I'll have Baby Kesa tomorrow, but if I can bring her with me, I'll come."

"Of course, definitely bring Kesa. And Lydia, if you want to bring the twins, that's fine, too. It would be a good thing for Emmy to interact with other kids at home. Thanks, y'all."

As the women murmured their acknowledgment and continued cropping pictures and applying them to their layouts, Mari walked over to the wall, which was covered in Peg-Board with silver hooks. A package of rubber stamps hung from each hook. At the end of the wall were several shelves on which sat rubber stamps that were mounted on wood blocks. Some were for babies, others for birthdays, deaths, seasons, celebrations. Picking a stamp of a gift off the shelf, she turned it over in her hand. This was what Andrea would be to her family. A true gift.

She had no idea why she and John were having such troubles getting pregnant again. They'd had very little problem conceiving Emmy. She had thought she was perfectly fine and very fortunate to have one pregnancy and one child. Many of her friends had experienced multiple miscarriages, but not Mari. Her first pregnancy had resulted in a bouncing, laughing, beautiful little girl.

And then it was like the well had just dried up. Try as they might, nothing they did resulted in a pregnancy. She supposed she should be grateful for the inability to get pregnant. It was probably better than getting pregnant and then miscarrying, but still she wished the doctors could at least find out what was wrong. Why had they been able to have one child so easily and then nothing?

She also knew that other people wondered why she couldn't just be happy with one. There were plenty of women who would give their right arms for the blessing of having just one child. They told her she was getting greedy and to be content with her one healthy child.

But her dream had always been for two. She didn't want Emmy to miss out on the fun of having an *hermanita*. The teasing and torture, the playing and laughter—she couldn't imagine what kind of mother wouldn't do everything possible to give that kind of childhood to her daughter.

She turned the stamp over again in her hand, running her thumb over the rubber image. Andrea would be a gift to all of them if they could ever get through the red tape required to get to her.

Staring at the stamp, Mari had a sudden inspiration. How about a cover page with this stamp in the middle and red tape tying it down to the page? It was the perfect illustration of their situation.

She took the stamp back over to the scrapping table, excited to have an idea that made sense. She could even do Andrea's birth announcements with the same theme whenever they brought her home!

"I need some help." The Sisters looked up at the excitement in her voice. "I want to do a page with this in the middle and somehow make it seem like the present is hard to get to because of red tape."

"Red tape?" Mac said.

"Like all the red tape we have to get through to get to Andrea."

"Oh! What a great idea!" Lydia slid off her stool and came over to Mari's side of the table. "We can stamp this twice, one in black, the other in all different colors. We'll put the black one behind the colored one and use a Pop Dot with the colored one to make it stand out. Put red ribbon running behind the whole thing, and it will look like the ribbon is running through the present!"

"I love that! I mean, I didn't get it all, but it sounds great!" Mari said. "Where do I get ink pads?"

Mac pointed to a rotating tower of ink pads in the center of the table that was sitting by two other rotating tool holders. "Any color you want should be right there." She began turning one of the other objects in circles. Mari thought it looked like her Tool Turnabout from Pampered Chef. "All the markers in here correspond to the same colors as the ink pads, so it'll all match. You can stamp it in black and color it in with these markers." She gestured toward shelves of paper in the corner of the room. "I've got every color in paper, too, so just help yourself."

Mari turned and stared at it all in wonder, for the first time getting an inkling of how it all worked together. Her head spun with all of the possibilities. "I wanna be you when I grow up," she breathed, and Mac cackled with laughter as they all turned back to their scrapbooks.

chapter 17

❋ · ❋ · ❋ · ❋ · ❋ · ❋ · ❋

Jane could hear her phone's trademark wildcat ringing as she neared her apartment door two hours later. She fumbled with the lock and made it to the phone as the answering machine clicked on.

"Hello?"

"Jane?"

"Bill?" *Why is my ex calling me?*

"Yes, it's Bill." Silence hummed across the line, and Jane began to worry.

"Is everything all right? Your parents? They're okay?"

"Oh, yes, they're fine. I'm sorry. Everyone's fine. Seeing you today . . ." He cleared his throat. "Jane, can we talk?"

No, we can't talk. I have a gorgeous neighbor, and life is looking up.

"What about?" She tossed her purse onto the kitchen table and pulled a bottle of water from the refrigerator.

"I don't know. I just feel like maybe we should talk. Things have changed in the past year. *I've* changed. I want you to know how sorry I am for what I did. I miss you. I miss us."

Jane held the receiver out and stared at it for a second. Who was the apologetic guy on the other end? Not the man she married who ended up yelling at her for invading his online privacy.

"Jane? Are you there?"

She put the phone back to her ear. "I'm here, Bill. But I don't think we have anything to say to each other. We're divorced. I think at this point the script says to go our separate ways."

"Since when do you do what you're told?" She laughed. Like it or not, the man knew her. "I don't want to pressure you into anything, just talk. I'm so sorry for what I did, and I want you to know that."

"I can know that by the fact that you just told me."

"But I want to tell you in person." He sighed. "I realize I have no right to even ask you to see me. Please. Give me five minutes to tell you a few things, and then I'll leave you alone. Forever, if you'd like."

Five minutes. Surely that isn't asking too much after all we've shared.

"Okay, Bill. When?"

"Are you busy tonight? How about dinner at the Green Hills Grille?" *My favorite restaurant for a dinner with my ex? No.*

"I'm not sure dinner is appropriate. Let's meet outside the

Davis-Kidd bookstore instead. There's a bench in the mall right by the store entrance. I can be there around six-thirty."

"Great. I'll meet you there. Thanks, Jane."

"You bet." She hung up. *I am the most idiotic person on the planet.*

"Hi, Bill." He stood from the bench to greet her, looking good. Why did he have to look good? Men who cheated in Internet chat rooms should be required to look bad for at least several years afterwards, if only to their ex-wives.

"Hi. How have you been?"

She sat down next to him on the bench. "Good." *Surprising, but true. Must have something to do with this new man I'm seeing.*

"You look great."

"Thanks. So do you."

They sat in uncomfortable silence for a moment. *I lived with this man for two years. I should be able to talk to him. But didn't he call this meeting?* "So you mentioned you had something to say to me?"

"I do." He turned to face her and took her hands in his. She let him, for no other reason than to let this scene play itself out. "I wanted to tell you how very sorry I am to have betrayed you and our marriage." The pain in his eyes was real, anyway. "I don't know what I was thinking. I got so caught up in the idea of a different relationship, and Vivien's vision of me sounded so much better than what you thought of me, I just had to go after it."

"So you cheated because I didn't think well of you?"

"No, no. That's not what I meant. This is not your fault in any way. I'm just trying to explain why it happened. Not that there's an explanation good enough, but I thought maybe you would want to hear it anyway."

She looked at him for a minute and considered that. It was good to know what had possessed him to do such a hurtful, foolish thing to her. Knowledge is power, at least that's what the bathroom walls always said.

"Jane, you have to believe that I'm so, so sorry. And I need you to know that it was never physical with Vivien. Everything happened online. Nothing happened in real life."

"It sure felt like real life."

"The virtual spilled over into the actual, yes. I don't know how it got so out of control, but it's over with me and Vivien. And I know we're divorced and you've moved on, but I've been thinking about you so much these past few months. And then, seeing you today, it made me realize I have to tell you." He took a deep breath. *Walk away while you still can.* "I love you, Jane. I've always loved you. Since high school. It's always been us. And if you can find it in your heart to forgive me, I'll spend the rest of our lives proving to you how much I love you."

The ticking of the clock on the end table sounded like a jackhammer as Jane entered her apartment and walked down the hall toward Wilson. *My ex-husband did not tell me he loves me and wants us back together.* The walls of the room began to waver ever so slightly, and she knew she had to get some Midrin in her fast before the migraine took over. She'd been in a fog since leaving the mall, not even sure how she'd made it home.

The latches on Wilson's crate sounded like explosions as she released them. Standing back up was too hard. She crawled to the bathroom and reached underneath the sink for the medicine basket, rummaging around in it, ignoring the sound of the bottles clanging together. The amber-colored bottle with a big red *X* on top finally, magically, came to the top. Sometimes the headaches caused blurred vision, so she had learned to mark the bottle with a big *X* to make finding it easy even when she couldn't see clearly.

The pain of pushing down on the lid felt like hot needles running up her arm and into her brain. The light in the bathroom was too bright; she was squinting now and praying for the relief of the medicine. The pounding in her head was so loud even Wilson was barking at it. *No, that can't be right. Wilson can hear my head pounding?* It took a minute to realize someone was pounding on the front door and calling her name.

The room swam as she tried to stand back up, so she sank back down to her knees. Crawling down the hallway, her pleading whispers to Wilson to hush went unheeded. His barking was going to make her head split right down the middle. Whoever was on the other side of the door was hitting it hard enough to make the frame shake. She felt linoleum on her knees and knew she had finally made it to the entryway. Moving her eyes to see the door hurt too much, so she lifted her hand and felt around until she found the doorknob. She heard the snick of the latch just as stars exploded behind her eyes and everything went blissfully quiet.

chapter 18

He watched her breathe, timing his own breath to hers, praying with each intake of air, sighing with every release. Seeing her face that white, yelling her name, begging her to open her eyes had all taken about ten years off his life. Thank God she had still been clutching a bottle of Midrin when she collapsed.

His gaze took in Jane's pale face. Her eyelids fluttered, and he came to kneel beside her, taking her hand in his. "Jane?" He spoke softly in case any traces of the headache remained. Her eyes came fully open then, and he sent up a prayer of gratitude at the life in their green depths.

"Jake? What are you doing here? What happened? Is Wilson—"

"Shhh, Wilson's fine. He's right here." Wilson put his front paws on the edge of the couch and licked her face. "I think you passed out from a migraine. You managed to open the door for

me before you went out, though. How long have you been getting headaches?"

She pulled her hand from his to pat Wilson on the head,
and he missed her touch. "I had them constantly in college. I
only get a couple a year now."

"Did you take the medicine before you blacked out?"

Her face scrunched up as she thought, and he smiled at the
little-girl cuteness of it. "I don't think so. I was trying to get it
open when I realized the door was pounding. Or you were
pounding on the door."

"That's because Wilson was barking, and I couldn't hear
you hollering at him to hush. I figured something was wrong,
so I started pounding."

"Thank you for that. I kept trying to get Wilson to hush,
because his barking was going to split my head open, but he
wouldn't. So I tried to get to the door to tell whoever it was to
go away, but I blacked out before I could say it." She put her
hand to her head and looked at the ceiling.

"Well, then, thanks for letting me come in. Can I get you
anything?" He tucked a lock of hair behind her ear, grateful
beyond words that she was okay. "How much water have you
had to drink today?"

"It's just a migraine, Jake. I'm fine." She sat up, and he
reached to steady her as she wobbled.

"Oh yeah, you look fine." He ignored the rebuke in her
eyes at his sarcastic tone. "How much water?"

"A couple of glasses, I think. Why?"

"Dehydration can set off a migraine. Sit tight."

She called out to him as he went around the couch and into the kitchen. "How do you know so much about migraines?"

He searched the refrigerator and grabbed a couple bottles of water. "I used to get them a lot." The cap clicked as he unscrewed one, handing it to her and indicating for her to drink. "I had to give up sugar for a while to get them under control, but it was worth it. Only get two or three a year now." Taking a long gulp from the second bottle of water, he sat back down in the other chair. "Mine were usually triggered by stress or sugar. Looks like yours might be lack of water."

Sounds better than Excess of Ex-husband.

"Were you coming over for a reason?" She took another drink as he stood and walked around behind her.

He began kneading the muscles in her neck. "Just to see when you were free for our second date."

If you'll keep doing that, we can have it right now. Oh, but my ex-husband just informed me he'd like to marry me again. Will that be a problem? "Anything particular in mind?"

"I had a few ideas to run by you. Have you had dinner?"

"As a matter of fact, I haven't." His hands moved up her neck to her head, and the tension began to seep away from her brain.

"We could go get some dinner right now, or order in and watch a movie if your head still hurts."

"It's feeling better, but I think I'd rather stay in." *So long as your hands don't stop.*

"Pizza or Chinese?"

"Pizza, please."

"My place or yours?" *Considering my ex-husband could call or drop by at any moment,* "Yours. You've got the better TV."

He chuckled. "So you're just using me for my superior taste in electronics."

"Mm-hmm."

"Glad we're clear on that." He pulled his hands away, and she turned to see him.

"I'll go back home and order our pizza. Do you need me to walk Wilson, or you feeling okay?"

"I'm good, thanks. I'll be over in a few minutes."

"Good. See you in a few."

Wilson went to the hall closet and whined as soon as Jake walked out the door.

"Okay, buddy. I hear you." She snapped on his leash and headed for the lake.

"Wilson, your momma's got to get some perspective, and fast." The dog's ears perked up as he trotted along beside her. "Your old dad wants back in our lives and, while I'm inclined to dismiss him out of hand, I think a smart woman would consider it for a second before saying no. Would you agree?" Wilson huffed at her and bent his head to sniff the ground.

"Good. Then let's consider." They were halfway around the lake by now. She slowed her steps a bit. "Bill and I had a great friendship. Or what I thought was a great friendship before he cheated on me. That doesn't make for solid friend status. Still, it's the only time I'm positive he betrayed me, not including the night before our wedding, which I never asked him about. If I'm giving the benefit of the doubt, and I should since he didn't cheat any other time for our entire dating or married life, then this boils down to whether or not I've forgiven him and he's changed."

She stopped as Wilson did his business and looked out across the lake. Two ducks were trailing along, leaving a wide *V* in their wake and earning a short bark from Wilson as he finished. She began walking again. "I know I've forgiven him. Whether or not he's changed remains to be seen. And then there's Jake to consider." They finished their circuit of the lake and walked back toward the apartment. Wilson stopped at Jake's door and sniffed at the edge.

"Come on." She tugged his leash. "No terrorizing Major Carter tonight, mister."

The door suddenly opened, Jake filling its space. "All done?" He knelt down and scratched behind Wilson's ears.

"Oh! Um, yeah. Just finished. I'll go put him back in his crate."

"How about bringing him on inside?"

"You've got a death wish for your cat?"

He chuckled. "No. But they seemed to get along well the other day. I thought it might be time for round two."

She considered for a minute. This could help her decide if Jake was a long-term presence in her life. *Long-term? You're having a second date here, Jane. Little early for those thoughts.* He stood back up, and she watched those tall legs straighten. *Now, those are long-term.*

"I suppose we could try."

"Great, then you two come on in." He stood back, and she entered the apartment, an eager Wilson leading the way. Major Carter watched warily from her perch on the back of a club chair.

"Major Carter, we've got company." Jake went over to the cat and picked her up, petting down the fur that had risen on her back. "You remember Mr. Wilson, right? He won't hurt you."

"There *was* the unfortunate tree incident." Jane said. "But I don't think we'll be having any more of those, right, Wilson?" He glanced up at her, then focused again on the cat in Jake's arms and pulled against his leash. "I'm not convinced this is a good idea. What if he hurts her?"

"Please. She's just as likely to scratch his eye out than he is to bite her head off. They've got to learn to coexist at some point."

She started and looked at him, but he was staring at the animals. "Coexist?"

He looked up and smiled. "As neighbors, of course."

"Oh, of course." *You idiot. He's not thinking long-term, either.*

Major Carter growled low in her throat, and Wilson went onto his belly. He began crawling across the floor, pulling himself along with his front paws.

"Now, there's something I've never seen a dog do. He looks like a soldier crawling under barbed wire or something." Jake laughed.

"I call it his Osama crawl. Not sure where he picked it up, but he does it when he's trying to make nice with me."

"So this is a good sign?" He knelt down, keeping Carter in the crook of his arm. The cat's eyes stayed locked on Wilson.

"Definitely." They watched as Wilson neared Major Carter, then rolled over onto his back, all four paws up in the air, long tongue hanging out the side of his mouth.

"I think he's ceded authority to her tonight." Jane smiled. "Or at least for the next few minutes."

"Smart dog." Jake sat Carter down by Wilson. They sniffed each other for a second; then Carter turned on one paw and walked away, tail in the air.

Jake stood up. "I guess she's decided he can stay for a while."

"That went better than expected."

"Yeah, I thought we'd get a little fur flying before it was all over."

"The night is young." *Oh, that's it. Sound suggestive.* She glanced up at him to see his reaction.

His eyes were the color of dark chocolate. *How did eyes get that dark? Could I live with a reminder of chocolate staring me in the face all my life? Quit thinking long-term.*

"What are you thinking?" Amusement filled his voice, and she noticed the laugh lines around his eyes again. He put his hands in his back pockets.

She shrugged. "Oh, nothing."

"Well, keep thinking it." He came to stand in front of her, close enough for her to smell his aftershave. She breathed in deeply as he ducked his head down to catch her eyes. "I like that look."

"I have a look?" *A look, but no breath left in my body.*

"Yeah, you do." He smiled, and the lines grew.

"Oh."

He reached a hand around her waist, and she let him, feeling tingles when his warm hand came to rest on the small of her back. He tugged her across the step between them, and she tilted her head back to keep his face in view.

"It's a look that says you're thinking about me, I think," he whispered.

"Oh." *Wow, you're sounding like a genius. Pick a different word.* "Good."

"Good?" He traced her jawline with his finger.

She swallowed. "Yeah." *Wait, did that make sense? What are we talking about again? Just kiss me already!*

He gave her a quirky smile. "Good." He bent his lips toward hers, and she closed her eyes in anticipation.

"Oof!" She fell against his chest with a thud as the doorbell rang and Wilson leaped toward the door, taking her leash-holding hand with him. They fell to the floor before she realized what was happening and let go of the leash. He jumped up on the door, short barks reverberating off the walls.

"Wilson Wellington, hush!" Her face was hot with embarrassment. *Lydia was right. I'm killing this dog.* She scrambled over to him and grabbed his collar. They backed away from the door. "This is not your house. Be quiet." His ears laid back, and he whined at her. He looked back and forth from her to the door. "Don't cry at me, you big baby." The deep sound of Jake's laughter made her face flame further.

"I'm sorry."

"Don't be." Jake got up, and she enjoyed the show. He looked through the peephole and back down at her. "Pizza's here."

"How about I put him in the bathroom until the dangerous stranger is gone?" *And give my face time to return to its normal color.*

"Sure." She felt his gaze on them as they walked down the hall. She entered the bathroom with Wilson and sat down on the toilet lid with a sigh.

"I suppose I should thank you," she whispered. "I don't need to be kissing Jake until this thing with Bill is cleared up anyway." Wilson laid his massive head on her knee, and she ran her hand over his black and tan fur. *Not that Bill ever made me forget to breathe.* "But you cannot be acting out over here. You embarrass your mother."

The door cracked open, and Jake's head came through. "All clear."

She stood up. "I think I'll take him home and come back. He's a big beggar during dinner."

"Are you sure? It's fine if he stays. Carter begs too. We'll just have an audience while we eat."

She laughed. "I'm sure. Let me run him across the hall, and I'll be right back."

"You're the boss." He opened the door wide and stepped aside into the hallway for them to pass. His big hand snagged her elbow as she walked by. "Hey, Jane?"

She stopped and turned to him, eyebrows raised in question. "Hmm?"

"Don't be long." He kissed the top of her nose. "Pizza'll get cold." He grinned at her, and her stomach did double flips.

"Right. You bet. Be right back." She hustled out of the

apartment and across the breezeway to her own door. A thousand thoughts ran through her brain, not the least of which was the memory of her ex-husband sitting on a bench in the mall, begging her for another chance.

"Crate, Wilson." As she followed his wagging tail down the hall and into her bedroom, she caught her image in the mirror over the dresser. Her face was flushed, her eyes were dancing, and she was almost positive her nose was burning where he had kissed it. *Bill never made me feel like this.*

She bent to work the crate's latches and realized Wilson was still wearing his leash. "Sorry, boy." She unsnapped it and tossed it to her bed. "Momma's brain isn't all here tonight." He circled around on his pillow and settled down with a "hmmph."

"Man, I'd like to curl up in there with you. What am I going to do, Wilson?" He gave her one dismissive look, then closed his eyes. "Oh, fat lot of help you are. And to think I give you the best in kibble and treats."

She turned and headed back to Jake's apartment. *Honesty is the best policy. Just tell him you saw Bill today.*

Her hand was shaking as she reached up to knock on Jake's door. *Calm down. Tell him, and you'll feel better.* Her shoulders straightened with resolve, and she rapped on the door.

"Come on in. It's open." *His voice is even sexy through wood.*

He was setting an ice bucket and two glasses beside a pizza box and two-liter on the coffee table. "Wilson all squared away?" He grinned at her, and she willed her knees to keep working.

"Mm-hmm. Probably falling into la-la land as we speak."

The ice cubes clinked against glass as he fixed her a drink. "Good. I think they made progress tonight." He nodded toward a sleeping Carter on the back of his chair.

"They didn't kill each other. I'd say that's progress." She took the drink he offered, ignoring the tingle where their fingers met on the cold glass, and sat down. "So if this is our official second date, I think there's some spilling to occur." The soda burned on its way down her throat.

He sighed. "You're right. I promised spilling, and I'm a man of my word." He poured his own drink. "But, as a wise woman has said, the night is young."

"Oh no." She wagged her finger. "You're not getting away with that again. Spill, mister."

He sat down in the chair beside her and took a sip. "Getting away with what?"

"You know what. Waiting until the end of the night, then telling me you'll just share your story on our next date. That worked for the first date. Not tonight. I want to hear all about your sordid history as a bouncer."

"A bouncer?"

"Hey, I don't have a whole lot to work with here. You'll learn that leaving things to my imagination is not a good idea."

"I've never been a bouncer."

"Rodeo clown?"

His laugh warmed her right down to her toes. "'Fraid not."

"Bad actor in an off-off-Broadway play?"

"Never."

She looked around the room. "Furniture dealer?"

"Nope. Mom and Meredith helped with this."

Major Carter looked at her with lazy interest. "I've got it!"

"This should be good."

"Cat saver! You went around town in the dead of night in a superhero cape, rescuing abandoned kittens. That's how you got Carter."

He threw back his head and laughed. She drank her Coke and watched his Adam's apple move under a tanned throat.

"You're actually close with that one."

Coke seared her throat as she choked. "What?" she sputtered.

"Minus the cape, of course."

"You rescue cats?"

"Cat, singular." He held up one finger.

"The big, bad past story you didn't want to share with me until our second date was that you rescued a cat? I think I'm missing something."

She watched as he took another drink. "Wait, *why* this particular cat?"

He pointed at her. "There's the question." He sighed.

"And the answer?" *Do I want to hear this?*

"Major Carter was a woman's cat. A woman I was seeing."

His pained expression made her want to stop him, but curiosity got the better of her. "And why would this woman give you her cat?"

His eyes seemed to be begging her for understanding, but she didn't know why.

"Because her husband was allergic."

Her breath caught. Her husband? No. He was not a cheater

like Bill. *Why is every man I fall for a cheater? Are any of them loyal at all anymore?* "Oh, I see."

"No, you don't. Get that look off your face."

"What look?"

"The one that says you think I'm a cheater. She was separated when I met her."

Her heart started beating again. Separated wasn't divorced, but it also wasn't married.

"Okay. I'm listening."

"Her husband had cheated, and she was planning on divorcing him. I met her three months after she'd moved out."

"Didn't you think that was a little quick for her to start dating?"

He shrugged. "She said she was divorcing him. I believed her. We started seeing each other. Six months later, she told me he was sorry and in counseling and she had to take him back." He snorted and shook his head. "Six months, and all it took was one phone call from him with the right words."

Or one conversation on a bench at the mall.

"The only problem was that she had gotten a cat, and he was allergic. Thus, Major Carter."

"Ah, it's all becoming clear now." *That there's no way I can tell you I talked to Bill today.*

"Yeah. When I met you, I thought, 'Here I go again.' But it's a little different since you're already divorced." He took a drink. "No big decision about signing the papers or anything."

"Nope. Signed, sealed, and delivered a couple of months ago." *Which doesn't keep him from trying to get me back.*

"So, we're okay?"

"Why wouldn't we be?"

"I was worried, with your history with Bill, that you'd think I was a cheater."

"You said she was separated when you met her, right?"

"Yeah."

"Well, separated is not divorced, and she had no business dating anybody until she had signed those papers, in my opinion, but I don't think you were cheating, no. She may have been, though. I'm not sure. Haven't thought about it enough." She nibbled a fingernail and considered.

He blew out his breath. "At least you're not running from my apartment. That's better than I'd hoped for."

She laughed. "You were really worried, huh?"

"I was." He leaned forward, setting his glass on the coffee table. His hand covered her knee. "I'm glad I didn't have to be, though. I like that we can be honest with each other."

"Honesty is good." *Is it dishonest not to tell him?* She cleared her throat. "So, what are we watching tonight? Tell me there's not a sci-fi marathon."

He grinned and stood up. "You're safe. Tonight is your decision. I've got a couple hundred DVDs to choose from." He opened the door of what she'd thought was an armoire. It was packed with movies. "Take your pick."

Setting her glass down, she walked over to the armoire. "My word. You're a veritable Blockbuster."

He grinned. "I like movies."

She ran her fingers along the spines. *Stargate, Star Wars*

collector editions, *Galaxy Quest, Spaceballs, The Matrix* entire boxed set. "Your sci-fi freakishness is on display here."

He looked over the movies. "Yeah, I guess it is."

Gladiator, The Patriot, Braveheart, Gods and Generals, Lethal Weapon I–IV, We Were Soldiers, Patton. "And your love for fighter movies."

"Fighter movies?"

"Yeah, look at these." She pointed to the titles. "You either love fighter movies or Mel Gibson. Since your mom and sister decorated this place, I'm assuming you don't harbor a secret love for men. So I went with fighter movies over Mel."

He pointed at her. "You'd be dead-on."

"Good. Another crisis averted." She pulled out *Must Love Dogs.* "I think this is appropriate considering the start to our night."

He looked at the cover and laughed. "Good choice." He put the DVD into the player, and they settled back into their chairs.

He turned to her as the FBI warning came on the screen. "Hey, Jane?"

"Hmm?"

"Thanks for understanding about Carter."

"What's there to understand? You shouldn't have worried about telling me." *Since now I have to worry about telling you Bill wants me back.*

"All the same, thanks."

"You're welcome. Now, hush. The movie's starting."

chapter 19

❀ · ❀ · ❀ · ❀ · ❀ · ❀ · ❀

A few neighborhoods away, Lydia stared into the mirror, turning every way possible and sucking in her stomach. No matter which way she looked, though, the pudge and bulge were still there. Combine that with the stretch marks from the twins and she was pretty sure she had lost her mind the day she had placed the order for this orange thing. It had looked much better on the online model. Airbrushing.

At least this shade of orange was her color. She smoothed down the see-through mesh over her middle and appreciated the way it contrasted with her olive skin and dark hair. Maybe if she kept her hair all down, Dale would be mesmerized by that rather than the saddlebags on her thighs and the baby fat still hanging onto her frame. She turned in a circle and watched the orange feathered edges swing with her.

"They couldn't have made the thing four inches longer?"

she muttered, feeling the soft feathers slide on her bare skin. Just four inches and those thighs would be covered. She looked in the mirror again and squared her shoulders. She could do this. Oliver and Olivia were over at Mac's. Dale was sitting out there in his recliner, watching a rerun of the Tennessee–Alabama game right now, and didn't have to be at work for another two hours. Second shift had its good points. It was the most perfect timing she was going to get anytime soon. He had seen that game a million times. And if he had already watched it, then there was a pretty good chance he'd be willing to turn his eyes from it long enough to take in her orange getup.

"And if he chooses an old ball game over me in this outfit, then I quit." She whipped around and marched out of the bathroom.

She made it halfway into the living room before Dale dropped his remote. "What are you *wearing?*" She tried to believe he was overcome with passion rather than hear the outrage in his voice.

"Something I'm hoping will get your attention off that TV and onto me." She pointed at the television and then put her hands on her hips.

"Do you know the windows are open? If the neighbors look in here, they're going to see you!" He got up off the couch and went over to the bank of windows, frantically closing the blinds. "What were you *thinking?*"

This was *so not* happening. She was not standing in her living room, clad in orange feathers and UT symbols in very strategic locations, while listening to her husband talk about the neighbors. He was supposed to be jumping her. Maybe next time she should get something . . . What was she thinking? There would be no next time. She stamped her foot, knowing it was a childish maneuver and not caring one whit.

"Dale Pritchett, I can't believe you're over there closing the blinds when I'm standing here in this—this—" She sputtered and tried to come up with a dignified word, but failed miserably. "This *getup*."

"Well, I can't believe you're parading around our house in that *getup*." He finished closing the last blind, and she saw red. Crimson Tide red, she thought with satisfaction, and her eyes narrowed.

"I'm parading around our house because you've done nothing for the past two months but sit there in front of that stupid television and watch sports," she said in the steeliest voice she could manage. "But I can see that my effort is completely unappreciated, and so let me assure you such a gesture will never—and I do mean *never*—be made again." She turned and stomped from the room with all the dignity she could retain while orange feathers were swirling around her legs.

The stomping carried her all the way into the bedroom, where she slammed the door and locked it with complete satisfaction and rage. She tore the offending garment over her head and threw it in the garbage can by the bed, then snatched up the phone and angrily punched in Mari's number.

"He told me the neighbors were going to see." Her voice shook with fury.

"Lydia?" Mari asked. "What? What about your neighbors?"

"Not the neighbors. Dale. I walked into the living room in that . . . that *getup*." She pointed at the offending article of clothing in the trash can and then realized Mari couldn't see her over the phone. "And all he did was tell me the neighbors were going to see."

"He didn't make a move on you?" Mari's voice was full of disbelief.

"Oh, sure, he made a move." Lydia jumped off the bed and paced back and forth with angry, short steps as she talked. "Directly over to the blinds, where he closed them so fast it made my head spin. Then he asked me what in the world I was thinking."

Dale knocked on the bedroom door and asked Lydia to come open it. She yelled back at him to go away.

"Oh, Lydia, I'm so sorry." Sympathy poured through the phone line. "Want me to come beat him up for you?"

Lydia plopped back down on the bed, tired and defeated. "No, I want you to come and knock some sense into me. I'm pretty sure I've lost my mind." She ran her hand through her hair and sighed. "Dale, go away. I'm on the phone," she yelled at the bedroom door. "At least he didn't comment on my wrinkles or baby fat."

"Way to look at the bright side. See? There are lessons to be learned here. What else can we take away from this?"

"That my husband has no desire for his wife at all?" She threw an angry glance at the door as Dale's knocking turned to pounding. "Go away!"

"No," Mari continued. "That your husband has a very deep

concern for what parts of his wife the neighbors see. That could be a good thing." Silence hummed over the line as both women thought about that. Lydia had to admit that Dale hadn't exactly rejected her. He had rejected her in front of the neighbors. Okay, so he was concerned about others seeing her in the orange getup. If she wasn't so mad, that would be endearing. She looked at the door and waited for another knock from Dale. He seemed to have given up.

"You're right." She sighed again. "His problem was that the blinds were open."

"So go back out there and make sure they're still shut."

"No ma'am. Wild horses couldn't drag me back out there. Do you know the color of humiliation? It bears a remarkable resemblance to my face right now." Besides, there was something degrading about having to work this hard to get her husband interested in her. They hadn't been married long enough to warrant all this effort.

"At least go out and talk to the man. He's an *hombre*, which means he has no idea what's in your head and is thinking incredibly wrong thoughts right now. Go set him straight before this gets to be a bigger mess."

Lydia picked at the polish on her fingernail and considered Mari's words. She was right again. If left to his own devices, Dale would think of every reason in the world Lydia had done this other than the correct one.

"Okay, I'll go."

"Good for you. Call me afterwards and tell me what happened, 'kay?"

"'Kay. Wish me luck."

"You won't need it. You've got his ring, his last name, and his kiddos. He loves you. Go talk to him. And remember he's a man. One thought process at a time. It's just how they're wired."

Lydia chuckled. "Thanks, friend."

"Anytime."

Lydia hung up the phone and pulled on her jeans and a sweatshirt. This wasn't going to be a fun conversation, so she might as well be comfortable having it.

She opened the bedroom door and peeked outside, but Dale had taken her command to go away at face value. He was nowhere to be seen. She opened the door the rest of the way and walked toward the living room, noting with a smile that all the blinds in the house were now closed. Dale was nothing if not thorough.

She saw the wariness in Dale's expression the minute she stepped into the living room. His eyes took her in as if she were some unknown thing moving through his house—determining whether she was friend or foe.

His shirt felt soft beneath her fingers as she patted his shoulder. "I'm sorry I freaked you out. That's not what I had intended."

The furrow in his brow deepened. "What did you intend?"

An exasperated sigh escaped her lips. "I thought I made that clear when I came out here dressed up in your favorite team's logo." She went and stood in front of the television, waving her hands around as she talked. "I'm sick of this television, Dale. All you do is watch sports and eat. You don't play with Oliver or

Olivia, you never walk Otis, and I can't remember the last time you looked at me for any reason other than to ask what we were having for a meal."

"That's not true! I walked Otis last week."

"When I put the leash in your hand." She rolled her eyes at him. "And even then you waited until whatever game you were watching was over. The poor dog sat whining by your recliner for fifteen minutes."

Dale looked around the room as if trying to find the whining Otis. "No, he didn't."

"Yes, he did." She put her hands on her hips. "See what I mean? You're not even aware anymore of what's going on around you."

"Of course I am, Lydia. You're being difficult."

"*I'm* being difficult?" She pointed to her chest. "I just walked into my own living room in the bright of day wearing orange *feathers* for you! And all you could do was tell me the blinds were open. And you sit there telling me I'm difficult? Talk about the pot calling the kettle black."

Dale's confused look turned to one of anger, and Lydia knew she had lost whatever opportunity had been there to fix things.

"Look, I don't know why you felt the need to do that, but don't get mad at me for not knowing what's in your mind. I'm not a mind reader. If you want something, just say it." He threw up his hands in frustration and sank back into the recliner. "Why can't women be more like men? We want something, we just go get it or ask for it."

Lydia stared at him. He wasn't that dumb. He just didn't

want to understand. And if he didn't want to, there was nothing she could say to make him. She hung her head in defeat and sighed. "Fine, Dale. Enjoy your game." She walked out of the room and headed toward her scrapbooking room. Maybe there was some paper that needed tearing or distressing.

The thought of how many stamp sets she could have bought with the money she'd spent on orange feathers made her mad all over again. Well, that was it. She had tried to get her husband to notice her, and it hadn't worked. He was more interested in stats and scoreboards than what was going on under his own roof. Angry steps carried her past the scrapping studio and into the kitchen.

And she could learn to be okay with his disinterest. He was a good provider. He would never raise a hand to her. He would never leave her. There were a lot of women walking the planet who would be very grateful for what she had. And here she had to go and rock the boat. She should be happy with what she had. If she wanted more, then too bad.

The kitchen sink was stacked with dirty dishes. She sighed and began running a sink of water. The phone rang, and Lydia snatched up the cordless.

"Hello?"

"Hey, how'd the talk go?" Mari said.

"He asked me why women can't be more like men and just ask for what they want."

"You're kidding me. *Dale es un chico loco.*"

"If you just said he's crazy, you've got the wrong spouse. I had to be crazy to think that would work."

"This is not your fault. Dale has marbles for a brain. Want me to have John talk with him?"

Lydia thought about the option for a second. Dale would get really offended that she had been discussing their bedroom life with another person.

"Not yet, but thank you."

"You're welcome. The offer is always there. So can I do anything to help?"

"Find a new brain for my husband?" Lydia laughed.

"I'm on it. I'm sure somebody's selling at least one on eBay right now. I can find anything on eBay."

Lydia laughed again. Mari was right, though. Buying things on the Internet auction powerhouse site was just too fun. Quite a few of her scrapbooking supplies had been purchased through eBay, along with her camera.

"Thanks. Let me know if you find a good deal."

"Will do."

Jane stretched as tall as possible and reached to the back corner of the shelf in the top of her closet. "I know you're up here. Come on out." Her fingers closed on a corner of hard leather. She grabbed it and tugged. Mittens and scarves fell down around her feet as her wedding album popped free.

"I *knew* I had put you up there." She made her way to the bed and crawled to the middle of it. Opening the album, pictures of the day she pledged to love and cherish Bill Sandburg forever played out before her. There they were, saying their vows, cutting the cake, sharing a first dance. Feelings buried for a year came flooding back with each new layout. Bill was a comfortable kind of love. Never surprising or exciting like Jake. Bill was steady, dependable. *Boring.*

That wasn't fair. Dependability and familiarity shouldn't be dismissed out of hand. *But how dependable is he if he cheats on you?*

It was just the one time. Every marriage had hiccups, didn't it? Perhaps Bill was right. They should have waited a while longer before calling it quits.

He cheated, Jane. That's more than a hiccup.

And yet he seemed genuine at the mall. Did he deserve a second chance? *No, that's not the right question. Everybody deserves second chances.* Was she willing to give him a second chance with her? *That's the right question.*

Would she be more willing to consider it if Jake wasn't in the picture? *Well, it'd be easier if I didn't lose my breath every time he came around. That never happened with Bill. Never happened with anyone. Shouldn't that mean something?*

Yeah, it meant she was letting her physical attraction to Jake outweigh her marital commitment to Bill. *Not that I have a marital commitment to Bill anymore.*

She turned the last page of the scrapbook and saw an 8x10 of Bill holding her close, their smiling faces turned to the camera, the wedding party surrounding them. Life was full of possibility *and* disappointment that day. Her constant friend through high school and college had become her husband. Her other constant friend had walked out the door as the ceremony began, convinced Bill Sandburg was a cheater.

Lydia was right then.

Jane grabbed the phone off her night table and punched in Lydia's number.

"Hello?"

"Did I wake you up?"

"No. I'm in here looking at the Sisters, Ink site. What's up?"

"Bill called me this week."

"Did you hang up on him?"

Now, why didn't I think of that? "No, I met him."

"You what?!"

"He begged me, Lyd. Wanted to tell me how sorry he was, that he'd changed."

"Couldn't he tell you that over the phone?"

"That's what I said, but he asked me for five minutes, and I thought, after all our history together, I could give him that."

"I think you gave him more than enough."

Jane sighed. Maybe she should have called Mac or Mari. "Do you want to hear this or not?"

"Sorry, sorry. So you went to meet him?"

"At Davis-Kidd. I stayed long enough to hear his apology and, um, his plea for a second chance."

"Please tell me you turned him down cold. That'd serve the cheating—"

"I didn't say anything. I walked away."

"Well, that's something." There was silence for a minute. "Wait, don't tell me you're actually considering his request."

"I'm not sure. I—"

"Jane Sandburg, you get your head outta your rear end right now. A tiger can't change his stripes. It just is what it is. That man cheated on you the night before your wedding *and* while he was married to you. What are you thinking? Why would you give it a moment's thought?"

"You don't think people can change?"

"I don't think Bill Sandburg has changed. People, I'm not sure about."

"But you didn't see him, Lydia. I think he was genuine."

"Good for him. Why isn't he off being genuine with his new woman?"

Jane bit her lip. "I don't know. I didn't ask."

"I'll bet she left him."

"That'd be rich."

"Why else would he come running back to you?"

"Hey, I'd like to think he might just want me back."

"Jane, you know I think you're a gift for whatever man you end up with. But Bill Sandburg is a thoughtless idiot who couldn't recognize a good thing when he had it. Forgive me if I don't think he saw you at the store and suddenly realized what he'd lost."

Jane sighed. "That's how it happens in the movies."

"Welcome back to reality, Sister."

"Reality sucks."

"Not yours. I seem to recall a gorgeous man making you a beautiful dinner. Has something happened?"

"No, we had dinner again tonight, and it was great."

"Well, there you go. Why give that up for a man who betrayed you?"

"Jake's not pure as the driven snow, you know. He told me tonight how he got Major Carter." She relayed the story to Lydia.

"That doesn't make him a cheater like Bill, Jane. That woman had left her husband and was living somewhere else for months before Jake got involved with her. Plus he was under the impression that she was in the process of getting a divorce. I don't think that can be compared to Bill sitting in the study of the home he shared with you and sharing sleazy instant messages all night."

"Ouch, okay, don't remind me."

"Somebody needs to, don't you think? Before you decide to welcome it back into your life?"

"Yeah, I suppose."

"Good. Quit thinking of a cheating slimeball and focus in on Mr. Gorgeous across the hall. You coming to church tomorrow?"

"I think I'm going to Mac's church tomorrow."

"Be sure you wear comfortable shoes."

Jane laughed. Mac's pastor wasn't short-winded by a long shot. "I hear you. Thanks, Lyd."

"You're welcome, Sister. Anytime. See you at Mari's house tomorrow, okay?"

"Yeah." Jane hung up and looked at her wedding scrapbook again. Lydia was right in a lot of ways. Bill had cheated on her, and the magnitude of that shouldn't be forgotten. But if she believed what they said in church, people could change. And that included Bill, whether Lydia wanted it to or not.

She ran her finger across the picture of their wedding party, wishing Lydia's face was smiling among the rest. Maybe it was time to toss this scrapbook. She got up off the bed and padded into the kitchen in her houseshoes.

The lid of the trash can popped up when she stepped on its pedal. Inside were the remains of an orange, tea bags, and some old popcorn. *Doesn't seem right to put my wedding memories in there with all that messy garbage.*

Outside Dumpster. She went back to her bedroom and exchanged house slippers for tennies. Not bothering to tie them, she carried the album out to the big metal container at the corner of her building.

Cold wind whipped her hair around her face as she stood by the Dumpster, willing her hands to do what needed done, what should have been done a year ago. She flipped through it again, the streetlight letting her see all the long hours of finding just the right paper and embellishments, the smiling faces frozen in time.

I'll deal with it tomorrow. She hurried back to the apartment.

chapter 20

Jane shifted on the hard pew, hearing it creak, and wondering if that was a commentary on her weight. At least this time her shoes were comfy. *Live and learn.*

Between the caffeine at Jake's house and memories of her wedding day flashing fresh through her dreams all night, sleep had been elusive. She shifted again and tried to focus on the sermon.

"You've got to watch out for the enemy," the pastor thundered.

"Preach, brotha," a man called from the back.

"He'll weasel his way into your life with just a little lie. Maybe not even a big lie. Maybe you just don't tell somebody the whole truth."

"You know that's right, preacher."

Great. The pastor's been spying on me, and the congregation's out to get me.

"And before you know it"—he snapped his fingers—"you're caught up in a web of deceit." Sounds of amen sounded around the congregation. Jane slid down in her seat.

"But it's not too late, sister."

"No, sir!" yelled a woman in the front.

"It ain't too late for you to turn around and tell that ol' Satan where to go!" The pastor pointed his finger at the floor.

"Tell him where he belongs!"

"Go on." A few in the crowd stood to their feet.

"Tell him he ain't got no business up in your life. Can I get an amen somewhere from God's people today?"

A lady in a white dress covered in big purple flowers stood. "Amen, preacher. Tell it!"

There's nothing like church with Mac. They keep it real.

"Come on, children of God! Tell the enemy where he can go when he tries to get you to lie." He paced back and forth across a stage covered in red carpet. "His power over you is GONE, I say." He wiped a handkerchief across a sweaty brow.

"GONE, Jesus says." Tambourines shook, and the drummer beat a staccato rhythm.

"GONE in the precious blood of the Savior." Robed choir members stood as one in a loft behind the stage, and the congregation started clapping.

"GONE under the power of the Cross." The choir hummed, and a soprano "Hallelujah" floated out across the stage.

"GONE, nevermore to return! Sing your PRAISE to the God who SAVED you from the power of His enemy!!"

The choir burst out in song, and the congregation joined in. Jane looked around at faces wet with tears, shining with joy. Beside her, Mac was singing praises at the top of her lungs. Tabby hadn't shown up, but Mac didn't let that stop her own worship.

Jane thought about life with Bill. It would never be this full of emotion. Had never been. But was a lack of emotion, of passion, enough to tell him no? It hadn't been three years ago when she stood at an altar and vowed only death would separate her from Bill.

But that was before she knew what she was saying no to. *Jake.* Her heart fluttered at the thought of his name. Sometimes in his presence she couldn't breathe. He made her knees lock and her brain register feelings she didn't know existed.

I know now. And I'm not sure I can—or even should—walk away from it.

"Church family, hear this truth." The people quieted and sat down at the reverend's hushed tone. "You ain't never gonna know the powerful life He means for you to lead when you're lettin' the enemy hold sway over you. He'll keep you down in a pit of lies or hold you back by denyin' the richness of this life. Be aware, brothahs and sistahs. Be aware. The devil comes to destroy you. Jesus comes to save you. God tells us to be wise as the serpent, but gentle as the dove. Don't you let that ol' devil trick you into thinkin' you gotta settle for somethin' God don't intend. You ask for direction, and then you listen when He gives it. Pray with me now."

Jane stared straight ahead, certain this preacher had a camera in her apartment and a crew following her around. Would it be settling for something God didn't intend if she gave Bill another chance? But wouldn't the God of turn-the-other-cheek and second chances encourage her to try? She shook her head in confusion. The preacher was asking God to give them direction and, right then, that sounded like a good idea.

Two hours later, Jane, Lydia, Dale, Mac, Mari, and John all sat back from the dinner table. Empty bun wrappers and crumbs littered the table. All that was left on the hamburger and hotdog platter were bits of charred grease.

"That was one fantastic meal," Mac said. "I don't think I've eaten that much since Thanksgiving."

"Ugh, me either." Jane rubbed her stomach. "I feel like I'm going to pop. How are we supposed to move baby furniture now?"

Mari chuckled. "You're right. We should've moved the furniture first. I wasn't thinking."

John stood up from the table and picked up the empty platter. "Maybe if we get rid of the evidence, we'll feel better."

Mari stood as well and began helping him clear the table. "Good idea. How about y'all go on into the living room and let all that food settle? John and I'll join you in just a few minutes, as soon as we've put the dishes and food away."

"Here, let me help with that." Lydia got up.

"That's okay. We've got it. Go on to the living room. I'm

going to need all that energy from you getting the baby furniture down." Mari gathered up the bun wrappers, ketchup bottle, and jar of mayonnaise and nodded toward the hallway. "Go on."

Slowly, they began moving and making their way out of the dining room. John came around the table and kissed Mari.

"I love you, you know," Jane heard him say.

"I love you too. Now, let's get this table cleared. We've got a roomful of adults willing to move furniture. Let's not waste it."

John laughed. "Right, I'm on it."

Jane made her way into the living room with everyone else. Mac was already rocking Kesa in the recliner, the chair creaking with each backward motion.

"Did she wake up?"

"Yeah, but I don't think she meant to." Mac smiled and kissed Kesa's curls. "I'll just rock her on back to sleep."

"Are the twins still asleep?" She looked over at Lydia.

"You bet." Lydia looked at her watch. "We've probably got another hour or so before they wake up."

"Okay." Mari clapped her hands as she and John came into the room. "Then let's get to it. Sisters, to the attic."

Lydia and Jane stood and followed her up the stairs, Lydia grabbing her camera from the end table on the way.

"So, Dale, you like sports?" Jane heard John ask as they left the room.

"Do we have a game plan?" She followed the Sisters up the stairs.

"*Sí*. I thought first we'd go to Emmy's room and move her furniture. When we've made space, we'll go get the things out of the attic that were hers as a *bambina* and move them into her room as well. *Está bien?*"

"Sure. What'd Emmy say when you told her?"

They stopped at the top of the landing and waited for her answer. "She was thrilled."

"Oh, good," Lydia said.

Mari nodded. "It was a huge relief. She was almost giddy, and she told everybody at church this morning how her baby sister is coming to live in *her* room. It was adorable."

"I wonder how adorable she'll think it is when Andrea's up crying in the middle of the night," Lydia said.

"Well, Andrea might be past that stage by the time we get her. We won't know until she's here. She'll have been on a schedule at the orphanage. They have to so they can keep order with lots of babies and very few caregivers. Anyway, the attic is through here." She pushed open a door in the middle of the hallway, and the women stepped through. "Be sure you only walk where there's plywood. Wouldn't want anyone poking their foot through the ceiling," she joked.

"Which way to the baby aisle?" Jane said.

"Over there." Mari pointed to the far corner of the attic, and all the women cooed over the white baby cradle there.

"That is so precious," Lydia stepped over and around boxes as she made her way to the cradle.

"I remember when we brought Emmy home from the hospital and laid her in it. She seemed so tiny. We probably won't need it for Andrea, though, since she'll already be over that age by the time we get her."

"How old will she be?" Jane said.

"She's nine months old now, according to the file they sent, and it will be at least a couple of months before we get to her, so she'll be about eleven months to a year old when we bring her home."

"Wow, close to the first birthday."

"*Sí, sí.*" Mari took a deep breath. "I hope we don't have problems bonding, with her having spent all that time with the caregivers at the orphanage."

"I'm sure everything will be just fine." Lydia patted Mari's arm in comfort.

Mari nodded. "Anyway, all this talk isn't getting the furniture moved. Let's go rearrange Emmy's stuff." She turned, and they followed her out of the attic, down the hallway, and into Emmy's room.

Bunk beds were set up in one corner with a bright pink toy chest beside. A butterfly rug decorated the floor at the base of the bunk's ladder. Pink and red butterflies adorned the walls.

"This is beautiful." Jane turned in a circle to take it all in. Mari beamed.

"It took John and me two months to get everything perfect, but it's been like this since Emmy was a baby. I asked her if she wanted to change it, but she's always loved butterflies."

Lydia lifted her camera and took a picture.

"Well, we have our 'before' shot. Let's move some furniture!"

For the next twenty minutes, the women tugged and pulled things around the room, making way for a crib and diaper changer. Lydia snapped pictures just about every time they moved anything, going through an entire roll of film before they even started moving the baby furniture in. "I think I'm going to need that electronic camera soon," she said.

She snapped another roll as they put the baby furniture in place. When it was done, all the women sat on the floor in the middle of the room and craned their heads to take it all in.

"This looks good." Jane nodded. "It looks like two little girls live here."

"Yeah," Mari said. "It does, doesn't it?"

Mac came up the stairs and into the room, a sleeping Kesa on her shoulder. "Wow, Sisters, this is beautiful."

"Thank you," Mari said.

"You ready to be a mommy times two?"

Mari looked around the room. "*Absolutamente.*"

Dale came into the room carrying both twins. "Lyd, I think we need to head home." He handed Olivia over to Lydia. "I'm guessing she's going to be hungry in about two minutes."

As if on cue, Olivia's little face scrunched up, and she let loose a cry.

"There's no way she's going to make it all the way to the house," Lydia said. "Mari, do you have a room where I could feed her?"

"Sure. Just go in my room. Or feed her right here. I don't think anybody in here is going to be offended." She glanced at Jane and Mac, who both shook their heads. Lydia sat back down on the floor and arranged Olivia in her lap. She offered the baby milk, and Olivia latched on.

"You want me to take him back downstairs?" Dale asked and lifted Oliver.

"I'll take him, if that's okay." Mari lifted up her arms, and Dale handed a wide-eyed Oliver over. "I'm guessing he'll need feeding right after Olivia?"

"Yeah," Dale said. "Just holler when you're finished, honey. I'll go get their stuff together." He left the room, and Mac sat down on the bunk bed, still holding Kesa.

"He seems awful helpful for a man with no interest in you," she said.

"Oh, he's great whenever there's not a TV around. Plus I think he feels bad about the orange feather incident." She filled Mac and Jane in on the outcome of the lingerie. "The man won't open any blinds in the house anymore. I tried to open them after I got off the phone with you"—she looked at Mari—"and he told me to leave them alone. I think he thinks I'll try it again."

"Won't you?" Jane asked.

"I'm not sure yet," Lydia admitted. "I dug it out of the trash can, so it's a possibility. I'm waiting to see how long he keeps the blinds closed." She grinned. "If he makes it two more days, I just might put the silly thing on again."

"Let me know if you decide to," Mac said. "I'm always happy to watch the twins."

"Yeah, but if you try it again, let's go get something new for you to wear," Jane said. "Mari, didn't you say there was a store down on West End?"

"Sure is."

Lydia jumped in to interrupt them. "If the first outfit works, we'll go get more. I'm not spending any more money on that stuff when I could be buying scrapping supplies."

"You know, since you're feeding them right now, you've got a four-hour window in front of you," Mari said. "And Dale's not watching television."

"Oh, I don't think so," Lydia said. "Rejection is still fresh in my mind."

"Come on, Lyd," Jane said. "Aren't you supposed to get right back on the horse if it throws you?" Her eyes twinkled as she grinned.

"I just can't. I'm not sure I *ever* want to put that thing back on, much less this afternoon."

"Then skip the lingerie," Mari said. "Just take him home and jump him."

"How romantic."

"Which are you wanting, romance or sex?"

Lydia thought about it. "Both. We don't have either right now. But I want the romance first."

"Okay, then leave the twins with me, and take him to the park for a walk," Jane said. "Or go see a movie. Do something just for the two of you."

"Are you sure you have time to watch them?"

"It's either that or sit around my apartment trying to figure out my life. I choose twins any day."

"I suppose we could leave you our car so you'd have car seats in case you want to go anywhere."

"I'm not going anywhere. Just bring them over, leave me what I need, and go reconnect with your husband."

"I don't think there are enough diapers in their bag, and I know we didn't bring any frozen milk. I'll run home and get those things, then swing by your place. Is that okay?"

"Sounds fine." Jane stood up. "I'm going to head toward home, then. Do you need anything else here, Mari?"

Mari looked up from a cooing Oliver in her lap. "Nope, I'm good. Thanks for your help with the furniture and everything."

"Anytime. Lyd, I'll see you at my place?"

"Yep," Lydia nodded. "We'll leave here right after I feed Oliver." She handed a now-satisfied Olivia over to Mari and took Oliver. "I'll call you when I leave the house."

"Sounds good. Bye, girls." Jane waved as she left the room.

Thirty minutes later, Lydia found herself once again standing in front of the television in her living room, hands on hips, arguing with her husband.

"But we have *four whole hours*. We could go see a movie or go for a walk or anything." She threw her hands in the air. "And all you want to do is watch *television!*"

"You should have asked me first, Lydia." Dale's patient tone made her even madder. "It's March Madness. These are important games. I need to watch them."

"More important than your marriage?"

Dale stopped trying to see the screen behind her and looked Lydia squarely in the eye. "That's a stupid thing to say. Of course it's not more important than my marriage. But you *didn't ask me.*" His voice rose, and she felt better. Let him lose his temper, too.

"Well, I didn't know I had to *ask* my husband to spend time with me."

"You do when it's in the middle of March Madness." He gestured to the TV. "Now, could you scoot over so that I can see the game? I don't know why you're so mad anyway. I missed the whole first half so we could go over to Mari's, and did you hear me complain? No."

Lydia turned and headed out of the room, refusing to stay and beg for her husband's attention any longer. "Fine. You've got the twins. I'm going to Jane's for a while."

"Why can't you take them with you?" Dale swiveled around and looked at her over the back of the couch.

"Because they're asleep, Dale." She turned on the baby monitor that was sitting on the end table. "They won't be hungry for four hours. I'll be back long before then." She walked out of the room, ignoring his protests.

"Oh, sweetie, I'm sorry," Jane said when Lydia explained what had happened. "What is his problem?"

Lydia blew out her breath. "I don't know." She shook her head and flopped back into Jane's couch cushions. "I really don't know."

"At least he's not rejecting you this time. He just needed to be asked before you arranged to do something together."

Lydia rolled her eyes. "I thought the point of being married is that I didn't have to worry about being rejected for a date anymore. Silly me."

Jane went into the kitchen and grabbed a couple of bottles of water from the fridge. She came back into the living room and offered Lydia one.

Lydia took it and unscrewed the cap. "Enough about me. How are things with the hunky neighbor?" She drank from the bottle.

Jane sank down onto the other side of the couch, folding her legs up under her. "I haven't told him about Bill."

"Why not?

"I used to think I knew a lot about men. If Bill taught me anything, it's that I don't know nearly as much as I'd thought. I'm not sure how Jake will react to the news, and I don't know if I'm ready to risk telling him."

"I'm beginning to think I'll never figure out men." Lydia jumped when Wilson barked.

"You need to go outside, buddy?" Jane asked, and Wilson went nuts at the word *outside*. "Okay, let's get your leash." Wilson ran to the hall closet door and began dancing around it, jumping on it and turning in circles.

"He knows where the leash is now?"

"Yeah, he's learning more and more things these days. He even knows Jake's cat's name."

"You're kidding me."

"Nope. Watch this." Jane leaned down to eye level with Wilson. "Major Carter." Wilson barked a short, sharp bark.

"That is hilarious!"

"And proof that being with Jake won't be as easy as we might think." Jane sat down in one of the kitchen chairs and pulled on her shoes. "Wilson would never quit barking."

Lydia rose from the couch and joined Jane at the door. "I'm sure that could be remedied if you set your mind to it."

Jane stood up and grabbed the end of Wilson's leash. "I'm sure you're right. They made headway last night." She opened the door and allowed Wilson to pull her toward the grass. Lydia followed along behind. "Lydia, will you tell me again what you saw the night before my wedding?"

"Why torture yourself with that old news?" They came to a stop under the giant oak, and Wilson began sniffing around.

"Because I'm trying to figure out if it was just a harmless flirtation at a bachelor party or something else." She looked at Lydia. "Bill asked for forgiveness, and I gave it to him. But he wants to try again, and I don't have an easy answer for that."

Lydia scrunched up her nose. She looked a lot like Olivia when she did that.

"Okay. I was driving home after your bachelorette party and stopped at the red light by Cadillac's. I heard a lot of people laughing and looked over to the parking lot. Are you sure you want to hear this?"

Jane blinked in surprise. "Yes, why?"

"Because knowing this isn't going to undo the affair he had while you were married. Do you honestly think you should go back to him?"

Jane sighed and shrugged her shoulders. "I don't know.

Jake makes me happier than I've ever been, but you know me. Being right matters a whole lot more than being happy because, most of the time, doing right leads to being happy."

Lydia nodded. "I'll agree with you there. I just can't figure out why you think going back to Bill might be the right thing to do."

The wind kicked up and blew Jane's hair in her face. She reached up and tucked it behind her ear. "I guess it's more that I don't want to do something wrong than that I think taking him back might be right. Does that make sense?"

"Only if you're making Jake the wrong thing. What are you scared of, Jane?"

"Well, look who I have the pleasure of running into." Jane ignored the thrill Jake's voice sent through her and turned to see him coming across the grass in a black T-shirt and jeans, Major Carter in hand.

"Jake. What good timing. I'd like you to meet my friend, Lydia Pritchett. Lydia, Jake."

"Nice to meet you, Jake." Lydia held out her hand, and Jake shook it as he joined them on the grass. "I've heard a bit about you."

"Oh, really?" Jake smiled, letting Lydia's hand go and looking at Jane. "Here's hoping she didn't tell you I was too awful. I realize I'm at a disadvantage because of the sci-fi shows."

"She hasn't been too rough on you, no. And this must be Major Carter?" She reached out and scratched the cat between its fluffy ears.

"In the fur." He looked at Jane. "Think Wilson would eat her alive or run her up a tree if I let her down?"

Jane thought about it and shrugged. "Only one way to find out." She circled Wilson's leash on her hand a couple of times to give him less slack and tightened her grip. "I've got him if you want to try."

Jake leaned down and deposited Major Carter on the ground, and she promptly took off to the other side of the lake. Wilson watched the cat and then plopped down into the grass with a sigh. Jane laughed.

"We've graduated to indifference," she said.

"Progress." Jake nodded. "Pretty soon we'll have them eating out of the same bowl."

Lydia cleared her throat. "Well, Jake, it was a pleasure meeting you. I've got to be getting back home. I have two twins who will be waking up soon and wanting their mommy, I'm sure."

Jane shot her a murderous glance, and Lydia smiled.

"Nice meeting you, too, Lydia. Take care."

Lydia hugged Jane. "Bill who?" she whispered in Jane's ear before pulling away. "See you at Mac's on Saturday."

Jane tugged on Wilson's leash. "Come on, boy, time to go." Wilson hauled himself up off the ground and obediently came over to her.

"Don't leave on my account," Jake said.

"Oh, I'm not." She felt the blush creep up her neck to her cheeks. "I've just got some things that need to be done and, um, I need to go do them." Could she sound any more lame?

Jake grinned at her. "How was church?"

"Fun. I went with Mac today."

"Who's Mac?"

"She's one of the Sisters I scrap with."

"So she's Lydia's sister?"

"No, I mean, we're all part of a company we started called Sisters, Ink." She explained the concept to him.

"I thought you already had a business that organized fund-raisers."

"I do. Sisters, Ink is a new business."

"So you don't like to sleep?" A smile played at the corners of his mouth.

"Sleep's for the weak." She chuckled. "I learned how important girlfriends were during my divorce. I wanted to help other women reconnect with that."

"Good for you." His praise warmed her heart.

"Thanks." They watched the animals in silence for a moment. "I'd better take Wilson back inside."

"What's your rush?"

"The mountain of projects on my desk and a never-ending to do list."

He reached out and snagged the hand that held Wilson's leash. "Working on a Sunday? Never a good idea. Come walk around the lake with me."

Might as well go. Tell him about Bill and get it over with.

"Okay." She fell into step beside him as they circled the water, loving the heat of their hands together. The sun's reflection danced on the ripples of the lake and the wind kicked up again. *It's too beautiful a day to ruin. I'll tell him about Bill later.*

chapter 21

❀ · ❀ · ❀ · ❀ · ❀ · ❀ · ❀

"Hush, Wilson!" Jane called to the barking dog as she made her way to the front door on Monday. "Hush! I've got it!" Wilson switched to his high-pitched whine. This was one of the moments she wished she'd let Bill have the dog.

She opened the door to Bill's smiling face.

"Hi." He held out a bouquet of tulips. Tulips? With a sigh, she took the flowers and stepped back to allow him entrance into her apartment, sneaking a peek at Jake's door. Was he watching?

"Bill, what are you doing here?"

"I saw those in the florist's window, and they reminded me of you, so I thought, what the heck, bring 'em on over and show her you were thinking of her." He looked at her with eyes full of hope. It was a little insulting that he'd seen droopy tulips and thought of her, but maybe he meant the bright colors were a reflection of her. She'd give him the benefit of the doubt. *I seem to be doing that a lot lately.*

"Thank you. They're beautiful," she lied and went to find a vase for them. He followed her into the kitchen and watched as she laid the flowers down in the drain board and rummaged around under the sink for an appropriate container. Something tall to help with the droopiness. Jake was tall. *Focus on Bill, not Jake.*

"So, I was wondering if you had any thoughts to share about us," Bill said, and she came up so fast that she banged her head on the cabinet.

"Ouch. Ouch. *Ouch.*"

He took a quick couple of steps toward her and rubbed her head. "Are you okay?"

The mix of pine and coffee scents coming from his shirt reminded her of the years they'd shared. Hadn't she read somewhere that smells were the strongest memory trigger in the world? She leaned forward out of habit and breathed in the scent of her old home. His hands felt good as they worked their way into her hair. *What? Why are his hands on me?* She stepped back.

"Bill. I'm okay."

"Are you sure?" He tilted her face up to his, and she would have laughed at the seriousness in his eyes if she could have put together a thought that wasn't jumbled up with past and present. "Your pupils aren't dilated. That's good."

"Of course they're not. I just bumped my head."

"All the same, you know the old remedy." Before she knew it, his lips were on hers, and she was responding by rote memory. He felt like friendship, like lazy afternoons and routine and safety. *And I'm kissing him back.*

"A loving kiss to make it all better," he whispered against her mouth and kissed her again.

What am I doing? She pushed against his chest and backed up to the other side of the kitchen.

"Jane?"

"I'm sorry, Bill, I shouldn't have—"

"Yes, you should, but it's fine. We can go slow. I don't want to rush you."

"Bill, I didn't mean to give you the wrong impression. I haven't had much time to think since I saw you." She crossed her arms over her chest.

"Okay, let's talk it through now. I love you. I messed up. I'm as sorry as I know how to be. But I've changed this past year, Jane. You've got to believe that."

"Changed how?"

"Losing you made me realize how selfish I had become. I mean, all those years we shared, and I threw it away because some woman thought I was the best thing since apple pie. I should have asked why you no longer thought of me that way and fixed the problem between us, but it was easier to run away from you, from us."

She shook her head. "I don't understand. Before I found out you were cheating, I didn't think anything bad about you. I thought we had a pretty good marriage based on a solid foundation of trust and friendship. What you did, though, showed we didn't have either of those things."

He spread his hands out in front of him. "But we did, Jane. We've been best friends for over half our lives. From passing notes on the bus in junior high 'til right now. Do you want to walk away from that?"

"I didn't walk away, Bill. You did."

"You're right. But who's walking away now?"

"I wasn't aware there was anything left to leave."

He sighed. "I've never been as good at word games as you."

"This is a game?"

"No, that's not what I meant. I think I'm making things worse."

"It's been a long day. How about I agree to think about your offer and you give me a few days to do that?"

He smiled, a smile she'd known almost forever. "All right."

chapter 22

❋ · ❋ · ❋ · ❋ · ❋ · ❋ · ❋

Tuesday dawned bright and crisp as Jane sat by the living room window, casting a glance up every three seconds to see if Jake was outside with Carter. Her wedding scrapbook lay open in her lap.

Wilson came and rested his head on her knee. "Hey, buddy. Your momma is messed up in the head. Why can't I just tell Bill no?"

Wilson turned his head on its side, offering her his neck. She obliged with a scratch. "What do you think? Do you like Bill or Jake?" She ran her fingers through his fur. Bill and Wilson had never meshed. Though Bill had gotten Wilson to be "their" dog, it was obvious after a couple of days which one of them the dog preferred. "This would be easier if I thought of them one at a time instead of comparing them, I think."

She slapped the wedding album closed and stood up.

"Maybe I shouldn't think of either of them at all. Come on, boy. We've got to get some work done."

She worked for two solid hours on Sonya's jungle-themed event, feeling much better about its status as check marks were placed down the to do list. *At least I can still do my job well.* She walked back out to the living room and looked through the window again. The lake was as empty as ever. Not even a duck swam upon its glassy surface. Her sigh woke Wilson from his sleeping position in the reading chair.

Mari sat in her office at Wachovia Bank, rereading the Google alert for the twentieth time. She had set a news alert for Chile as soon as they'd made the decision to adopt from the country. Each day, an e-mail popped into her in-box with all the day's headlines for her second daughter's home country. Tensions had been escalating between the people and their leadership for years. No one had expected anything to come of it.

And yet the words on her screen refused to change. There had been a fire at the orphanage where her Andrea lived. No further news was available, not even the knowledge of how many or if there were survivors. Her telephone warbled, and Mari snapped out of her trance.

"Marinilda Morales."

"Mari? Honey, have you heard?" John's voice broke. Her resolve to never show tears in the workplace flew out the window.

"John, I can't find out anything. It just says there was a fire. Is she alive?"

"I don't know. I've called the agency, and they can't get in touch with any of their workers in the area. They're sending someone down in the morning. We'll know by tomorrow. Sit tight. I'm on my way to your office."

She nodded and hung up, staring again at the screen in front of her as tears coursed down her cheeks. Was God playing some cruel cosmic joke? First she can't get pregnant. Then she can't find a reason for her infertility. Then the months and months of filling out paperwork, sending it off, and waiting by the mailbox. They were in the homestretch. No more snags, the agency worker said. It's just a waiting game now. You've done the hard part.

She read the story again. Nobody could have seen this coming.

But surely Andrea was okay. God would not have let them come this far, crossed this many hurdles, only to yank their little girl from them in the eleventh hour.

She looked up as John walked through her office door, his face devoid of color save for the red of his eyes from too many tears. "Mari, we have to believe she got out." He came around her desk and took her in his arms. "We have to believe."

She nodded against his hand stroking her hair, then heard the click of the laptop as he closed it.

"Come on, honey. Let's go home. The agency will call us as soon as they know something, but it may be a few days before their worker can get there, make his way to the orphanage, and get back to a communications center."

She let him pull her up from her chair and walked in a daze out of the office, barely seeing the concerned expressions on her coworkers' faces. The sunshine outside seemed inappropriate somehow. Her little girl may have died today. What right did the sun have to shine?

John's hand at her elbow was a welcome anchor in the midst of mental turmoil. He walked her to the car parked at the curb, opening the door and placing her inside. She stared straight ahead, certain that this was all a nightmare.

Mac snapped the oven door closed on a casserole for Alice Turnbow at church, humming all the while. Alice's cancer was responding to treatment, but she still needed some help feeding a family of six in a two-bedroom house. Not everyone in the Brentwood/Cool Springs/Franklin area of Nashville was as rich as the rest of the city would like to think.

The phone rang, and Mac walked over to answer it.

"Hello?"

"MacKenzie? It's John, Mari's husband."

Mac's senses, honed from years of weathering life's storms, went on high alert. "Hi, John. Somethin' wrong with Mari?"

"The orphanage in Chile, where Andrea is, has burned down."

"Oh, sweet Jesus, help us."

"We don't know about Andrea yet. We don't know anything. The agency's sending down a worker, but they won't be able to tell us what's going on for at least four days, and Mari's just sitting there, staring at the wall. I don't know what to do for her, Mac, but she came home from your house last week so happy to have found you girls that I thought maybe you'd have some ideas. She's scaring me, and I don't want Esmerelda to see her like this."

"Of course not, John. You doin' the right thing. I'll call the Sisters. We'll be right there."

"Thank you, Mac." Relief filled John's voice.

"Ain't no thanks needed. This is a Sister thing. We'll be right there. You just hang on." She hung up and snatched the receiver back off the cradle. Punching in Lydia's number, the feeling of losing someone you loved to a sudden death came back over her. "Jesus, hold 'em in Your hands."

"Hello?"

"Lydia?"

"Hey, Mac. What's up?"

Mac told her about the fire.

"Oh, my word. I'll call Jane. Get on over there. We'll meet you." Mac hung up, grabbed her keys, turned off the oven, and was revving her engine in ten seconds flat.

Jane stood in front of Jake's front door, working up her nerve. He had given her honesty about his past. It was only fair that she tell him Bill had come back into her life. Which wasn't going to be taken well, considering his past. Taking a deep breath, she bit the bullet and knocked on his door. *Think of it like a Band-Aid. Rip it fast and it won't hurt as much.*

"Hey there. I was just thinking about you."

"Good thoughts, I hope?"

He swung the door open and motioned her in. "Always."

"Were you busy? Did I interrupt something?"

"Nothing that can't wait a few minutes. Ah, the joys of working from home, right?"

"Right." She fidgeted and looked around. *How do I start this?*

"Is something wrong? You look a little out of sorts." He took her elbow and guided her to the chairs in the living room.

He sat, and she followed suit. "I'm not sure. But I need to tell you something, and I don't want to."

His forehead wrinkled. "That's cryptic."

She smiled. "Sorry."

"I want you to know I appreciate your honesty with me about your past."

"You're welcome."

"And because you were honest with me, it feels like I should tell you what happened yesterday."

"Sounds fair."

She sat in silence. *This is a bad idea. Just tell Bill no, and Jake never has to find out. You don't have to make him go through this again.*

He leaned forward and took her hand. "What is it, Jane?"

"Bill called me Saturday." *Band-Aid, think Band-Aid.* "I ran into him at the store on my way to Mac's on Saturday, and he called me later and asked me to meet him, and I don't know why, but I said yes, and so I saw him out at the mall for, like, two seconds, but that was long enough for him to tell me

233

he's sorry and has changed and wants me back, and then he came over yesterday with flowers and told me again that he's sorry, and I don't know what to do with that or what to say or how to feel or what this means for us, and I hate that this has happened."

Her cell phone vibrated on her hip, and she grabbed it, grateful for anything to stop her torrent of words. Lydia's name was on the caller ID. It could be anything from another fight with Dale to a kiddo in the emergency room.

"And even though this is the most inopportune time in the history of the universe to take a phone call, I have to answer this." She flipped open the phone. "Jane Sandburg."

"Jane, it's Lydia. We've got to get to Mari's. The orphanage in Chile burned down, and they don't know if Andrea made it out."

"What? When? How?"

"I don't know anything other than that they won't know about Andrea for several days, but John is freaked out because Mari's just sitting there staring at the wall. He called Mac and asked if we could do something. Mac's on her way there now."

She glanced up at Jake. His eyes showed compassion, but he had let go of her hand at some point in her diatribe. He was now sitting back in his chair. "I'll be there in five minutes. Grab your tea bags, and I'll bring some valerian root. She's probably in shock, but once that wears off, she'll need something to calm her nerves and help her sleep."

"Good. Good. I've got the tea in my hand. See you in five. Be careful."

"You too." Jane snapped the phone closed. "The orphanage one of the Sisters is adopting from burned down. They don't know much of anything. I've got to get over there."

"Of course. Go on." He shooed her with his hands, and she remembered how much that had irked her the day they met in the parking lot of The Savvy Scrapper. Now it seemed kind.

She stood and walked to the door, anxious to get to Mari. "I'm so sorry to dump this on you and run."

He smiled, but the sadness in his eyes unnerved her. "That's life."

Jane decided that was good enough and dashed into her apartment to put Wilson up and grab the natural sleeping aids she kept under the bathroom sink. Mari was more important than the mess of her love life.

Mac's cell rang as she was pulled into Mari's driveway. She thought about ignoring it, but years of raising a child who'd just as soon break the law as abide by it had taught her better.

"Hello?"

"Mrs. Jones?"

"Yes, this is MacKenzie Jones." She rolled her eyes, assuming it was a telemarketer.

"Are you the mother of Tabitha Jones?"

Her spine straightened. Only doctors, judges, and police officers used that tone of voice.

"Is she hurt?"

"No, ma'am. This is Officer Kent Tucker of the Nashville

Police Department. She's fine. We're holding her in our lockup along with a bunch of other kids we found in a meth lab out on the east side of town when we responded to a disturbing-the-peace call-in. Are you familiar with a boy by the name of Antonio Cooper?

Mac sighed. "Yes, I am. And, yes, I understand he's gotten into meth. Was Tabby using?"

"No ma'am, I don't think so. But she was there, and we brought everybody in who was in the house. Figured we'd sort it all out when we got down here to the station."

"All right. How late can I come and get her?"

"Before midnight would probably be best. She's at the station down by the Titans stadium. You know where it is?"

Mac sighed again. She knew the locations of too many police stations in this city.

"Yes, I know just where it is. I'll be there soon's I can. Thank you, officer." Mac hung up and opened her car door. Tabby's latest shenanigans took a backseat to the real pain and suffering happening behind that red front door.

chapter 23

❀ · ❀ · ❀ · ❀ · ❀ · ❀ · ❀

Jane pulled up behind Lydia's van and shut off her engine. Nothing about this would be easy. She walked up to the front door, feeling heavy sadness in the air. Had they gotten more news?

She pushed the small circle of light and heard a doorbell ring inside the house. Lydia answered it. "Hey, girl." Her tone was hushed. She stepped aside, and Jane entered Mari's house. Every wall had pictures of Mari's family members. She had seen them when they were here on Sunday, but they'd been too busy arranging furniture for her to ask questions about Mari's heritage. From wedding portraits to the standard school photos to candids, the walls were an intricate display of Mari's love of family. A Puerto Rican flag hung on one wall above a large black-and-white wedding portrait.

"Hey, do you know if Mari is from Puerto Rico?"

"Yeah. She lived there through elementary school. Then her family moved here. Her grandparents and cousins are still there. That's her parents in the picture." Lydia pointed to the wedding portrait.

"Got it. So how's she doing?"

Lydia shook her head. "She's said a couple of words to us, but not much. John says it's an improvement. Until Mac and I got here, she hadn't said a word since he brought her home from the office."

"Poor Mari. I can't imagine what she's going through."

"Me, either."

"Where's Emmy?"

Lydia walked toward the back of the house and pointed out a window. "Outside with John, playing on the swing set. He's trying to keep her away from Mari until she snaps out of this."

"Good idea." Jane followed Lydia down a hallway. "Do you have hope of that happening anytime soon?"

Lydia looked over her shoulder as they stopped in front of the master bedroom door. "I believe in miracles."

As they stepped into Mari's bedroom, Jane noticed the closed blinds and darkness. Mac was sitting on one side of Mari, her big arm around Mari's waist. She was humming one of the songs they'd sung in church yesterday. Jane sat down on Mari's other side.

She picked up Mari's cold hand and sandwiched it in hers, rubbing a bit to warm it up. "Mari, I need you to talk to me, honey. Tell me what happened."

Mari turned her head, and Jane's heart broke at the vacant

look there. "Andrea's orphanage. It burned." Her voice was no louder than a whisper, and Jane leaned in to catch it all.

"When did that happen?" *Keep her talking.*

"Today. They're only an hour ahead of us. While I was eating breakfast, her home was burning down." Mari turned back toward the wall.

"Honey, look at me." Mari obeyed. "Do you know what caused the fire?"

Mari shook her head. "We don't know anything. They're too far away."

"John says the agency is sending someone. Is that right?"

Mari nodded. "But the orphanage is in the mountains. It'll take days for us to know."

"Then we'll sit here and talk for days."

Mari blinked, and her eyes focused on Jane. "You're going to sit here for days with me?"

"You better believe it. We all are." Lydia came and knelt down in front of Mari.

"You're not alone, Sister," Jane said. "We're here, and we're walking this road with you."

Mari looked at each of the women. "Y'all barely know me."

"Don't matter if we met you five minutes ago. You's a Sister. That's enough."

Tears tracked down Mari's face. Long minutes passed in silence. Jane worried Mari had retreated back into her silent shell.

"Thank you," Mari whispered.

"Ain't no thanks needed."

Jane let go of Mari's hand and rubbed her shoulder instead.

"I'm glad you're talking to us. We were a little worried there for a bit."

"*Lo siento.* It's just that we don't know anything. And we can't know for *days.* How am I supposed to walk around here, going through the motions, not knowing if my daughter is dead or alive?" Mari swiped at her tears.

"It's hard; you're right." Mac's big black hand covered Mari's small olive one. "I 'member when Saul was off fightin' the war and I had to go to bed ever' night not knowin' whether he was breathin' Earth air or heavenly scent. But you got the same reason I had to keep on keepin' on. Mine's name is Tabby. Yours is Emmy."

"Oh, Emmy. Has John—"

"He hasn't told her yet," Lydia said. "He wanted to talk with you first. He thinks you might want to keep her in the dark until you have something sure to tell her."

Mari nodded. "*Muy bien.*" She sniffed and sat up a little straighter. "I need to go to Emmy."

"No rush. John's outside on the swing set with her."

"*Está bien.* I'm okay now." She took the tissue Jane offered and blew her nose. "Well, as okay as I can be, not knowing what's happening with my daughter. You're right, though, Mac. I've got to keep on for Emmy and for John." She stood up and went to the window, opening the blinds.

"They need me right now, and what kind of mommy would I be for Andrea if I let her *familia* down, right?"

"Right."

"So what can we do for you?" Jane said.

Mari smiled, sadness tugging part of her smile down. "You've done so much more than I deserve already. I can't believe you all dropped what you were doing to come over here. How'd you even know what happened?"

"John called me. That man loves you like the dickens."

Mari looked at their wedding picture on the wall by their bed. "He called you?"

"Mm-hmm. Told me you's sittin' on your bed, starin' at the wall and not sayin' a word. He didn't know what to do, but he's smart enough to know when to call a woman."

Mari smiled again. "Thanks, Mac."

"Stop all this thankin' business, now. I done told you. You's a Sister. That means you ain't doin' life by yourself. You're stuck with us."

Lydia walked over to Mari. "Thick or thin, good or bad. We're in it together."

Jane joined them. "Because there's nothing in the world like girlfriends."

Mac completed the circle. "Preach it, Sister."

chapter 24

Two days later, Jane found herself once again sitting by the living room window in the early morning sunshine, wedding scrapbook in hand. They'd stayed by Mari's side for two days, but no word had come from the agency worker. Mari had said not to come today, to give her some time with her family.

Jane looked out the window. It almost seemed trivial to worry about her love life when Mari and John didn't know if Andrea was dead or alive. Thoughts of Bill and Jake, though, wouldn't leave her mind. *I've got to decide this thing and get on with it.*

She turned a page in her scrapbook and looked at the smiling faces of her family and friends. *Why didn't I throw this out months ago?* She turned another page and read the journaling in her own hand of the day's events. It had been fun to marry Bill, to fulfill the expectations of everyone around them. After staying together through junior high, high school, and college, it was inevitable that they would get married. Their engagement announcement in the paper was met with not a ripple of surprise.

Did I marry him because I was expected to? Or because I wanted to? When Bill proposed, refusing him was not an option. Saying yes to him was a habit by that point. Other guys had tried to come into her life through the years, and a few even succeeded in taking her out a couple of times, but she always ended up going back to Bill. His steady presence, demanding nothing of her, was easier to fit into her busy life than a man who wanted hourslong dates to sit around and talk about nothing or, worse, see how far she'd let him go.

Wilson jumped up onto the footstool and nudged his wet nose under her legs. "Hey, buddy." She reached down and scratched his ears. "Do you have an opinion to share? What should your momma do?" Wilson woofed at her and laid his head back down, tail wagging. "That's no help, mister."

She looked out the window and saw Jake and Major Carter out by the lake. They hadn't had a chance to talk since she ran out of his apartment to get to Mari's. She'd gone by several times, but her knock went unanswered.

Is he avoiding me? Or am I just being paranoid?

"There's one way to find out, right, Wilson? Let's go outside." At the word, Wilson leaped down and went to the closet. She got out his leash and slipped on her tennis shoes. She had no idea what she would say to him when they got out there, but two days was long enough to have this cloud over her head. Was he mad that she had talked to Bill?

She opened the door and stepped into the breezeway, hearing a woman's laughter. *Ugh, these walls are thin.* It was probably someone's television turned up too loud. Wilson set off toward the lake, and she followed along, shooting a glance at Jake's door. She stopped cold when the laughter sounded again.

Did that come from his apartment? "Hang on, Wilson." A quick glance showed her Jake and Carter were on the far side of the water. She stepped back a bit so he couldn't see her standing there and strained to hear. Bits of sentences floated through the doorway.

". . . fine . . . again . . . as last time . . . Carter." There was silence and then the woman's laughter again. What was a woman doing in Jake's apartment? This was too much. First Bill makes a play for her; then she spends two days by the side of a woman whose child may or may not be alive, and now Jake is seeing someone else. She shook her head. Those things were not on the same playing level, but they all combined in one ball of stress that began pounding behind her left eye. She reached up and massaged her brow bone, hoping to stop the pain before it spread and turned into a migraine. Little white stars danced at the edges of her vision, though, telling her to get to a bottle of Midrin fast. Her feet felt sluggish as she walked to the edge of the concrete and let Wilson do his business. Jake was seeing someone else. She racked her pain-addled brain for another explanation but couldn't come up with one.

His business done, Wilson pulled on the leash toward the water and trees. She pulled back. "Not right now, buddy. Momma's got a headache." He came with her, glancing back to

244

the trees, and she fumbled with the key in the doorknob. This one was coming on fast.

Footsteps sounded on the concrete. *Please don't let it be Jake.*

"Hey, Jane." His voice kicked her pulse up, and the pounding in her head increased. *Stupid key. Come on!*

She turned her head a bit, not trusting herself to look at him. "Hi, Jake. Good to see you. Gotta run." The key finally hit home and she turned it, falling into her apartment with Wilson in tow.

"Hey, are you okay?"

For a woman whose head is splitting open and whose boyfriend is seeing someone else and whose husband saw someone else and whose shoulder just rammed home onto her entryway, I'm groovy. "Fine, fine." She squeezed her eyes shut against the light and scooted back across the floor. "Just a headache."

"Can I help?" *Yeah, tell the chippy in your apartment to go home.*

"No, I'll be fine, thanks." She kicked the door closed, not caring that it was rude, and went to the bathroom. Some Midrin and a long nap might make her believe this had been a bad dream.

Mac bustled around her kitchen, ignoring the angry looks Tabby sent her way. Morning was always the best time for cooking.

"Momma, I didn't do anything wrong. The officer told you so."

Mac pointed with a wooden spoon. "That officer told me you didn't break the law. Don't mean you didn't do nothin' wrong, chile." She went back to stirring cookie dough.

"So what'd I do wrong? Tell me."

"If I have to tell you, you think it's gonna stick in your mind? You smarter than that, Tabitha Jones. Tell me why you ended up in a jail cell *again*."

"'Cause they brought everybody in, but I wasn't doin' nothin'."

"How many times I got to say it? 'Nothin' don't land you in a jail cell."

"They only took me because I was with folks who—oh, you tryin' to get me to say my friends are all bad. I get it."

"No, you don't, but you're gettin' there." She pulled out a cookie sheet.

"Momma, how'm I supposed to walk away from all my friends?"

"Nobody said it would be easy, chile, but things that matter usually ain't." She dropped dough in rounded heaps on the pan. "Tabby, you got a baby girl to worry about now. You got to stop all this foolishness."

"Everybody's got babies, Momma."

Mac put the sheet of dough in the oven. "Everybody ain't you, Tabby. What do you want that baby to think of her momma when she's big, hmm?" She pointed down the hallway to the nursery where Kesa slept. "Want her to tell everybody her momma runs around with dopeheads? How you gonna tell her to finish her education and go to college if you don't?" Mac sighed and came over to the table. She sat down in the chair beside Tabby's. "I know it's hard, Tabby. Lord knows I do. But you got to get a new set of friends."

Tabby stood up from the table in a huff. "I got to go for a walk. You mind watchin' Kesa for a while?"

Mac sighed, knowing where that walk would probably take Tabby. "You know I don't."

Tabby stalked out of the room, and Mac went to the sink to wash up the dishes.

The phone rang, and she snatched it up.

"Hello?"

"Mac? It's Lydia."

"Hey, Sister. Any word from Mari and John?"

"Nothing yet. What's going on at your house?"

"The usual, Tabby's mad at me 'cause I told her to get new friends, and Kesa's sleeping in the next room." She plunged her hands into the soapy water. "How 'bout you?"

"The usual. I'm sitting here wondering why I slept in bed by myself last night while my husband's out in the living room snoring in his recliner."

Mac chuckled. "He slept there all night?"

"He does it at least once a week now. He was watching some game, and I guess it went longer than his attention span. He was asleep when I got home from Mari's. What am I gonna do, Mac? I feel like I'm losing my husband."

"You know, I just read a good book that might help you out. Hang on. Lemme run find it." Mac laid the phone down on the kitchen island. Drying her hands on a kitchen towel, she went to the living room and snatched the book she'd been read-ing the night before up off the coffee table.

Going back to the kitchen, she settled the phone between her ear and shoulder. "Here it is. *The Five Love Languages* by Dr. Gary Chapman."

"Love languages?"

"Yeah, he talks 'bout how we all speak love in five dif'rent ways." She flipped through the book. "Acts of service, touch, words of affirmation, gifts, and quality time. Those are the languages."

"I don't get it."

"Well, the way I understand it, everybody's got one or two main ways they like to be told they's loved. Me, I'm an acts-of-service kinda woman. I do stuff for people so's they know I care about 'em. Like these cookies I'm makin' right now for Alice Turnbow's family. Now, if I just went and bought cookies and took 'em over to Alice, it might be more of giving a gift than doin' a service since all's I had to do was get some cookies when I was at the grocery store."

"Okay, I think I understand. So what were the other three?"

"Words of affirmation. That's for folks who need to hear praise, like "good job" and "I'm glad we're together" and stuff. Quality time and touch are the other two."

"And you think this will help me how?"

"Well, when I was readin' this, I got to thinkin' 'bout you and Dale and the rough time y'all headin' into, and I thought maybe you and he ain't speakin' each other's language."

"Hmm. You may have a point there. What do you think Dale's language is?"

"Sister, I don't have any idea. How 'bout tryin' each one out and seein' which he responds to the best?"

"Nothing ventured, nothing gained, I suppose." Lydia sighed. "I think words of affirmation might be the easiest. I'll start with that one."

"Look on the bright side. If none of 'em works, just cut off the cable." There was silence on the line for a second, and Mac cackled with laughter. "You're considerin' it. Good for you!"

"If I did that, would I have to pay a reconnect fee?"

"Who cares, if it gets you some time with your husband?"

"Good point. Maybe I should try both."

"Hedgin' your bets?"

"Something like that. I'm telling you, Mac, if this man doesn't start paying more attention to me than that stupid television, I'm going to go nuts."

Mac chuckled. "Then cut off that cable, girl."

"Okay, Mac. I feel better now that I've got a plan."

"Call and let me know how it goes."

"Will do."

Mac hung up and smiled at the phone. Kesa's cry sounded through the baby monitor. "I'm comin', precious," she called and left the dirty dishes soaking in the sink.

Lydia stared in her own mirror and marveled at the difference a complete night of sleep could make on a person's looks.

"Can you believe they slept through the night, Dale?" she said as he joined her in the bathroom. "Isn't that amazing? I feel like I could conquer the world!"

"Mmm-hmm," he mumbled and leaned over the sink to splash water on his face. "Think they'll keep doing it?"

"I don't know. I sure hope so." She looked across the mirror at him in his boxers. Maybe if she just jumped him right now, she could bring that spark back to life. "You know, I've got a ton of energy this morning. I've got to find some way to burn it off," she hinted.

"Glad to hear it. Wish I could say the same. That recliner doesn't sleep too well." He stretched. "The garden's got to get tilled if we're going to plant it next month. Think you could get started on it this afternoon?" He walked behind her and turned on the shower.

Okay, maybe subtlety wasn't a great idea. Perhaps telling him in plain words how she felt would do the trick.

"I'll see if I can put some time into that, sure." She turned from the mirror and watched him step under the hot spray of water, then close the clear glass shower door. "You know, you look really hot under all that water." Not the best line in the world, but it was a start.

"I like hot showers. You know that." He began soaping up his hair.

"Right, right." She cast about for something else to say, but everything that popped into her mind sounded like it came from a cheesy X-rated film. Maybe words of affirmation weren't his thing. He rinsed the suds from his hair and reached for the soap.

"Lucky soap," she said.

"What?" He turned to look at her through the shower door, and she froze.

"I said, 'Lucky soap.'"

"How'd you know that?"

"What?" Now she was confused.

"How'd you know this was my lucky soap?"

Oh, great. "Um . . ."

"I've been using this kind of soap ever since the Vols beat Alabama. How did you know?"

"Lucky guess."

He looked at her warily. "You sure are talkative this morning."

"Guess it's just from getting so much sleep. All that extra energy, you know."

"Yeah." He rinsed and turned off the water. Stepping from the shower, he pulled the towel from its rack and began to dry off. "Maybe I'll call the guys and we can go play some football or something at the park."

Perfect. Here she was trying to get him in bed and he was thinking of sweating it out at the park, fighting over a pigskin. She gave up. "Good idea. Well, I'm going to go check on the twins." She felt him watching her back as she left the bathroom and put a little extra sway in her hips. It wasn't words, but it was all she had at the moment.

She was sitting in the rocker in the twins' bedroom, playing smiley face with Olivia, when Dale hollered up the stairs, "Lydia! The cable's out! Did we pay the bill?"

With a grin, Lydia stood up and put Olivia on the floor with Oliver. She blew her beautiful kiddos a kiss and went to see if she could find some other form of entertainment for her husband.

The vibration of Jane's cell phone woke her from a Midrin-induced sleep. She pulled it off her hip and looked at the caller ID. *Ugh.*

"Jane Sandburg."

"Hey, Jane, it's Bill."

"Mm-hmm."

"I'm sorry to bother you in the middle of the workday, but I was wondering if we could have lunch." She sat up and looked at the clock on her nightstand. Yep, her "nap" had lasted four hours.

"Oh, Bill, I don't think I have time. I've been asleep—migraine, you know—and not gotten a thing accomplished all morning."

"What if I bring something over? I bet we could eat in fifteen or twenty minutes. Come on. You've got to eat anyway, right?"

She thought about it. Jake might see him coming to her apartment, but who cared at this point? He was probably over there having fun with his floozy anyway. "Why not? Can you be here in about an hour?"

"Sure, no problem at all. Anything in particular you want for lunch?"

"No, whatever's fine."

"Okay, then I'll see you in an hour."

She hung up and stared at the phone. *Did I just tell my ex-husband I'd have lunch with him?*

Her sock feet made a shuffling sound as she padded into the bathroom and splashed cold water on her face. The shock woke her up a bit. *Should have done that before answering the phone.*

But this could be a good thing, in the end. Jake had moved on. There was no reason for her to ignore Bill's offer of reconciliation. Even if Jake wasn't in the picture, Bill's words were deserving of at least a moment's thought.

A knock at the door caused Wilson to leap into frantic barking mode. "Hush, dog." She walked to the door and peered through the peephole. Her breath caught in her throat at the sight of Jake standing there with his arm around a beautiful woman. Did he want to rub her face in his new romance? Was he that mad she had talked to Bill?

He knocked again, and Wilson started his barking. Had Jake heard her tell Wilson to hush? If not, pretending she wasn't home looked like a very good option. She stood silently at the door, watching them through the peephole. The woman had thick, wavy red hair and was tall. Jake turned to her and said something. She shrugged her shoulders, and they walked off toward the parking lot.

Don't they look cozy.

Why was Jake already seeing another woman? Her mind

couldn't wrap itself around the timing as she sat down at her laptop. The little beep sounded as it booted up. Was there any other explanation?

She could be his sister, but her luck with men wasn't that good. Besides, what would his sister have been doing at his apartment on a workday morning? No, might as well face the facts. Telling Jake that she had talked to Bill had scared him off.

And if he ran off because I was honest, then I don't need him anyway.

She glanced at the clock on her laptop. Bill would be here in less than an hour, wanting an answer. Did she have one?

She slapped her hands down on the desk. Sometimes being a strong, independent female just sucked. As a wife, if her brain was tired after a long day of work, she could leave the decisions about dry cleaning and dinner to Bill. He always supported her like that, taking on tasks when she was at her wit's end. He never complained about it, just silently brought her a plate of food while she sat at the computer, working to meet a last-minute deadline.

I miss that. Having someone to help me. That was another reason she married him in the first place. He was always there, helping her at the right moments, turning the ringer off on the phone when she needed some peace and quiet, taking care of little tasks, like changing lightbulbs or getting extra keys made, that she never had time to do.

He sounds more like a butler than a husband. But wasn't marriage supposed to be about serving each other? Loving another person enough to put her needs and wants above your own?

Now that she thought about it, there weren't too many of Bill's needs and wants to know. The only thing he'd ever asked of her that she wasn't ready to give was her hand in marriage. But he had done so much for her, never asking for anything in return, that it only seemed right to marry him.

The perspective of a year on her own made that logic seem a bit warped. Had she let Bill guilt-trip her into marriage? Why would he want to marry a woman who wasn't in love with him? *And be honest, Jane: you never felt for him what it took Jake two seconds to make you feel.*

Did Bill think she was in love with him? Did Bill love her? Or was she just as much a safety net for him as he had been for her all those years? It was easier to stick with a buddy than jump on the roller coasters of romance and love.

She needed to move around, get the blood circulating again. "Hey, Wilson, how about a quick trip outside before Bill gets here?" He barked and wagged his tail, running back and forth from the closet to the front door. She snapped his leash on and opened the door.

Wilson pulled her across the breezeway and down to the water. As he sniffed at the water's edge, she thought back to her wedding day.

So many of their friends had come to wish them well. Old teachers and bosses from high school jobs sat right beside current friends and family. When they'd opened wide the sanctuary doors, she could see Bill was startled to see her face rather than Lydia's coming down the aisle. He never asked her where Lydia had gone. She'd assumed he didn't want to hurt her. But, with the hindsight of experience, now she wondered if Bill knew Lydia saw him at Cadillac's. *Something to ask him when he gets here.*

Because, if they were getting back together, there would be no unspoken words between them this time. No acting as if it was normal to marry someone she wasn't in love with or pretending to be in love with him for the sake of their families. Playing house was no longer an option.

Wilson finished his investigation of the bank and let her pull him back to the apartment. She saw Bill walking down the other end of the breezeway as they came up to her door.

"Hey, good timing." He held up two bags from Chick-fil-A.

"Yeah. I thought I'd walk him and put him in his crate so we don't have an audience while we're eating." She pulled out her key and unlocked the apartment.

He went to the kitchen table and began pulling out food.

"Crate, Wilson." The dog obeyed, and she followed him to her bedroom, rewarding him with a dog biscuit.

"Wish Momma luck." She scratched his nose through the wires.

The smell of fresh chicken greeted her as she came into the kitchen. "So, what are we having?"

"Thought you might want some chicken tenders and a few waffle fries. Is that still one of your favorites?"

"Yep. Good memory."

"It hasn't been that long, right?"

She smiled at him. "Right."

"How's your day going?" He handed her a salt packet.

She tore it open and dumped the white crystals on her fries. "I think I'm about caught up today. And you?"

"You know how March can be for accountants. I'm snowed under with work from people who wouldn't know a receipt if it stood up and slapped them in the face." He grinned at her. "But I'll muddle through."

She took a sip of the lemonade that Chick-fil-A was famous for and returned his smile. "Glad to hear business is going well."

"Thanks."

They ate in silence for a minute or two.

"Have you thought any more about us?" Bill said.

"I've been thinking about it a lot." She swallowed her chicken. "And some questions came up."

"Like what?"

"Well, why did you propose to me?"

He stopped chewing. "What?"

"Why did you ask me to marry you, the first time?"

"What kind of a question is that?" He resumed eating.

"The kind designed to elicit a response. I've been thinking about our years together, and we've got a lot of history, I'll admit. But I can't find a time when our friendship turned to anything else."

"Why did it have to turn into something else?"

"You mean you're not in love with me?"

"Wait, I thought we were talking about our friendship."

"We were. Are. Just answer my question. Why did you want to marry me?"

He shrugged. "Why would I not? You're beautiful, intelligent, successful, and I've known you more than half my life."

She listened hard but was almost sure he hadn't said the one thing that mattered.

"But isn't that true for you and Lydia as well? Or any one of our friends?"

His face screwed up in distaste. "Lydia? No. None of our friends compared to you. I've always been closer to you than anyone else."

Now we're getting somewhere. "What do you mean 'closer'?"

He set his sandwich down and tilted his head in thought. "I mean closer. I've spent more time talking with you and being with you than anyone else in my life."

"And that made you want to marry me?"

"Yes." He nodded and went back to his lunch.

"So you married me because I was your friend, not because you were in love with me."

"Why are you all of a sudden so focused on being in love?"

"I guess my question is, why *aren't* you?"

"Why would I be? That kind of stuff has never mattered to us. We've got trust and respect and history. Those are three things the vast majority of marriages in America can't claim."

"I'm not so sure about the trust part. That flew out the door right behind you."

He winced. "You're right. I need to build trust with you again. But that will come with time."

"And it doesn't matter to you that I'm not in love with you and you're not in love with me?"

"No. I think you're putting too much stock in emotions."

"Maybe you're right, but we should have talked about this before we got married. I thought you loved me."

"I do love you. I've told you that."

"I didn't mean that kind of love. I meant the kind men fight wars over or die for."

"I think that's just in the movies."

"So did I, but now I'm thinking I might have been wrong." *Since I met Jake. I'd fight a war for that.*

"What changed your mind?"

"Oh, I don't know. Meeting people. Talking to them." Sharing Jake with him seemed too personal. "Anyway, it's something to think about."

"Why?"

She blinked. "Why what?"

"Why think about it?"

She threw up her hands in frustration. "Why not? People think about this stuff all day. They make soap operas about it, and movies and songs. It's a real emotion, Bill. And most people get married to other people they have this feeling for."

"But it's not the only reason to get married."

"No, though I think it has to be *a* reason to get married."

"So because I don't feel some emotion, you think we shouldn't try to work things out between us?"

"That's not the only reason, but it's a big one." *I guess I've made a decision here.* "We can be friends, Bill. But that's all we were ever meant to be."

He looked at her for a thousand lifetimes. "Can I do or say

anything to change your mind?"

"I don't think so. I want you to have someone who's in love with you *and* is your friend. I want that for all my friends. And for myself." She wadded up her trash and put it back in the Chick-fil-A bag.

"Have you found it?"

Her hands stilled. "I thought I might have, but it's over."

"What happened?"

"I told him about you."

"What about me?"

"That I ran into you, that you called, that I went to meet you. He's had this happen before. I think he decided he'd rather pull away than risk losing me to you."

"Sounds like this passion and romance stuff can get very complicated and messy."

"It can. That's what's so great about it."

He stood and put his trash in the bag as well. "The feeling is worth the mess?"

She thought about the tingling in her hand when Jake held it. The way her heart fluttered when he looked at her. "Yeah, it's worth it."

He put his hand over hers on the table. "Then I hope you get him back."

"Me too."

"I'm comin', I'm comin'," Mac called to the ringing telephone as she bustled across the kitchen floor.

"Hello?" she said, out of breath.

"MacKenzie Jones?" The voice was hesitant, unsure, nothing like a police officer or doctor.

"Yes, this is MacKenzie."

"I'm not sure if you'll remember me. This is Cecil Cloar. From the jail the other night? I spent some time talkin' with Tabby."

"Oh, sure! I remember you. And I got your nice e-mail, too. Thank you for sendin' it." Not that she'd had any idea how to respond to it.

"You're more than welcome, of course. I was just callin' to see how Tabby is doin'."

"Oh, she's fine. Still tryin' to walk the straight and narrow and findin' it's a bit harder than she bargained for, you know."

Cecil chuckled. "I sure do know. She told me she had a baby?"

"Lands, yes, a beautiful little chile named LaKesa. She's the spittin' image of her momma. Least, that's what I'm tellin' her 'til she knows otherwise. No need in her knowin' she got some of her features from her druggie daddy, right?"

"Right. Well, I guess I'll be lettin' you go. I'm happy to hear Tabby's doin' okay."

"Well, thank you so much for callin'. I'm sure you're busy as ever with all those crazies down at the jail."

He chuckled again, and it reminded her of Saul.

"Unfortunately, they do keep a steady stream comin' in here. But not so steady as I couldn't find time to have a cup of coffee sometime if you'd be interested."

Mac sucked in her breath. Was this man asking her out? It'd been so many years since she even thought about romance for herself, the whole idea seemed foreign.

"I'd like that," she heard herself say and wondered what she was getting into. Didn't she have enough to worry about with keeping Tabby on the right path and helping raise Kesa?

"Well, thank you. They're bringing somebody new into the jail right now, so I need to go see about that. But I'll call you again and we'll figure out the details. All right?"

"All right. Thank you for callin'."

"Thank *you* for answerin'."

She heard the click of the phone and pulled it away from her ear, staring at it in wonder. Cecil Cloar. Now, that had a nice ring to it.

chapter 25

❋ · ❋ · ❋ · ❋ · ❋ · ❋ · ❋

That night, Jane decided she needed the Sisters. All three of them had more experience than she did with this love stuff. They could tell her how to fix things with Jake.

She picked up the phone and called Lydia.

"Hello?"

"Hey, it's Jane."

"Hey, what's up?"

"I need a Sisters meeting. You busy tonight?"

Lydia giggled. "Not too much. I should be able to get away for an hour or so."

"What so funny?"

"The cable's off at my house."

"And that's funny?"

"Let's just say it's had a good effect on my marriage." Lydia hushed someone.

"Not having cable had a good effect on your m—oh! Am I interrupting something? Geez, woman, turn the ringer off. You don't have to answer every time the phone rings."

"No, no, it's fine. Why do you need a Sisters meeting?"

"Bill came over for lunch. I told him I didn't want us back together."

"That's good. Turnabout's fair play. So why the meeting?"

"Jake has another woman."

"No, he doesn't."

"Yes, he does. I saw him with her."

"Jake is not seeing another woman. He can't be. I would have to kill him if he were, and *murderess*, though a very pretty word, is not something I aspire to."

"I'm telling you, I saw him with a beautiful redhead."

"It's his sister."

"Do we need to reevaluate my luck with men? It's not his sister."

"Did you ask?"

"No."

"Go over there and ask."

"Oh, sure, why didn't I think of that? I'll just waltz up to his door and ask if his sister is a drop-dead gorgeous redhead, and when he says no, he'll ask how I know he was with a redhead. At which point I will have to admit that I was, indeed, home when he dropped by to introduce me to the new love of his life, but I hid in my bedroom until he left. Sure. That's the perfect way to handle this."

"He brought her to your apartment?"

"Lydia!"

"Okay, okay, you're right. We need a Sisters meeting. Call Mac. I'll call Mari. Say, nineish? The twins will be in bed by then."

"Nine is great. I'll call Mari. Do you think it's all right to bug her with this right now?"

"She'll probably welcome the distraction. I talked to her a couple of hours ago, and they still hadn't heard anything."

"Okay, see you at Mac's."

She hung up, then dialed Mari.

"*Hola.*"

"Hi, Mari. It's Jane. Any news?"

Mari sighed into the phone. "No, nothing yet. The agency says not to worry, though, that it can take several days to reach the orphanage, then get back to somewhere with a working phone."

"How are John and Emmy?"

"We haven't told Emmy anything's wrong. No sense worrying her over nothing, right? John's holding up well. Thanks for asking. I think we're both driving each other crazy, sitting around here waiting on the phone to ring."

"That's the other reason I'm calling. I wondered if you could come out to Mac's tonight around nine."

"I suppose I could. That's after Emmy's bedtime. Why so late? Are we still meeting on Saturday?"

"Yeah, Saturday is still on. I just have something I need your help with, and I thought it'd be easiest to get us all together at Mac's. It's okay if you need to stay home. My love life isn't nearly as important as hearing something about Andrea."

"No, it's fine. John will be happy to get me out of his hair for a little while, and I'll have my cell in case the agency calls."

"Thanks, Mari."

"No thanks needed. You're a Sister, right?"

"Right."

Jane hung up and looked around her apartment, her gaze landing on the wedding scrapbook sitting by her reading chair. *I guess I should toss the thing out now.* She went over and picked it up. "Our Wedding" was embroidered in silver thread on its black background. This scrapbook had taken six months to complete, and she was proud of the hard work she'd put into it.

Do I have to throw all that work away?

Light played off the page protectors inside, and she tilted the book to see the pictures. There were all her aunts and uncles together, smiling for the camera. When would they ever get together again? And here were the cousins. One had died since this picture. One had gotten married. Her roommates from college, old friends from high school, everyone from her life was captured in these pages.

Is the scrapbook about the people in it or the story of myself I want to tell?

She snapped the book closed. The Sisters could help her figure this out, too.

"Okay, ladies, let's get to what we came here for." Mac clapped her hands, and all the women looked up. Lydia, Mari, Mac, and Jane all sat around the scrapping table. Eyelets, paper, stamps, letters, embellishments, paper, and pictures lay scattered about, giving testament to their passion.

"Jane, give us all the scoop." Mac grabbed a cookie off the plate in the center of the table and sat back on her stool.

"Okay, here's the deal," Jane said, and took a deep breath. Thank heaven for girlfriends. "I decided to be honest with Jake earlier this week, so I told him that I had run into Bill at the store."

"When did that happen?" Mari asked.

"Saturday, when I was on my way over here. I stopped to get a tape runner, and Bill was there."

"Why didn't you tell us?"

"I didn't think it mattered. We live in the same city; it was bound to happen sooner or later. But then he called and asked if we could get together."

"And you said yes."

Jane nodded. "I did. I met him at Davis-Kidd, and he said he had changed this past year, was very sorry for what he'd done, and wanted me back."

"What'd you say?" Mari said.

"I didn't say anything. I just left him sitting there on the bench. And then he dropped by with flowers."

"What kind?" Lydia said.

"Does it matter?"

Lydia rolled her eyes. "Everything matters. What kind?"

"Tulips."

"Ugh. Droopy flowers?"

Jane grinned. "I thought he might have liked the bright colors. Anyway, we talked for a bit, and he kissed me."

"He kissed you?!" Mari said.

"Yeah."

"Did you kiss him back?"

"Sort of."

"Now, it's been a long time since I kissed a man, but I can't remember it ever bein' a 'sort of' kinda thing."

"Well, I kissed him back, but it was more out of habit than desire. Does that make sense?"

"No, but go ahead," Mari said.

"I had dinner with Jake that night at his place, and things were really starting to take off."

"This is when you told him about Bill?"

"No, that didn't happen until Tuesday."

"Why'd you wait three days to tell him?"

"I tried to tell him the day it happened, but I didn't know how. See, the woman that Jake was with before me was separated from her husband. She'd been living on her own for a few months when Jake met her, and she was in the process of getting a divorce. They started seeing each other, and he fell pretty hard for her, I think."

"Why isn't he with her?"

"She went back to her husband. He got left with the cat."

"That's her cat?" Lydia said.

"His cat now. Her husband was allergic."

"No wonder you didn't want to tell him about Bill. That had to be awful for him to hear."

"Exactly. I had just told him about Bill coming over when my cell rang and it was Lydia with news about the orphanage. I haven't seen Jake since."

"You haven't seen him at all?"

"He came over with this gorgeous redhead on his arm, probably to rub my nose in the fact that he had found someone new. I didn't answer the door."

"How do you know it wasn't his sister?" Mari said.

"Thank you very much. I said the same thing." Lydia smiled.

"I still believe my luck in men would dictate that she's his new girlfriend." Jane held up her hands to stop their protests. "But let's assume it may just as well be his sister. That doesn't change the fact that it's been four days since I told him about Bill, and he hasn't called or come over except for that one time."

"At all?"

"At all."

"Don't he have your cell?"

"No, I never gave it to him, but I have an answering machine that would have caught his call if I was out, and I've checked the caller ID about four thousand times, and his number's not on it."

"So no contact for four days other than the one time. It's not looking good for the home team."

"You've got it."

"Before we get too far into this, are you absolutely certain it's over between you and Bill?" Mari said.

"Yes. I had lunch with him today at my place. We had a

good talk. I'm not mad at him—I think I've moved past that point. It's more now that I feel sorry for him. He's never felt what I feel for Jake for any woman, which is why he's happy to settle down with me."

"So there was never any passion or romance in your marriage?" Mari said.

"Not really. I thought that was just movie stuff. You know, a Hollywood invention to sell tickets at the theater."

"But now you've changed your mind." Mac smiled.

Jane grinned back. "Yeah, I guess you could say that. Jake makes my world stand still. When I see him, my breath just goes, and I get all excited and tingly. Does that sound crazy?" She looked about, hoping for affirmation.

"No, it's not crazy, honey," Lydia said, and Jane sighed with relief. "It's called being in love and it's scary as all get-out."

Jane pointed at her. "You hit the nail on the head. It's scary beyond belief. No wonder people fight wars and conquer kingdoms over this feeling. But won't it go away? I mean, we're talking about a major change in my entire belief in marriage. If you marry for the zing, what happens when the zing goes away?"

The women looked at one another, and Lydia spoke up again. "You fight for it," she said in a small voice. "It doesn't have to die. It might go down to a low simmer, but the undercurrent of passion and romance can always be there if you pay attention to it. If you don't, you're right—it'll take a hike. And when that happens, you have to fight doubly hard to get it back." She grinned. "You'll do illogical things, like have your own cable cut off."

The Sisters laughed.

Jane remembered Lydia and the orange feathers, and it all began making sense in her mind. "But, assuming I can get him to talk to me, forgive me, and have a relationship with me, how do I take care of the zing?"

Mari piped up. "You figure out what makes him feel loved, and you tell him what makes you feel loved. If you need to hear the words, tell him that. If you need hugs and kisses, tell him that. And ask him when he feels loved by you. Is it when you're doing things for him, like taking care of Major Carter? Or is it when you bring him things? You know, he *did* bring you that bag of CDs to smash. If that's the way he shows he cares, it's probably the way you can show him you care."

"Okay, *now* we're getting somewhere." Jane said and rubbed her hands together in excitement. They could do this. They'd figure out a way for her to be with Jake. "So you're telling me I need to take him a gift, and he'll get that I care about him."

"You think he don't already know you care?" Mac asked and chuckled. "He knows you care; he just thinks you care more 'bout Bill."

"Right." Jane wrinkled her forehead in confusion. "But if I tell him what happened, then he'll know I'm not going to be with Bill, and we can move on, right?"

"I doubt it's as easy as just telling him," Lydia said. "What exactly did he say to you when you told him about seeing Bill?"

"Nothing. As soon as I got the words out, I got your phone call."

"Hmm. That doesn't give us much to work with." Lydia tapped her finger against her lip.

Mac slapped the table. "No more of that talk," she said. "Bible says love never fails, and that's the truth." She pointed at Jane. "So we ain't gonna have no negative talk around here. If it's love, it won't fail."

Jane went around the table and hugged Mac. "Right. You're totally right. Okay, Sisters, we need the best present ever, and I need a groveling speech." She took a deep breath. "Ideas?"

"A good gift doesn't have to cost a lot of money if that's his love language," Mari said.

"Love language?"

"Yeah, it's in *The Five Love Languages*."

"You read that, too?" Lydia said. "Mac just gave it to me. I'm on the second language right now—touch—trying to figure out how Dale speaks love."

Mari laughed. "John and I read it before we got married. I know it made us better communicators."

"What is this book? Why hasn't anyone given it to me yet?"

"Because you don't read nonfiction." Lydia stuck out her tongue at Jane. Jane returned the favor.

"People speak love either with words, by giving gifts, doing acts of service, touching, or spending quality time. Jake is probably a gift person, since that's how he showed you he cared about you."

"That is so smart," Jane said.

"Yeah, it helped me and my marriage a ton," Mari said. "So it doesn't matter if you spend a lot of money on Jake's present.

It just has to show that you really thought about the person you're giving it to. What kinds of things does he like?"

"Sci-fi, Major Carter, computers." Jane ticked the things off on her fingers that she knew about Jake.

"And you," Lydia added and Jane grinned.

"Yeah, and, hopefully, me."

"We can work with that," Mari said. "What else does he like?"

"Helping me kill the Internet?" They all laughed.

"What is something you could give him that would have a major impact? Something he's wanted before but couldn't have?"

"If he still has feeling for me, I guess that'd be me."

"Right, and what's a tangible way we could give him the gift of you? Something he can hold in his hand to look at and know that you know him and love him."

Jane thought for a second as the women watched her. She threw up her hands. "I have no idea. But while we're figuring out my life, can someone please tell me what to do with my wedding scrapbook?"

"Why wouldn't you just throw it out?" Mari said.

"I was going to do that today, but I looked through it again and I don't want to lose the pictures inside it. Some of my family members are in there who aren't even alive anymore. Plus, even though my marriage is over, it did happen. It's a part of who I am."

"If Jake had a scrapbook full of pictures of the cat woman, would you want him to have it?"

"I don't know. I guess it depends on whether or not he had closure with her. If it was over. It would also depend on how he told the story inside. Like, does it stop with her, or does the story continue with him finding me?"

Lydia snapped her fingers. "That's your gift idea!"

"What?"

"Why didn't we think of it before? It's perfect!"

"Great. We're thrilled you've come up with something. Mind sharing with the rest of the class?" Jane said.

And she did.

Lydia walked inside, carrying the sleeping twins. She was still excited about her gift idea for Jake. *Maybe that's my love language. Gifts.* She'd have to remember to talk it over with Dale.

The memory of their time together before he left for work made her smile. She glanced at the clock on the microwave and saw it was a few minutes past time for him to be home. "Dale?" She didn't call too loudly, trying not to wake the twins.

As she walked through the house to the stairs, she saw the glow of the television from the living room. "Dale?"

She walked in, and there he sat, remote control in hand. "Cable's back on. I called the company, and they said they'd gotten an order to turn ours off. Stupid cable people. Don't know what they're doing." He pointed the remote and clicked to a different channel.

Lydia's heart sank. "Oh, glad it's back on."

"Me too. Just in time for the games this weekend."

She didn't say a word, just carried the twins on up to bed.

chapter 26

✽ · ✽ · ✽ · ✽ · ✽ · ✽ · ✽

Jane took a deep breath as she stared at the phone hanging on her kitchen wall the next night. He might hang up on her before she could get the words out. Or he could let her get the words out and then hang up on her. Or he could listen and agree to meet with her. Or the redhead might answer the phone. Those odds sucked.

Knocking on his door could be a better idea. Though having a door closed in her face would hurt a lot worse than hearing the dial tone over the phone. So would having the door opened by his new woman. At least being hung up on would occur inside her own home, where no one else could be watching her humiliation.

But putting it all on the line was the whole point here. The Sisters had told her that she had to go all out to make this work—really be honest with him, let him know she was offering her heart. Which was terrifying, but made sense.

She glanced at the gift lying on the kitchen table, wrapped in white paper with a huge red bow on top. They'd spent half an hour on the bow alone, but it was perfect. And the gift inside was perfect. All she had to do was figure out the perfect timing and the whole thing should go off, well, perfectly.

Except this was Friday night, which meant Jake was over there watching sci-fi. Maybe tomorrow night would be better.

No, there was no way she could endure this torturous waiting for another twenty-four hours. She walked over to the living room and flipped on her TV, surfing through the channels until she hit SciFi. She'd just wait for a commercial. As soon as it started, she'd have at least four minutes to go over there, knock, plead ignorance, beg forgiveness, and hand him his gift. Four minutes. That was good.

The first three segments of *Stargate SG-I* passed by before she got up her nerve. As a commercial for the latest stuffed-crust pizza came on, she grabbed the gift off the kitchen table and turned to Wilson. "Wish me luck, boy." Wilson gave a bark that she swore sounded like encouragement.

The night air was chilly and made her shiver as she crossed the breezeway to his door. Cold air and nerves. Not a magic combination. She waited what seemed like an eternity, and then there he was, standing before her with a bewildered expression on his adorable face, and she longed to reach out and touch him.

"Jane?"

"Look, I know you're mad at me, and it's fine if you want to slam the door in my face. I just wanted to bring you this." She held up the gift as the peace offering it was. "We don't have to talk or anything; the commercials are probably over." She gestured inside to the TV. "I'll just go back over here and, um, live." She turned and walked back toward her door, certain that there were a million ways she could have said that better, but also certain that the hounds of Baskerville couldn't get her to turn back around.

"Jane, wait." Hounds, no. His voice, yes. She stopped and turned to face him.

"Yes?"

He came across the breezeway. "Thank you for this, but I don't take gifts from ladies involved with other men." He held the gift back out to her. "I'm sure you understand."

"Oh, I'm not involved."

"I thought you were going back to Bill."

"Yes, um, I forgot you didn't know about that. Turns out I just don't love him." Jake's eyebrows shot up. "Which I know sounds crazy, because I married the guy, for heaven's sake, but I didn't know the kind of feeling you were supposed to feel for somebody you were marrying, because I had never felt that, and now I know, so I asked Bill if he felt that way for me, and he said no, and I asked him why he would want to be with someone he wasn't in love with, and he told me he didn't value that, which tells you a lot about our marriage and even more about why I'm not going back to him."

Somebody shut me up. This was beyond embarrassing. When had her tongue decided to develop a life of its own?

"So you're not going back to Bill, and you've brought me a gift because . . ."

"Oh! Yeah, I guess you would wonder, right? Sorry. I should have explained. I mean, I know it seems out of the blue and all, but . . . um . . . you brought me a gift, remember? And so I thought maybe you liked gifts, and I tried to think of a gift that would be perfect for you, and I made you this." She gestured to the beautifully wrapped package.

"You made what's inside this box?" He held it up to his ear and shook it.

"I had some help from the Sisters, but I did the entire first part of it by myself."

He smiled at her. "It's cold out here, and you're shivering. Why don't you come inside and I'll open it?"

Did she want to be there when he opened it? Who cared? He was inviting her over! "Sure, um, that's fine. It's just—" She glanced over her shoulder at her apartment door. "Wilson is loose in there, since I didn't think I'd be gone long, but I'm sure he'll be fine, so, okay, let's go."

"Are you sure he won't tear anything up? You can bring him over if you want."

"Oh, I don't think Major Carter would love that too much."

"Carter's in the back bedroom, hiding under the bed, letting me know how mad at me she is for not sharing dinner with her. Go get Wilson."

"Okay, if you're sure it's not a problem. I mean, I don't want to intrude or anything, and I may not even be there long, but, okay, I'll get him." She turned and made a beeline for her door, anything to stop this inane chatter she seemed to have lost control over. What was wrong with her?

She opened the door, and Wilson trotted out, going over to sit down at Jake's feet.

"Smart dog," Jake said. "Shall we?"

Not trusting herself to open her mouth again, she nodded and silently followed him into his apartment. Wilson walked over to the fireplace and collapsed in front of it, making himself right at home. She followed Jake over to the chairs and sat down.

Jake sat down in his chair and, pulling a knife from his pocket, gingerly slit the ribbon holding the bow in place. He tore the wrapping paper from the box and looked at her in question.

"Did you get me the entire DVD collection of *Galactica*?" He smiled at her, and she relaxed a little.

"Thought about it, but it would have taken too long to get here."

He lifted the lid on the box and turned to her in confusion. "This is your wedding scrapbook?" He pulled it out and set the box aside.

"Something like that. Just flip through all the way to the end." She scooted to the edge of her seat and watched his face as he turned the pages, seeing the pictures of her and Bill at the altar, her and Bill dancing at the reception, cutting the wedding cake, then waving good-bye as they drove off to their honeymoon.

"Jane, I don't understand."

"Just turn the page."

He did and laughed out loud. An 8x10 print of her standing in front of a pile of CDs with mini-sledgehammer in hand was framed in royal blue paper. The headline read "The Party's Over." On the right-hand side of the layout was another blowup of her, this time smashing the CDs. Little bits of silver were in the air all around her, and the camera had captured the look on her face as she brought the hammer down on the stack.

"Those turned out well."

"Yep. Keep turning."

He turned the page. "Is this my front door?"

"It is. Read the poem on the right." She'd worked so hard on it, she had every line memorized. He read it out loud.

For years I walked in blissful death, not knowing of the light
I walked my path not knowing the depth of day or night
Each hour passed and with it came a bit more certainty
That life consisted only of what you or I could see
I told myself that things like love were fables in the mist
Not knowing that for all my life I had not been truly kissed
And yet one day a man arrived whose lips were full of life
He shared with me a mystery and with that thought came strife
How ever could my life be based on such a well-placed lie?
How great the mind and body's vast power to deny
Today I believe and toss my heart into a ring of love
At last I know there is a gift given only from above
Though movies, stories, songs, and books have told the tale for years
Today, this hour, the truth of love's existence brings me tears
For I knew love when first I looked into your blessed face
Yet I ignored the thought, the lancing pain of it erase
And caused instead your countenance to fall on love's proffered door

So that you chose at that very hour, to love and long no more
I pray, my love, that once again you find it in your heart
To offer me a love in which I now joyfully take part
I give this book to you because it's all I have to give
And I no longer want the memory of the time before I lived.

She was going to faint at any moment, she just knew it. Did he get it? Or had she made it too vague? This was a dumb idea. She should get up and walk out, taking what little dignity she could muster with her.

He looked at her, and all the air left the room. His eyes—those beautiful, precious, dark chocolate eyes—were all she needed to see. He got it.

"This is the best present I have ever been given," he said.

She let out her breath. "I'm sorry it's not the DVD set of *Galactica.*"

He laughed. "It's so much better than that, Jane. Did you write this?"

"Like I said, I got a little help from the Sisters."

"It's amazing."

"Thanks."

"So you love me, huh?"

Her cheeks flamed, and she ducked her head. "I wouldn't trust my judgment. I don't have a whole lot of experience with this."

He came up out of his chair and knelt before her. "I do," he said and kissed her. She held his face in her hands, loving the rough feel of his cheek that let her know he hadn't shaved since that morning. His lips on hers caused the now-familiar tingle, all the better because she was acknowledging it now.

"I love you, Jane. I know we haven't known each other long enough for that, and it sounds crazy. I get that. But I want you to know I love you." He kissed her again.

"So this is what love feels like, hmm?" She kissed him back.

"Yes ma'am."

"Then what's with the redhead?" He leaned back, keeping his hands on her knees.

"What?"

"The redhead I saw you with. Who is she?"

He laughed. "That's Meredith, my sister I told you about."

"You could have mentioned she's gorgeous."

"Sorry, I forget about her looks. To me, she's still Meredith on the playground. When did you see her anyway?"

Her blush started again. "The night you came over."

"You were home?"

"Yeah. I thought you wanted to introduce your new girl-friend."

"You're kidding me, right? Even if I was mad at you, I don't move that fast."

"What was that you were saying earlier about it being too early to love?"

"Okay, I only move that fast with you." He grinned and kissed her. "I love doing that."

"I love it when you do that."

"Then we're going to be an awfully happy couple."

She turned serious. "Not if we don't take care of this thing we have. Lydia's having to fight for it with Dale. I don't want us to do that."

"What's wrong with Lydia and Dale?"

"He's more interested in the zing he gets from SportsCenter than what he gets from her." She tilted her head. "Though having her cable shut off may have turned the tables."

"She had her cable turned off?"

"Hey, desperate times call for desperate measures."

"Feel free to tell me if I'm ignoring you before cutting off the cable."

She grinned and gave him a short kiss. "So, what now?"

"What do you mean?"

"Well, in books, this is where everything ends, and they all live happily ever after. Since this is real life, what happens now?"

"Now we figure out a way for Wilson and Major Carter to coexist." Wilson gave a short, loud bark, and they jumped.

"Sorry. He has a tendency to get riled every time I say the cat's name."

"You're kidding me." Jake looked over his shoulder at the dog still lying in front of the fire. "Major Carter." He laughed as Wilson barked. "This is going to be one very noisy relationship."

She sighed and wrapped her arms around his neck, pulling her to him. "Good thing I like loud."

"Yeah, a very good thing." He kissed her, and she leaned into him, loving the fact that he was hers and she was his.

"They'll get used to each other eventually," he said, and she smiled at his confidence.

"If you say so."

"I do." She shivered at the words. Funny how two little words could hold such deep meaning if coming from the right person.

"Are you still cold?" He ran his hands up and down her arms, then reached over to pull a throw off of his seat.

"Just a little." He tugged her from her seat to sit on the floor with him and laid the blanket across her lap. "There, now you're all warm and snuggly for the rest of sci-fi night."

She rolled her arms and punched him in the arm. "You're going to make me watch sci-fi? I give you my heart, and this is what I get in return?"

Before she knew it, his arms were around her and his lips were teasing hers. "No," he whispered against her mouth. "This is what you get in return. Anytime, anyplace you need somebody there with you, I'm in."

"I don't know," she whispered back. "It's not going to be this easy all the time. I'm going to get mad and yell, and you're going to get frustrated with me. What then?"

"Two shoulders, no waiting, remember?" He looked into her eyes. "I'm here for you, babe, no matter what it is. You need to cry, call me. Wanna yell? No problem. Need to smash some CDs?" She laughed, and the smile she was growing to expect came back again. "I'm your man. I'm here for you through thick and thin, for better or worse."

His eyes were sparkling at her, and she looked hard into them, thrilling inside when all she saw there was honesty. He meant it. He was in this for the long haul.

"Just so long as I don't find you in any Internet chat rooms."

He held up three fingers. "Scout's honor."

"Were you even a scout?"

"No, but I figured it was a universal proclamation of honesty." She laughed again.

"Seriously, I have to work with computers all day long. I have no desire to use them for personal pleasure. Why would I? You're just across the hall." He grinned at her and wiggled his eyebrows, and she pushed him back.

"Yeah, well, just so you know that's where I'm going to *stay*, mister."

"Your honor is safe with me." He started to make the scout sign and caught himself. "Honest."

She leaned forward and kissed him, falling into the magic and stars behind her eyes.

"Unless, of course, you're going to keep doing that. And then all bets are off."

She pulled back and hastily arranged the blanket around her lap. "No, no, keep your bets on." She blushed as she realized how that sounded. "And everything else, for that matter."

He took her hand in his and rubbed his thumb against it. "Thank you again for my present."

"No problem." She gave him back his standard reply and settled into the crook of his arm as they leaned back against the chair, ready to watch the rest of sci-fi night.

"And thanks for watching sci-fi with me," he said.

"You were right about it," she admitted and twisted her head to look up at him. "It's amazing how much better these shows seem when I watch them with good company."

He pulled her to him, squeezing her shoulders and placing

a light kiss on the end of her nose. "That wasn't the only thing I was right about," he said, and she laughed, loving the feel of his strong arm around her, knowing she'd finally found the love for which wars were fought and people died.

"It *does* exist," she said and watched his face soften in acceptance.

"Yeah, it does," he said, and kissed her as Major Carter came to lie in her lap, purring all the while.

chapter 27

❀ · ❀ · ❀ · ❀ · ❀ · ❀ · ❀

Mari sat in her bathroom, staring at the stick in her hand. The irony was too much. Two little pink lines stared back at her, confirming her suspicions. At first, she'd thought it was just nerves over not knowing about Andrea. Nausea and exhaustion were normal for someone under as much stress as they had been for five days.

But the unthinkable, the impossible, had happened. They were pregnant. They were finally *pregnant*. God must have one heck of a sense of humor. What would John think? They'd be a family of five now if Andrea had made it out of the fire. Her mind stopped at that thought, but she forced the unthinkable to the dark recesses and focused again on the white plastic stick in her hand. It blared out the miracle of life to her again, the pink lines seeming to glow out of the window.

One of the girls at the office was always joking about not

having the third children because then you're outnumbered. But that didn't seem like it would be a problem. All her life, all she'd wanted was a big *familia*. She looked again at the stick. He might be very excited about this.

Or it might be the stressor that pushed him over the edge. They were walking a very thin tightrope that grew more taut as each day went by with no word from the orphanage. Every morning, John woke up and picked up the white phone by their bedside. They knew the agency number by heart—he had even put it on speed dial. And every morning, Mari would watch John, her own hope building as he listened to the ringing, phone pressed tightly to his ear. He'd watch her, pat her hand, and then ask the question when someone finally picked up. Was their Andrea okay? Had she been found? Was the orphanage a total loss?

And each day for five days, he had turned to her with a sorrowful, frustrated expression. The light in his green eyes, dulling bit by bit as the days passed with no news. Would they find out something today? Would they hear that their Andrea was alive?

She rubbed her tummy and looked again at the stick. She had to be careful not to stress too much. It wouldn't be good for the baby growing inside her to have a mom who was scared all the time for her big sister in Chile.

Mari smiled. They'd done it. She was *pregnant*. The thought thrilled her all over again. The toilet paper holder squeaked as she wrapped up the stick. She put it at the back of her makeup drawer. John wouldn't look there. As soon as they got word about Andrea, then he could learn about this news. Either it would be icing on their family cake or a balm that would soothe his soul. She pushed that thought away again. Andrea would be okay.

The shrill ring of the phone made her jump. She looked into the mirror, wondering if John would see the joy there amidst the agony.

"Honey!" John's strong voice bounced off the hallway walls. "It's the agency!"

The phone rang, and Jane rolled across the bed with a moan. Who was calling her at—she sneaked a peek at the alarm clock— seven in the morning on a Saturday? If it was a telemarketer, somebody was about to see her bad side.

"Hello?"

"Jane? Are you asleep?"

"Yes, Lydia. Like the majority of Americans who do not have to get up and till the fields, I'm asleep on a Saturday morning at seven a.m."

"Well, get up. Mari just got a call from the agency down in Chile."

Jane sat straight up in bed. "I'm awake. What'd they say?"

"The phone cut off just as he said he'd found Andrea. They're waiting by the phone in case he's able to make contact again. Mari asked that we come on over. I'm getting the twins ready now. Dale's coming with me to keep John occupied."

"I'll call Jake. I'm sure he'd want to come."

"So the gift went over well?"

"Like a dream. I'll tell you all about it at Mari's."

"Okay, see you there. Be careful."

She pressed the button to hang up, then dialed Jake.

"Good morning." His gravelly voice did amazing things to her insides.

"Morning. Did you get some sleep?"

"Yeah, I've been asleep the whole four hours you haven't been here. I can't believe you're awake."

"Lydia called and woke me up. Remember when I said things might not always be easy?"

"Yep. Two shoulders, ready and waiting."

"The agent down in Chile called. The communication was cut off just as he was giving them details, so they still don't know a whole lot, but it sounds like she's alive. We're all going over to Mari's."

"I'll be ready in five minutes." She smiled. His words warmed her inside and she marveled at how seamlessly he fit into her life.

"Thanks."

"For what? I told you. We're in this together. See you in five." He hung up, and she made a mad dash for the shower.

"Please, God, look after little Andrea."

They sat in Mari's living room, watching the pendulum swing back and forth on a clock Mari's mother had brought with them from Puerto Rico. It had a black striped cat whose eyes went back and forth and who meowed every hour. Mari thought she might just scream if that cat meowed one more time before the phone rang. She looked at each of the people sitting in her house—people she barely knew a few weeks ago. Jake and Jane sat huddled together, his arm around her. Mari smiled at that. Lydia and Dale were in opposite chairs. Mac sat in the rocking chair, humming as she gazed out the window.

"Tell us again what he said, Mari," Lydia said and they all leaned in to try to glean meaning from the few words the agency representative and said before the line cut off.

"He said, 'The agency asked me to call you as soon as I had news. I've gotten to the orphanage and—' Then he was cut off."

Lydia slumped back into the couch cushions and sighed. "Okay, that's just nothing to go on. How long has it been since he called?"

Mari glanced up at the cat clock, but John jumped in before she could respond. "Forty-seven minutes," he said, his voice a monotone.

Jake leaned over and patted John's shoulder. "It's gonna be alright, man. Whatever happens, we're all here and it's gonna be alright."

Mari's heart twisted. Men in Puerto Rico rarely showed their feelings. It was one of the things that had drawn her to John—his willingness to be open about his thoughts and emotions. Hearing the defeat in his voice was just about her undoing, but Jake—bless Jake—he seemed to be throwing John the lifeline Mari couldn't find the strength to pick up.

John nodded at Jake and cleared his throat. "Anyone want

anything to drink? I think if I keep moving around, it won't feel like every minute takes an hour to go by."

Mari jumped up from her place in the big reading chair. "Good idea. John, there's a new box of soda cans in the garage. How about some food, too?" She went to the kitchen that had always been her haven from the world, but stopped short when she noticed Emmy sitting on the other side of the kitchen island. "Honey, I thought you were coloring in your room. What are you doing out here?"

Mari's breath caught in her throat at the serious look on Emmy's face. "Mommy, has Andrea gone to Heaven?"

Mari took a deep breath. Letting herself lose it in front of Emmy would only scare her daughter further. "Why do you ask that?"

"I heard you talking to Daddy and you said she was either with us or with Jesus and I you told me Jesus is in Heaven. But I thought we didn't come back from Heaven. That's what you said when Felix died. So is Andrea with Jesus? Because if she is, I'm mad at Him for taking my baby sister."

Mari gathered Emmy close and settled her back against the edge of the island. She ran her fingers through Emmy's silky hair and tried hard to get control of her emotions. "Oh, *bambina*. Do not worry. I'm sure our Andrea is safe and sound, we're just all waiting on the agency to call and tell us that." *Please God, let her be safe and sound.*

"If she's okay, then why do you think she's with Jesus?"

Mari kissed the top of Emmy's head just as the phone rang. "One minute, sweetheart. Mommy needs to get the phone."

She released Emmy and scrambled to her feet, dashing into the living room at the same time as John. They looked at each other and the pain in his eyes broke another piece of her heart. *Please, God, let this be good news.* Her ears filled with the sound of her own rushing blood and the room tilted a bit as she watched the love of her life walk to the phone. He picked it up and Mari's hands went to her mouth. *Please, God. Please, God.* John's head nodded up and down, but his face was to the floor. He wasn't asking questions. Wouldn't he be asking questions if she was alive? Asking about her condition? Where she was?

Mari felt Emmy lean against her leg and looked down. Emmy's eyes were huge saucers looking up at her. *Please, God.*

John hung up and walked over to her. His green eyes shined as he gently touched her shoulder. "She's fine. Our little girl is fine."

Mari's breath whooshed out of her and she fell into his chest. "Thank You, Jesus. Thank You." She murmured into the softness of his shirt, righting herself as her world righted itself. She pulled back and looked into his eyes. "Where is she?"

"She's with a family in a little village about five miles from the orphanage. We can go and pick her up as soon as we want. All the papers are in order—they were in order before the fire —but the agency didn't get word until the fire had broken out." Words tumbled from John's lips like water to a thirsty woman. She was alive! "Then they didn't want to tell us everything was final in case Andrea wasn't okay." He raked his hand through his hair. "But she is! She's fine!"

"So Andrea's not in Heaven with Jesus?" Emmy's little

voice cut through the haze of Mari's brain and Mari turned to her. She knelt down and took Emmy's face in her hands.

"No, baby. Andrea is not in Heaven with Jesus. She's just fine and we're going to bring her home."

"When?"

Mari laughed. "As soon as we can get on a plane!"

Emmy hopped up and down. "YAY! My baby sister is coming!" She bounced around the living room. "My baby sister is coming!" Everyone laughed at her exuberance.

Jane leaned forward. "You're going to be a family of four!"

"That's right! Because, right now, we're three." She pointed to John and Mari. "Daddy is one. Mommy is two. And I make three. But Andrea makes four. So now we have enough for teams!"

Mari grinned. *No time like the present.* "Well, we might have to talk about that a little bit, Emmy."

Emmy stopped bouncing and all eyes turned to Mari.

Mac stopped rocking. "Sister, you got somethin' you ain't sharin'?" Her wise old eyes bore into Mari.

"I'm not keeping secrets, Mac. I just found out this morning." She looked at John. "What do you think about a family of five?"

John's whoop was loud enough to wake the dogs. They started barking as the clock struck the hour and the cat began to meow. The Sisters came over and hugged her, patting her tummy and talking about baby names and due dates. Emmy came over and added her voice to the mix.

"So, am I going to have two baby sisters?"

Mari chuckled. "*Bambina,* we can't be sure yet. We know you have one baby sister in Andrea. But this baby might be a brother. We won't know for a long time."

Emmy crossed her arms over her chest. "Yeah, well, I'll just talk to Jesus about that. We don't want brothers here." She turned and marched down the hallway to her room, but turned back as she got to her doorway. "I'll teach Andrea to pray, too. Don't worry, Mommy. I'll make sure we get two baby sisters." She went in her room and shut the door as all the adults laughed.

Lydia's thoughts were a whirlwind as they pulled out of Mari and John's driveway. In one day, they'd faced death and won— twice. She had a headache from trying to take it all in.

"Hey, do you think your mom would mind keeping the twins a bit longer?" she asked Dale. A nap would probably knock this headache right out.

He shrugged. "You know she loves having them. I'm sure she won't care."

The silence stretched out and Lydia wondered again about the growing chasm between them. Watching Mari and John lean on each other had made her long for the days when she reached out to Dale and with he certainty that his arms would encircle her.

"You have some reason for not wanting to pick them up?" he asked. "Something maybe covered in orange feathers?"

She turned to stare at him. Was he actually expressing interest in her?

"Watch out!"

She jerked her attention back to the road and swerved to miss a pedestrian.

"Sorry, sorry. I think I misunderstood you."

Dale leaned over and laid a hand on her knee. "No you didn't."

The Kroger was just up ahead. Perfect parking lot for a discussion. She whipped into the lot and threw the car into Park.

"So now you *want* me to wear orange feathers?"

He sighed. "Lydia, I've always wanted you to wear orange feathers. You just took me by surprise is all."

"Mmm hmm. And right in the middle of a game. What rotten timing on my part, right?" He wasn't getting off the hook that easily.

"Well, yeah, it was rotten timing."

"Dale!"

"It was, Lydia! Seriously, what if I came in your scrapping room while you were in the middle of one of your layout thingamadoos and told you to stop, that I wanted you to pay attention to me. What would you do?"

She thought about it for a second. Okay, he had a point. But still.

"I'd ask you to wait a minute and then come see what it is you wanted."

He laughed and shook his head. "Oh, please. We both

know you'd finish that and start something else and forget I ever came in the room."

Sometimes being known wasn't a great thing. "Maybe."

He looked at her.

"Probably." She smiled. "But, Dale, I really don't think I spend as much time scrapping as you do in front of the TV."

"I think you do, Lydia."

"Then I guess we're at an impasse."

He shook his head again. "I don't think so. I've been thinking about this a lot. I know you've been trying to get my attention and," he leaned forward and ran his hand along her thigh, "I appreciate the effort. But I may have finally figured out an answer to our problem."

"What problem is that?" Because if he had finally figured out that she was sick of sports being more important to him than her, then there was hope here.

"The problem of our own personal interests being more important than our interest in each other."

Sheesh. Just when she thought she had him pegged, he came out with something like that and reminded her why she'd ever became his wife in the first place.

"You really think my scrapbooking is more important to me than you?"

He shrugged. "Sometimes. And I'm willing to admit that sometimes I've let the TV be more important than you."

"Wow, that's a pretty big admission."

"Well, seeing the heavy stuff Mari and John are dealing with kind of put things in perspective for me and I started thinking about all the time I spend on TV and you spend on scrapping."

She shook her head. "I just don't see it, Dale. I mean, yeah, I scrap with the Sisters a lot. But I don't think I spend as much time scrapping as you do watching that crazy television."

"Okay, then let's do this. For the next month, we'll chart how much time you spend scrapping and how much time I spend watching TV." He held out his hands. "Maybe I'm wrong. But I think this will help us figure it out and I think that, if we can agree to spend equal amounts of time on our personal hobbies, then maybe we can get past this, I don't know, *thing* between us."

She looked at her husband sitting there, asking her to step out and cross the divide between them. At least he knew there was a problem and was brave enough to acknowledge it. It was way more than she ever expected him to do and reminded her of the days he sent her flowers and balloons all the time. When he was still chasing after her heart.

His hand rubbed her leg again and a little frisson of zing went through her. "Okay, Dale. I'm in."

He grinned. "Really? Does this mean I get to see the orange feathers again?"

She laughed and swatted his arm. "I think they're off at the town dump by now. But there's more where they came from."

He held his chest and threw his head back. "Be still my beating heart."

She chuckled with him, grateful that the tension in their marriage was beginning to ease. It wouldn't be easy—and she might even have to cut back on her scrapping time for a while —but their zing wasn't lost.

He stopped laughing and looked at her. "I love you, Lydia Whitehaven."

She put her hand in his and squeezed. "I love you, too."

acknowledgments

Thank you to. . .

My dedicated mother, Linda DeBoard, who spent hours on her knees in prayer, securing protection for me as I walked life's difficult path. You were right, Mom. I'm a writer.

My gifted daddy, who worked his tail off to make sure we had food on the table and put his own dreams aside to ensure we could go after ours. I'm so proud of you, Dr. DeBoard.

My beautiful sister, Christie Ricketts, and my talented brother, Herman DeBoard. Each of you has spurred me on to greater creativity. Thank you to your families as well for providing fodder for my fiction.

My amazing husband, Charles, who shows me support and unconditional love every day. I don't deserve the love you give, and I'm so grateful you love me enough to ignore that.

Grace and Jim, who called with encouragement just as I

was ready to throw the laptop against the wall. Everyone should be blessed with such wonderful in-laws.

My best friend, Mari, for letting me use her baby and family names. I miss you, sister.

My girls, Danielle and Deonne, for the hours of scrapping in Nashville.

Ami McConnell, a lady who has more talent in her pinkie than I'll ever hope to have. Thank you for knowing what God made you to be and serving in that capacity. You've changed my life.

Beth Jusino, agent extraordinaire. Your grace and patience with me are a godsend.

Karen Ball, without whom this story would never have been told. You have a gift, my friend.

Allen Arnold, for showing me it's okay to be a fiction freak.

The staff of Glass Road PR. I know you guys have worked hard behind the scenes so that I could write this book. I'm grateful to have you on board.

Finally, my astounding heavenly Father. I'm so unworthy to be a part of Your plan for this world. Your faithfulness humbles me; Your love sustains me. Your mercies truly are new every day. Thank You.

reading group guide

✳ · ✳ · ✳ · ✳ · ✳ · ✳ · ✳

1. On her wedding day, Jane's best friend, Lydia, tries to talk her out of marrying Bill because she believes he is a cheater. Was Lydia right in speaking so forcefully—or do you think she should have kept quiet? What would you have done in that situation?

2. When Jane discovers her husband's on-line affair, she leaves him immediately. If she had stayed in the marriage and insisted on their seeing a counselor, would that have saved the marriage? Why or why not?

3. Lydia also has marital problems. What are they? What do you think of Lydia's attempt to solve one of their problems through sexy lingerie and cutting off the cable TV? What should she do to improve their relationship?

4. Jane and her scrapbooking friends discuss the importance of learning and speaking a person's "love language."

303

Which of the five love languages did Jane use to communicate her feelings for Jake? What is your preferred love language? What is your significant other's?

5. When Jane's ex-husband begs her to come back to him, she has to choose between a man who offers a marriage based on friendship and one based on romantic love. Which is more important when choosing a mate? Why? Can a good marriage be built on either alone?

6. With which of the characters do you most identify? Why?

7. Jane considers throwing away her wedding scrapbook, but instead decides to add some new photos and a poem. What does this signify about Jane's ability to deal with her past rather than bury it?

8. A major theme of *Prints Charming* is the friendship of women. What do Jane and her Sisters, Ink. friends offer one another that they don't find anywhere else in their lives? What ideas did this book elicit in you about the possibilities of a similar group?

tips & tricks

❀ · ❀ · ❀ · ❀ · ❀ · ❀ · ❀

Provided by Veronica Hugger, president and cofounder
of The National Scrapbooking Association

MANAGE YOUR MEMORIES: Use the FRAME method to manage your digital photos:
- Filter your pictures
- Reorganize by marking your favorites
- Archive pictures two times with two methods in two locations
- Make a print using archival materials
- Ensure backups are safe with an annual checkup
- For details, visit www.gotdigitalpictures.com.

THREE IS THE MAGIC NUMBER: Use the Rule of Thirds in photo-taking and scrapbook layouts. Simply divide your frame or page into thirds both horizontally and vertically and place your main subject in one of the four points where the lines intersect.

Use the Visual Triangle Rule, too, when composing your

scrapbook page. Place embellishments and accents in relation-ship to your photos to create a visual triangle.

(I got some of this info from http://www.digicamhelp.com/learn/shoot-pro/rule.php and http://www.scrapjazz.com/topics/Scrapbook_Basics/Layout_Design/189.php)

LET THE KIDS CLICK!: Strap your digital camera on your children and allow them to take plenty of pictures with their per-spective. Send them on an "assignment" to capture specific shots. Help them select their favorites and share the printing process with them. Set some activity time aside to scrap their images in albums they can share with their friends. Theme ideas include "All About Me," "In My Backyard," "My Favorites," etc.

EASY ENHANCEMENT: Paper tearing is a simple technique that can add interest to any scrapbook page. Paper has a grain, and it's easier to tear paper with the grain. To find the grain in a sheet of paper, hold it flat in the open palms of both hands. Bring your palms together to bow the paper into a "U" shape, and notice how the paper "gives." Turn the sheet 45 degrees and bow the paper in the same manner. The position with the least resistance indicates the grain. To tear, hold the paper in each hand and between your thumb and forefingers. Pull your domi-nant hand towards you to tear. Practice on scrap paper.

SCRAP FOR SUCCESS: Start a scrapbooking project with the end in mind. Beginner projects may include a mini-album or a pre-designed page kit. Create an album around a specific event or theme, like a recent vacation, and use a smaller format like an 8x8" album. One 4x6" can fill up a page, making it fast and easy to complete.

AVOID NIT-PICKING! GO FOR THE ENSEMBLE!: Manufacturers create beautiful and tempting products, so let their designs work for you. Stick within a specific product line. Select papers and accents within that line. The coordinating colors, embellishments, and papers take the guessing—and time—out of selecting the right "outfit" for your page. Think of it as Geranimals for scrapbooking!

TIME-SAVING TIPS: When you buy patterned paper by the sheet, also pick up one or two or the coordinating solid sheets. Buy double-sided papers; there's usually a coordinating design on the back that matches perfectly. After creating a page, make cards until all the scraps are used up. You'll have fewer scraps to manage and extra cards on hand!

SERVICE WITH A SMILE!: Your local scrapbooking store (or LSS) offers hands-on customer service and education, plus all the supplies to get you started. In addition to classes and product selection, most local retailers host retreats, crops, make-and-takes and many other fun activities to enhance your scrapbooking experience. To find an LSS near you, use the Store Locator on the NSA web site at www.nsa.gs.

Use the following sample pages
by Stacy Julian to capture
happy memories and celebrate
the people you love!

cousins

WHAT YOU'LL NEED:

- Seven to nine snapshots of family or friends
- Two sheets of cardstock in medium tone (this is your background)
- One sheet brightly colored cardstock (for your main photo mat and subtitle block)
- Medium- and small-sized letter stickers (white really pops!)

- A jumbo square punch
- Scraps of cardstock for punching squares
- A jumbo flower paper punch
- One black journaling pen (.03 point)
- Buttons for the middle of the flowers

ASSEMBLY TIPS:

Don't be afraid to trim your photos just a bit. This way you can fit more onto a page. Line up several pictures along the bottom of a layout, but always select one photo to emphasize and draw attention to it with color and accents. A square punches are versatile tools that you'll use over and over again. Punch squares of cardstock scraps to create a fun title right down the center of your page!

the halloween scene

WHAT YOU'LL NEED:
- Eight holiday snapshots trimmed to approx. 3½" x 3½"
- Two full sheets of patterned cardstock from a line of coordinated products
- Two sheets of white cardstock (for photo mats)
- Two other pattern papers cut into four thin strips
- An additional pattern paper cut into a title block
- Assorted chipboard accents and letters
- One black journaling pen (1.2 point for the title)
- One black journaling pen (.03 point)
- Assorted medium sized brads

ASSEMBLY TIPS:

This page pattern works great for almost any holiday. Try purchasing a themed kit of several products designed to go together. Don't line things up too much—just have fun!

On handwritten note in image:
Little Sister By Influence.

She's smart and savvy and all of a sudden grown up with a baby. Lucy's mom, my little sister, I'm wishing she didn't live so far away. I like that were friends.

Chandi Stacy 2005

little sister

WHAT YOU'LL NEED:
- One large (about 5" x 7") black and white photo
- Four different sheets of pattern paper—anything goes!
- One sheet of white colored cardstock (this is your background)
- One sheet of light colored cardstock
- Three short pieces of ribbon—mix it up with different colors and styles!
- One circle accent
- One silk flower accent
- One medium sized brad
- Acid-free glue stick or adhesive
- One bottle of acrylic paint
- One foam paint brush
- One dual-tip archival journaling pen, in a fun color (for the title)
- One black journaling pen (.08 point)

ASSEMBLY TIPS:

I call this layout design freestyle color-blocking and it's easy. Start by cutting one of your pattern papers into a big wide strip or square and adhere it to your background anywhere you want. Now cut another pattern paper into another square or strip and place it. Next, fill in the spaces that are left over—leave small margins in between blocks of paper and be sure to cut and include blocks of cardstock for your title and journaling. Add your photo, ribbon, accents, and words. As a final splash of color, use a foam brush to add paint to the sides of photo and edges of the page.